FORGOTTEN SECRETS

ALEXANDRIA CLARKE

In a hectic world, a moment of silence is worth more than money can buy. Data bombards us from every direction, from our televisions, phones, and worst of all, other people's mouths. Noise runs rampant these days. You're never truly alone, not when you carry the entire universe in the palm of your hand. A single piece of nondescript technology—the smartphone—connects all of us together. We're so accustomed to the cacophony around us that the value of silence goes unnoticed, until, of course, they started marketing that too with meditation and mindfulness apps. We hide our mountains of stress behind quirky tweets and aesthetically-pleasing Instagram posts, hoping our followers spend half a second to click on a tiny heart button that might gratify our need for validation. Shakespeare has never been more relevant than today. The whole world's a stage, and the people merely players. Social media has allowed us to expand our personal stage to reach greater audiences, a two-faced situation—

My pen tore through the cheap notebook paper, severing one entire corner of hasty handwriting. The offending piece hung on by a few last fibers, the word "two-faced" split right down the middle. I reached for my phone to take a picture, remembered I didn't have it, and set my pen aside. This blog post wasn't going the way I wanted it to. It was one thing to write a profound piece on the effects of social media. It was another to bash it mercilessly when the whole world—and my career—relied on it.

I rolled backward onto the bed and propped my hands behind my head. Buddha, embroidered on the curtains, gazed serenely over me. His expression seemed to say, *I've achieved inner peace. Why haven't you?* With my feet, I pushed the curtains aside. Dusky indigo light lay upon the simple room. There wasn't much here, just two beds, a wardrobe, and a side table. Beyond the terrace of the retreat center loomed the Himalayas, snow-capped peaks awash with mystery and adventure. If I squinted, I could make out the colorful prayer flags strung throughout the villages. My chest tightened at the thought of ascending those mountains. According to legend, monsters dwelled there.

A gentle knock sounded at the door. My roommate, a woman in her late thirties named Nahla, smiled at me. "Hey, Bex. One last sunset meditation before you leave?"

"I'll be there in a minute."

As Nahla retreated, I chewed on the end of the pen and stared at the words I had written. Then I set the pen to the page again.

I'm the first one to admit my addiction to social media. After all, it's the way I make my living. But it doesn't have to be all or nothing. If I've learned anything from this ten-day retreat, it's that taking time to disconnect is vital to the mind and soul. If you struggle with leaving your phone behind, I challenge you to complete my next Daily Dare. For the next ten days, turn your phone, computer, TV, tablet, etc. off for one hour. You'll be surprised by how much you can get done, and how deep your consciousness can reach, when you're not tending to technology every other second. Happy travels! Bex.

Sunset meditation had already begun on the tile terrace of the retreat center. The space next to Nahla was free, so I unfurled my mat and settled next to her. She opened one eye and squeezed my knee. Over the last ten days, she and I had simply enjoyed the other's companionship. Though the retreat center didn't require silence, Nahla and I had come to an early understanding that we both needed quiet. We communicated with gestures, expressions, and the occasional brief sentence. We didn't know anything about each other, but from the picture she kept near her bed, I surmised she was a mother of two and probably divorced; the man's face had been torn from the photograph. The comfortable silence between us came as a relief.

The meditation lasted an hour. The retreat center acted as a temporary home to roughly thirty tourists and travelers at any given time. A new batch had arrived that morning. They fidgeted and squirmed, unable to stay still and quiet for an entire hour. I knew the feeling. Before this, my thoughts crawled through my brain like skittering bugs. Over time and with daily practice, I learned to let distracting thoughts leave me. At least temporarily.

The sun set on the retreat center, and darkness fell across the terrace, signaling the end of the meditation session. Before the instructor released us, he reminded us to take note of the stillness we felt.

"Take it with you," he announced. "You'll thank yourself later."

As Nahla and I rolled up our mats, one of the new guys— a tanned twenty-year-old with floppy blond hair and a rainbow bandana around his head—let out a low whistle and stretched his joints until they popped.

"Wow!" he said loudly. "Is it always like this? I feel like my head is going to explode. It's so quiet."

"That's the point," I muttered.

"Sorry, what did you say?"

"That's the point," I repeated, enunciating each syllable. "It's meditation. It's for peace of mind and inner stillness."

Nahla laid a comforting hand on my shoulder. "Don't worry," she told the new guy. "It was hard for me to get the hang of it at first too. You'll learn, especially if you put in the work."

"Thanks." The new guy finished rolling his mat and offered me his hand. "I'm AJ. What's your name?"

Reluctantly, I shook hands. "Bex."

"Nahla."

AJ swept his hair out of his eyes with a subtle tilt of his head. "Nice to meet you both. I'm here with a few friends. Any chance you two want to join us for dinner? Show us the ropes or maybe share some tips?"

Nahla and I looked at each other. Her expression matched mine. Neither one of us wanted to "show the ropes" to a bunch of unwashed fraternity brothers. It was our last night at the center, and all I wanted to do was savor my remaining hours of silence. Then I remembered I'd used all of my meal vouchers and was low on cash.

"Actually, that sounds like fun," I said. Nahla raised an eyebrow. "On one condition. You're buying, AJ."

AJ grinned. "It's gotta be like that, huh?"

"Tell me you're not hiding a trust fund under those khaki shorts."

His blue eyes twinkled with mischief. "You're weirdly good at reading people. Anyone ever tell you that?"

"A couple times."

"Fine." AJ pulled several twenties from his pockets and laid them in my hand. "Let's do it. It'll be worth getting to know a few people. That's what this is all about anyway, right?"

NAHLA and I met AJ and his friends—Jason, Harriet, and Melanie—in the lobby of the retreat center then walked to a nearby restaurant. Nahla and I sat on the floor around a low table without hesitation, but the young tourists had trouble getting comfortable.

"Do you think they'd bring us chairs?" Jason asked. "My legs are kinda long to sit on the floor."

"Then you probably shouldn't have come to Nepal," Nahla answered. She patted the pouf beside her. "Come on down, pretty boy. You'll be spending a lot of time on the floor."

Nahla and I ordered for the table. As we waited for the food, the four newbies chatted. Without asking a single question, I learned that they were all from a university in Massachusetts and studying abroad for the fall semester. As I'd guessed, three of them came from affluent families. Harriet was the only one with a scholarship.

They checked their phones constantly between bites and conversations. Melanie refused to let us dig in until she'd taken a picture of the food. Jason jumped every time he received a new text, then hastily replied. Harriet scrolled through Instagram, and AJ posted several videos of the food and us to Snap-Chat. Finally, I batted the phone away from my face.

"You want to learn something from us?" Nahla asked. "Turn off your phones, or at least put them on silent."

They obeyed, but their eyes flickered back to the waiting screens. With expectant gazes, they stared Nahla down.

"That's it," she announced. "That's the lesson. Disconnect."

"Let me get this straight," Jason said. "Neither one of you has a phone?"

"I have one," I answered, "but not with me."

AJ spooned a heap of fried rice onto his plate. "Let me guess. You have a flip phone from 2007 because you think technology is evil."

I snorted into my food. "Definitely not. My whole life is my phone. I'm an influencer—ugh, I hate that word though."

Harriet's face lit up. *"That's* where I know you from! You're The Wanderer! I follow you on Instagram." She studied me from across the table. "You should post more pictures of your face. You're so pretty! Anyway, you're one of the reasons I wanted to do this trip in the first place. Is there anywhere you haven't been?"

"What is she talking about?" Nahla muttered to me.

"It's my job," I explained. "My social media handle is 'The Wanderer.' I travel around the world to take pictures and write blog posts."

"That's why you're here?" Nahla asked. "To get material for your blog?"

"Not exactly." A pea pod slipped from my chopsticks once, twice, three times. "I realized being glued to my phone wasn't the healthiest choice. I needed a break from everything."

AJ shoveled rice into his mouth. "Aren't both of you almost finished with your retreat? Where do you go after this?"

"Home," Nahla said wearily. "I have responsibilities, just like everyone else. Kids to feed, work to do" —she rolled her eyes— "an ex-husband to deal with."

"And you?" Jason asked me. "Do you have a home base?"

"Doveport, Oregon," I replied. "That's where I grew up, but I'm heading to India next."

Nahla rested her head on my shoulder. "When's the last time you went home?"

"About two years ago."

"Doesn't your family miss you?" AJ asked.

I finally picked up the slippery pea pod with my fingers and ate it that way. "My dad died when I was a kid, and my mom's memory isn't the best. I don't have any brothers or sisters, so no, my family doesn't miss me."

"Man, what a weird way to live," Jason said. "Don't you get tired of traveling all the time? Never sleeping in your own bed?"

I shrugged, jostling Nahla's head. "I don't mind it. It's what I do best."

Nahla rustled what was left of my dirty blonde hair. I'd shaved the sides a while ago, since it was easier to deal with when traveling. "This one's an expert," Nahla said. "She has a rule about how much she carries with her. Go on, Bex. Tell them."

"It's nothing. It's for convenience."

"It's brilliant," Nahla told them. "She only carries twenty-five things with her at one time. That includes her phone, wallet, clothes, backpack, and any other necessities. If she picks up something on her travels, she gets rid of one of the things she already has."

"I read about a guy who did something similar," I expanded. "It's helped me learn how little I need to get by. A pretty important lesson. Besides, the less I have to carry, the better."

"I could never do that," Melanie said. "What about makeup?"

"I don't use it. Sunblock, however, is a must."

"Shampoo?" Jason added. "Body wash or deodorant?"

I lifted my arms and pretended to waft my scent over to him. "I'm *au naturel*. Deodorants are full of harsh chemicals anyway. As for shampoo" —I mimed scrubbing the top of my head, where my hair was about two inches long— "I don't have much to maintain. I keep a bar of soap with me and use whatever stuff is provided at the places I stay."

Harriet took a hesitant whiff around me. "You don't smell though."

"I do shower," I assured her.

"Moisturizer?" Melanie asked.

"Coconut oil."

AJ snapped his fingers. "Toilet paper."

"Whatever's available," I answered. "Or if I'm desperate, I rinse with a water bottle."

"Ew," Melanie said.

I chuckled and shrugged. "It's no different than using a bidet, right? And that's considered fancy in France."

Harriet adjusted her seat so she could stretch her short legs. "What about all the products you post on your Instagram? Don't those companies sponsor you to use them?"

"I partner with companies that emphasize the importance of sustainability, reuse, and ethical practices," I replied. "For instance, my T-shirts are made of one hundred percent recyclable materials. Once I wear them out, they won't end up in a dump like cheaply-made brands. *And* they wick sweat to keep me dry, so they're perfect for what I do. I keep the companies happy too because my travels show how much I rely on their products."

AJ rubbed the sleeve of my shirt between two fingers. "Genius. I want a few of these."

"I'll send you a link," I offered. "Once I get my phone back."

"Me too!" Harriet said.

"Send it in a group text," Melanie added. "We could all use something like that."

Nahla plucked her shirt by the shoulders to show it off. "She convinced me. Good at her job, isn't she? And that's not all I admire her for. She took a vow of silence for the first five days of the retreat."

The newbies groaned and let out soft "wows" of awe and disbelief. For them, it was impossible to fathom being quiet for an entire five days. I, on the other hand, needed to be alone with my thoughts for a while.

"How did you manage that?" Melanie asked. "I couldn't be quiet for ten minutes. How do you communicate?"

"It's easier at the retreat center," I explained. "A lot of people do it there."

"But why did you do it?" AJ asked. "The point of the retreat is to learn meditation, right? You don't have to give up everything."

"It's another level of disconnecting from everything. I find it peaceful. Nahla helped too. She was always respectful." I tried my hand at another pea pod, clenching the chopsticks tightly around it. This time, the vegetable didn't slip between the utensils. "You all should try it sometime."

"No way."

"I couldn't."

"Me either."

I nodded at their phones, all sitting on the table. "From what it looks like, you all could use a break from those things. Take it from me. I know the value of a smartphone, but I also know the detriments. Do yourselves a favor and take a break."

"Is that a Daily Dare?" Harriet asked.

"Funny you should mention that," I said. "As soon as I leave the retreat center, I planned on making a blog post to challenge my followers with a similar dare. Turn your phone off for one hour a day for the next week and a half."

AJ made a show of powering his phone off. "I accept your challenge, Wanderer. What about the rest of you?"

Jason, skeptical, checked his screen again. No new text messages. He turned the phone off. "You know what? Why not? Bailey's ghosting me anyway."

"Girlfriend?" I asked.

"Ex," he muttered.

"This is the perfect way to get some detachment," I assured him. "Spend your time at the retreat center getting to know yourself again."

Melanie gazed lovingly at her phone. "An hour a day, huh? I guess that's not too bad."

"I'm in if you are," Harriet told her.

"Done."

They both switched off their phones. For a minute, I let them sit in the wake of their decision. Similar to the meditation earlier, they twitched and squirmed, eyes flickering toward the screens every few seconds. I beat my fingers lightly against Nahla's thigh, mimicking the newbies' restlessness, and she laughed under her breath.

"Now what?" Jason asked glumly.

"Now," I said, flagging down the server. "We order another round and enjoy the rest of our evening."

IN THE MORNING, I squeezed in one last sunrise meditation session, packed my belongings, and bid adieu to mine and Nahla's shared room. With a long look at the view of the Himalayas through the window, I headed to the lobby. Nahla waited for me there, her own belongings organized in one of those enormous backpacks people lug across Europe. She hoisted it over her shoulder when she saw me.

"Ready to blow this popsicle stand?" she asked.

"Let's do it."

We thanked the owner and staff of the retreat center and headed out into the busy streets of Kathmandu. Accustomed to silence, we walked without speaking. I touched the back of Nahla's hand to warn her of an oncoming vehicle. She guided me around the waist when we were almost separated by a group of rowdy tourists. As we reached the point where our paths diverged, my stomach sunk low. I would miss mine and Nahla's quiet sisterhood.

"Keep in touch, yeah?" she said as she brought me into a tight hug. "And I don't mean on Instagram. I'm not the social media buff that you are. Here's my phone number and e-mail." She gave me a torn piece of notebook paper folded in half. "Don't lose that. I expect to hear from you. If I don't, I'll be forced to stalk you like your followers."

I pressed the paper to my heart then tucked it into the front pocket of my backpack. "I promise not to lose it."

"You don't have to give up one of your possessions to keep that, do you?"

I cracked a smile. "Since you stole the paper from my notebook, I think I'm good."

Nahla winced. "I was hoping you wouldn't notice."

I pulled her into another hug. "I notice everything. Take care of yourself, okay? No matter how hard it gets."

She nodded against my shoulder. "You too, kid. This might sound cheesy, but you changed my life. Everything's so much clearer to me now."

"*You* changed your life," I told her. "I went along for the ride."

We parted ways, but after a few steps, I turned to watch as Nahla disappeared into the colorful crowd. Though she vanished, the bulky upper part of her backpack bobbed above the throng. As I watched, she raised a hand in farewell high enough for me to see. I waved back, and then she was gone.

"THERE SHE IS, THE STUPENDOUS WANDERER!"

Taj, who I'd called Beard Guy for an entire month before learning his actual name, rolled off his cot to welcome me back to the hostel we'd shared before I'd left for my retreat. When his hug engulfed me, my head bounced off his enormous pecs. He was over six feet tall and built like the buffest version of Adonis. He kept his shoulder-length hair in a bun most of the time, but when he let it down, it blended in with his beard. That along with his brilliant blue-green eyes made him look like a legendary sea prince. All he needed was a trident.

About a year ago, we met in Vietnam, and after randomly bumping into each other three times, it seemed fate was telling us to travel together. Since then, Taj acted as my personal bodyguard and most reliable companion. As a lone traveler, hustlers and jerks often tried to take advantage of me, but with Taj by my side, we hardly ever ran into trouble. Once, a sketchy guy grabbed my backpack, mounted a moped, and attempted to speed off, but Taj literally ripped the man off his vehicle. The moped skittered off and crashed into the jungle brush, and Taj landed one punch in the middle of the guy's face before he hastily conceded my backpack. With a bleeding nose and a nervous apology, the thief ran off, leaving his ruined moped behind.

"What's up, Beard Guy?" I said, throwing fake punches into Taj's stomach. He lowered into a crouch, put his hands up, and batted away my hands. "How did you survive ten days without me?"

"I didn't." He flopped onto the cot and dramatically laid the back of his hand over his forehead like an overwhelmed damsel from the middle ages. He put on a high, womanly voice that sounded bizarre with his natural Australian accent. "I'm nothing without you, darling. I've wasted away. Please" —he grasped his throat and gasped— "revive me!"

I kicked his knee and stifled a laugh. "Give me a break. Where's my phone? I need to check my messages."

He reached under the cot into his bag and tossed the phone to me. "I turned it off because it wouldn't stop ringing. You got a bunch of blank texts and missed calls from an unknown number. You think someone's stalking you?"

The hair stood up on the back of my neck. "It's probably nothing."

As soon as I booted up my phone, all of the messages, missed calls, and emails poured in. Taj beatboxed a rhythm to go along with the constant chimes and random sounds. When I turned the phone to silent, Taj ended with a improvised fill. I sat on the edge of his cot, and he rested his chin on my shoulder.

"Gah!" I swept him aside. "Your massive amounts of facial hair feel like Brillo pads on my skin. Get off me, you hobo."

"If I'd known you were going to call me a hobo, I would have sold your phone for a quick buck."

"I'm surprised you didn't."

"You know I only steal from the rich." He rolled over and propped his bare feet on the wall. "Where to next? I know we said India, and it's, like, right there, but I'm feeling somewhere Mediterranean. You ever been to Greece? I could go for some traditional spanakopita. Have you tried baklava? It's the food of the gods."

"I thought chocolate was the food of the gods," I said, scrolling through my missed calls list. "Or is it honey?"

"There's honey in baklava," Taj countered. "What say you?"

I tapped on an interesting-looking voicemail and put the phone to my ear.

"Hey, Bex. I'm not sure if you remember me, but this is Mr. Belford from Doveport High School. You were in my tenth grade English class. Anyway, I'm actually the principal now, and Career Day is coming up. I noticed you have an impressive social media following and thought it might make for a cool presentation. The kids needs to hear from someone who didn't follow a traditional career path so they know they have options. It's next Friday, so if you're interested, give me a call! Otherwise, I hope you're doing well. Hope to hear from you soon, Bex."

Taj drummed on my arm. "Who was that? You look weird."

"My old English teacher. He wants me to do a presentation for career day."

"In Oregon?"

"Yeah."

"When is it?"

I checked the date of the voicemail. It had come last week. "This Friday."

"Oh." Taj cleared his throat with a thin cough, something he did when he was uncomfortable or disappointed. "So you're going home then."

I checked my bank account and my airline reward points. I had plenty of money for a ticket home, and I could make it there by Friday for the presentation. It had been over two years since I'd seen my mother. Maybe it was time to stop in.

I pulled the band keeping Taj's hair in its bun and watched his luscious curls tumble around his face. I patted his cheek. "Don't worry, Beard Guy. I'll be back before you know it."

2

_____

*H*ugging Taj goodbye at the airport drop-off felt like leaving my long-lost brother behind. Once I made it past security, I turned around and saw him waiting for me to disappear into the crowd, just as I'd watched Nahla go a day earlier. We waved to each other, and he made a "get out of here" motion with his hand. I flashed him the peace sign and went on my way.

Hours later, after an overnight layover in China and a quicker one in San Francisco, my third plane in two days finally approached my home state. The floor rumbled beneath my feet, and my elbow slipped off the arm rest, sending my head off its perch. I jolted out of my nap and found myself face to face with the smiling flight attendant.

"Anything else I can get you before we land, dear?" she asked.

"I'm okay. Thanks."

"Sure thing, honey."

She continued up the aisle, pushing the cart full of drinks. I tapped the screen on the seatback in front of me and pulled up the flight map. We had an hour to go before we landed in Portland. From there, it would be another few hours' drive to my hometown of Doveport. The last leg of travel time always felt the longest. Seconds expanded into minutes, minutes into hours.

The line at the tiny bathrooms formed down the aisles, torturing my full bladder. The flight attendants kindly asked those waiting to return to their seats until the bathroom was open again. When I saw the occupancy light go off, I darted out of my row, danced past a middle-aged man as he struggled with his seatbelt, and slipped into the bathroom ahead of the others waiting. It was a dirty trick, but with all the time I'd spent on airplanes, I'd learned you had to make things go your way. Otherwise, you squirmed in your seat for the rest of the flight, made a run for the busy bathrooms in the terminal, and waited in line there anyway.

I rinsed the oils from my face and patted myself dry with coarse paper towels then checked myself in the minuscule mirror. A red blotch stretched across my cheek from where I'd been leaning on my hand. My eyes were bloodshot from hours of restless, inefficient plane naps. My hair stuck up in the back like a peacock's ruffled plumage. I wet my hand and attempted to flatten it down, but it stubbornly remained upright. Hat day, it was.

When I slid out of the restroom, the middle-aged guy with seatbelt issues glared at me as we exchanged places. I gave him my best grin and returned to my seat. Another rumble shook the plane, and the "fasten seatbelts" sign flashed on. The overhead system crackled on.

"Good morning, everyone," an even-toned, bodiless voice said. "This is your pilot speaking from the cockpit. We're heading into some turbulence, so please take your seats and fasten your seatbelts as soon as possible. Our ETA to Portland is about fifty-five minutes."

My stomach dropped with the next bump, and a few people exclaimed. In the row across from mine, a small child started to howl. His mother rocked him back and forth and whispered soothing nonsense into his ear, but the kid could not be consoled. The passenger in front of them threw a dirty look over her shoulder and rolled her eyes. As the child's cries increased in volume, the area around us echoed with annoyed huffs and disapproving mutters.

"Sheesh, how hard is it to control your child?"

"Probably tired, poor thing."

"Ugh, can someone get it to shut up?"

I kicked the seat in front of me, and its passenger—one of those with too much to say about the woman's parenting skills—glanced into the aisle at me.

"Can I help you?" he asked rudely.

"Yeah, I don't have a problem with the baby, but your voice is starting to grate on me," I told him. "You don't have kids, do you?"

His lip curled. "No."

"Then shut up and mind your own business."

The man opened his mouth to reply and thought better of it. As the child let out another anguished wail, he sneered and returned his gaze forward.

I ripped a sheet of paper out of my notebook and leaned across the aisle. "Hey, buddy! Check this out."

The child turned in his mother's arms to face me, the crying stalled by his shock that another human being was speaking to him. I waved the paper, and his attention snapped to the flapping sound it made.

"Wanna see a magic trick?" I asked.

With a series of flourishes, I made a show of folding the sheet of paper into a paper crane. When I was finished, I presented the origami piece to the child. His little cherub cheeks—pink with exhaustion—plumped up as he smiled. He took the paper crane in his tiny, chubby fingers and immediately shoved it into his mouth.

"Oh, gosh!"

I reached for the crane, but his mother was already on the ball. She plucked the paper from between the toddler's gums and stuck it in between his bare toes. As he busied himself with trying to free it, the mother smiled at me.

"He's at that stage where he wants to put everything in his mouth," she said. "Thank you, by the way. He needed a distraction, and I stupidly forgot to pack his favorite toy in our carry-on."

"No problem."

The woman nodded toward the man in front of me and whispered, "Thanks for speaking up too. Not many people would do that."

The toddler squeaked with joy as he pulled the paper crane from between his toes and crushed the wings in his tomato-sized fists. His mother offered him a container of mini graham crackers, and he tossed the crane aside in favor of the snacks. I grinned as he munched happily, the tear stains on his onesie forgotten.

"It's no big deal," I told the woman. "Some people are jerks. It was the least I could do."

"Do you have children?" she asked me, bouncing the boy up and down on her thigh.

"No," I replied. "But I like them, and they usually like me."

The boy tossed a graham cracker into my lap, laughed,

19

and reached his short little limbs out to me. I offered my arms, and his mother lifted him across the aisle.

"Are you sure?" she said. "He can be kind of a handful."

"I don't mind."

She passed the toddler to me. He grabbed the zipper of my hoodie and flung it up and down at the quickest pace he could manage, laughing hysterically the entire time. A few minutes later, he passed out in my lap. For the rest of the flight, he snoozed against my chest, silent except for the bee-like buzz of his breath.

I PARTED ways with my new friends at baggage claim, waving goodbye to the toddler with a goofy smile. As I headed to the pickup loop for arriving flights, I dialed my mother's number. It went straight to voicemail.

"Hey, Mom," I said. "It's Bex. I'm on my way out. Just wondering if you're here yet. See you soon. Can't wait."

On the curb of the pickup loop, I stretched my arms over my head then bent over to touch my toes. It was a busy day at the airport. Drivers honked and shouted as they fought for a spot closest to the curb to pick up their visitors. People heaved heavy baggage into trunks and backseats. They squeezed into hotel shuttles and minivans. An annoyed cop kept the traffic moving through the loop as best as he could.

While I waited, I checked my social media feeds. I hadn't posted anything since the beginning of my retreat in Kathmandu, and my followers were getting hungry for content. A few of them had already unfollowed me. The Internet was fickle that way. I scrolled through Twitter.

When will The Wanderer return from war?

Bex, we miss you!

Naturally, my home feed wouldn't be complete without a few dozen memes of my followers expressing their woes about my leave of absence. I liked as many posts as possible before my brain begged for me to look away from the endless timeline of other people's opinions.

I uploaded a series of photos from Kathmandu, typed up a shorter version of the blog post about my break from social media, and posted all of it to Instagram. Within seconds, the likes started pouring in, as well as a few comments.

You're back!

Glad to see you didn't get lost in Nepal!

Have you ever thought about competing on the Amazing Race?

I muted notifications. The constant vibrations drove me crazy if I left them on, but my phone buzzed anyway. I checked the screen. One text message from an unknown number. I tapped on it and found a single word: *m0m*

A little zap tingled through my brain, as if a tiny jolt of electricity had been administered to my skull. My phone buzzed again: *n0 m0m.*

I dialed my mother's number. Again, it went to voicemail. Without leaving a message, I hung up and dialed once more. This time, to my great relief, someone picked up.

"Mom?" I said before the other person had time to say something. "Is that you?"

"Hi, Bex. No, it's Melba. Do you remember me?"

"Mom's friend? Of course I do. Is everything okay?"

"Everything's fine," Melba said. "What about with you?"

"I'm at the airport," I told her. "Is Mom on her way? Did she forget her phone or something?"

A rustle echoed through the phone as Melba put her hand over the mouthpiece and called to someone across the room.

In a muffled voice, she asked, "*Lydia*, did you tell Bex you would pick her up from the airport today?"

If my mother replied, I couldn't hear it. Another rustle as Melba came back on the line.

"I'm sorry, Bex," she said. "Your mother forgot to tell me you were flying in today. Can you hire a car to drop you off? I'd come get you, but it's a long drive, and I can't leave your mother alone."

My face wrinkled with consternation. "Can't leave her alone? Did something happen?"

"Lydia, your appointment is next week," Melba called. "Next week! No, don't get in the car. We're not going anywhere—Bex, I have to go. See you soon!"

"Melba, wait—"

The phone clicked as she hung up on me. I stared at the blank screen until another brain zap made me wince and an incoming text message showed up: 0h n0.

"Shut up," I muttered and clicked the phone to sleep mode.

A FEW MINUTES LATER, I sat in the backseat of what was sure to be the most expensive Uber ride of my life. The driver, a guy in his early twenties with stretched earlobes and faded purple hair, checked the map on his phone.

"Doveport, huh?" he said. "This says it's two hours away."

"Yup."

"That's far."

"Uh-huh."

He looked to where I was sprawled out across the backseat. "My mom gets mad if I don't make it home in time for dinner—"

"Dude, I'm sure your app shows you the rider's destination before you accept the job," I interrupted. "So you're either painfully unobservant or you don't want to make it home in time for dinner. Either way, make up your mind because I have places to be. You wanna drive me or not? I tend to leave decent tips."

"Do you care if I vape?"

"Have at it."

He happily took a rainbow pen from the glove compartment, took a huge hit, and blew the vapor through the cracked window. Then he pulled off the curb and into traffic.

An half hour later, we got stuck behind a crash. As we inched across the asphalt, blocked in by a wall of other cars, the driver kept glancing at me in his rearview mirror.

"You look familiar," he finally said. "Do I know you from somewhere?"

"Instagram, maybe. Or Twitter."

"Nah, that's not it."

He continued to peer at me. The car crept toward the stationary one in front of us.

"Watch the road!" I scolded.

He slammed on the brakes and sent me flying forward. The car stopped a few inches from the next person's bumper. "Aha!" he said. "I saw you on the news, like, a hundred years ago."

My stomach clenched. "What?"

"Yeah, when all those kids went missing," he rambled. "I was, like, six years old. My mom went nuts. I told her, Mom, we don't live anywhere near that area, but she was all, Caleb, I don't care where we live, I'm watching you like a hawk. Anyway, it's not like anything happened to me, but weren't you one of the milk carton kids?"

"I've never been on a milk carton."

Caleb made a quick lane change to get around the slow-moving car in front of us. "Are you sure? I'm positive it was you."

"Six years old, huh? Childhood memories aren't the most reliable."

He took another long look at me in the mirror. "Yeah, you're probably right. Whatever. You said you're on Instagram? What's your handle?"

"The Wanderer."

"Oh, you're *that* chick! My girlfriend's obsessed with you." Another quick swerve into a different lane as we passed a bashed-up sedan. "She even made me stop wearing deodorant, but that didn't last long once she realized how gross I smell when I sweat."

As Caleb babbled on, I leaned my head against the window, closed my eyes, and wished he was taciturn and unsociable like most of the other Uber drivers I'd had over the years. No luck.

EVENTUALLY, Caleb's directional app led him off the main roads and into the shadow of the trees. The Pacific Northwest was as beautiful as I remembered it. With October soon approaching, the trees had just begun to turn colors. The green leaves were tipped with orange, yellow, and red. Misty clouds floated though the foliage, as low to the road as the car. If an elf or fairy stepped from the mysterious woods, it wouldn't feel like much of a surprise. As we crossed a bridge, Caleb gazed with wonder at a small waterfall as it cascaded from the rocks and into a river.

"Wow," he said. "I've never been up this way before. Is it always like this?"

"Magical? Pretty much."

"I love it."

We drove a little farther. One car passed in the opposite direction, but other than that, there weren't many humans besides us. Caleb shifted in his seat and checked his map again.

"Is this the right way?" he asked. "I feel like we're in the middle of nowhere."

"Doveport *is* the middle of nowhere," I told him. "Don't worry. We're almost there. As soon as the trees open up—"

The road widened as soon as the words left my mouth, the foliage thinned, and the world beyond the woods became visible again. Doveport lay beneath the forested hill, the only town on this little section of Oregon's coast. From where we were, I spied the short strip of buildings and restaurants we called downtown Doveport, and the neighborhoods that branched out from the center of town. The port itself was tiny and defunct. Once, the citizens of Doveport used it to ship materials in and out. Now, it acted as a nice place to spend a summery Saturday afternoon.

A wave of nostalgia washed over me as we descended into town. We passed the old logging station that had been turned into a collection of hip stores and counter service restaurants. Further up the road was Doveport High School. It looked exactly the same as it did when I graduated over ten years ago. The blue and white paint had recently been refreshed, as had the enormous portrait of our mascot—the Doveport Shark—that decorated the side of the gymnasium. Teenagers jogged around the track while the marching band practiced on the football field. The football players warmed up on the sidelines, eyeing the band with dubious expressions.

We drove through the downtown area. There was Dove's Pub, the locals' favorite place for fish and chips, burgers, and sports. Since it was a nice day, they had the garage doors open, exposing the pub's interior to the outside world. I caught a glimpse of a few familiar faces as we passed by.

The neighborhood houses were spaced far apart. Each homeowner had a yard the size of Texas to take care of. Some of them managed. Others let their lot grow wild like the woods. The bushes in my mother's front yard were so overgrown that Caleb drove right past the driveway.

"You missed it," I said.

Caleb put the car in reverse and backed up to the curb. He squinted through the bushes. "This is it? I can't see a house."

"It's behind all the trees." I pulled up my Uber app, added a large tip for Caleb, and climbed out of the car. "Thanks, Caleb. Get back to Portland safely."

"Will do. Take care!"

I hiked my backpack higher on my shoulders and vaulted the low gate that bordered my old house, avoiding the rusty lock that needed too much persuasion to open. Though Mom had never been particularly fond of gardening, this was over the top. The grass was knee high except for around the footpath. Rotting apples littered the ground beneath the trees. Weeds and wild vines crept up the spruces and firs.

My mother's car was parked in the driveway. It was coated in pollen and fallen leaves, as if it hadn't been driven since last autumn. Another car—Melba's, I guessed—was parked there too. The house itself, a pretty green cabin with a natural wooden wrap-around porch, blended in so well with its surroundings that I tripped over the first vine-covered step. The door was unlocked, so I walked right in.

It smelled different. My mother's favorite cinnamon scented candles had not been lit in a while, leaving behind the musky outdoorsy smell that I never minded and a hint of unwashed laundry that I minded quite a bit. The candles were gone entirely. There were none on the mantel, nor on the side tables beside the leather couch, nor on the bookshelf full of classic novels.

I checked the coat closet. My mother—who was a nurse at the local clinic—usually kept her scrubs hung here for easy access, but it was all winter coats and rain jackets. I pulled out a familiar fabric and found a coat of mine from several years ago. The sleeves were two inches too short. Why had my mother kept it? I laid it over the edge of the sofa to remind myself to donate it later.

"Mom?" I called up the stairs as I shrugged off my raincoat and hung it up. "It's me, Bex! Are you home?"

Footsteps pattered overhead, and my mother appeared at the top of the stairs. She beamed from ear to ear when she spotted me, but I couldn't return the expression. In two years, she had aged ten.

"My baby!" she exclaimed, tossing her arms around my neck and pulling me close. She smelled like talcum powder and old perfume. "I miss you so much during the day."

I gently dislodged myself from her embrace and held her at arm's length for a better look at her. Since the last time I'd visited Doveport, her brown hair had turned entirely gray, the lines around her eyes deepened to grooves, and she'd lost a tooth on the bottom middle of her mouth.

"Mom, what's wrong?" I asked. "Are you sick? You look—"

"Oh, I'm fine!" She waved my concern off and sidestepped

me. "Come on into the kitchen, hun. I made your favorite after-school snack: apples and peanut butter!"

Confused, I followed her to the back of the house, where the window over the sink looked out onto an amazing view. Behind our house, you could see all the way to the port, the water, and the mountains beyond. When I was a kid, I spent most of my time on the back porch with a pair of binoculars.

"Don't forget to wash your hands," Mom ordered, turning the water on for me. "Who knows what kind of germs you pick up at that high school?"

"I haven't done my career presentation yet."

"You have a presentation coming up, huh?" She opened and closed drawer after drawer, looking for something. "It's not a group project, is it? I know you hate those. Where are all the damn knives?"

I dried my hands and pulled open the silverware drawer. Spoons, forks, but no knives. The knife block that had sat on the counter since my birth was gone too. Hell, even the sharpened fork for serving roast was nowhere to be found.

My mother rinsed an apple in the sink and set it on the table, in front of the chair where I'd eaten all my meals growing up. "Guess you'll have to bite into it, kiddo. Sit down. Tell me how your day was."

I slid into my seat across from her, wondering what kind of weird alternate universe I'd arrived home to. Mom smiled at me.

"Well?" she prompted. "You haven't had any more trouble with that Lauren girl, have you? If I have to speak to her mother, I will."

I reached into the back of my memories to figure out who she was talking about. "Lauren Moore? Mom, I haven't seen her in ten years."

28

Someone cleared their throat, and I glanced over my shoulder to see who it was. Melba leaned against the archway into the kitchen. As a caretaker for the elderly, she almost always wore navy blue scrubs.

"Good to see you, Bex," she said.

"You too," I replied. "Is everything okay? Mom seems—"

"Off?" Melba asked. "It's because she thinks you're fifteen."

3

"*I*t comes and goes."

As Mom tended to her wild garden out back, pruning dead ends off the tomato vines, Melba and I rested in the Adirondack chairs on the porch. Melba sipped pink lemonade, but mine went untouched. Beads of condensation rolled off the glass and absorbed into the arm of the chair, leaving a dark ring on the light wood.

I rested my elbows on my lap and studied my mother, on her knees in the dirt. "How long has it been like this?"

"It started getting bad about a year ago." Melba drew her knit cardigan tightly to her body. Though the sun was out, the days grew chilly quickly at this time of year. "At first, she'd have moments here and there, but if I reminded her of what year it was, she snapped out of it. Now, she spends about half of her time thinking it's 2004."

"Why didn't you tell me?"

Melba inhaled deeply through her nose and out through her mouth. "Honey, you were almost impossible to reach. I'm not tech-savvy like all your friends. I couldn't reach you on

Instapic or whatever it's called. Every time I tried to call you, I either got your voicemail or a robotic lady told me the number was out of service."

My phone buzzed in my pocket, accompanied by the familiar twang of electricity in my head. I left the device where it was. "The candles are gone."

"She would forget she lit them," Melba said. "One of them fell over and caught the curtains on fire. Thankfully, no one was hurt and nothing else was damaged, but it was enough of a warning sign to get rid of them."

"And her job?"

"I persuaded the clinic to let her continue under supervision for a while," she answered. "I thought it was important that she stick to her routine, despite the dementia. The more she deteriorated, the less able she was to go into work, so I convinced her to retire early. Thankfully, Lydia was smart. She started a retirement fund as soon as she turned eighteen, so you don't need to worry about paying for her care."

"I wasn't worried," I said. "She was always good with money. So you're her caretaker now?"

Melba swept her hair from the back of her neck. "She wouldn't let anyone else in the house, but she'll let me do things for her because we were already friends." Her face fell, and she turned toward the water to hide it from me. "We met after you graduated. Half the time, she doesn't know who I am."

"I'm sorry." I drew abstract art in the condensation of my glass, whirling patterns of dewdrops here and there. "This is partially my fault. I should have come home more often."

"I'm not blaming you, Bex," Melba said. "It's tough, but I understand why this place makes you anxious, even though I wasn't around when all of those things happened."

31

My phone buzzed again. This time, I dug it out of my pocket and checked the messages with the hopes of discontinuing them. The first read: *fir3*. The second read: *us3L3ss*. I deleted both and turned off the device.

"Bex!" Mom waved a handful of tomatoes in the air. It was late in the season for tomato-picking, but the fruits looked perfect. "Look at these beauties! You can eat them right off the vine!"

"They look great, Mom!" I called back, raising a thumbs-up in her direction. "Keep at it." Mom buried her head in the vines again, and a heavy weight laid upon my chest. "What do I do, Melba? I'm only supposed to be here for a few days."

Melba rested a wizened hand on my knee. "Go about your business, honey. Give your presentation at the school then head out if you like. You have a life. No one's going to judge you for returning to it."

"I wasn't prepared for this."

In the garden, Mom whooped with joy as she plucked another plump, candy-red tomato from the vine and added it to the canvas bag at her feet.

Melba sighed. "No one ever is."

MELBA MADE fettuccine while I helped Mom prepare a salad with the fresh vegetables from the garden. The knives, it turned out, were hidden in a locked drawer, another precaution to keep my mother safe. As I sliced the tomatoes, she gave me pointers on how not to squish them, the same pointers I'd heard over and over as a teenager.

On the bright side, Mom was able to take care of herself. She showered, brushed her teeth, and dressed in pajamas without mine or Melba's help. Shortly after, Melba bid us goodnight to return to her own family. The house fell quiet except for the wind whistling through the trees outside and the faint whoosh of far-off waves.

I fell onto the couch with a cup of chamomile tea, switched on the TV, and lowered the volume so it wouldn't bother Mom. After ten minutes of watching a nature documentary about sharks, I remembered my phone had been off for the entire evening. When I switched it on, my notifications were blowing up. My followers responded to my most recent post with exaggerated enthusiasm. I scrolled through the comments and replied to the ones that were most creative, getting lost in the world of social media. It was easy to feel comfortable behind the mask of my adventures. No one who followed me knew the real thoughts coursing through my brain or about the little zaps that no MRI or CT scan could make sense of. I winced as another one hit.

B3hind u.

A pair of warm arms encircled me from behind and squeezed me tight. "Honey! Why didn't you tell me your flight got in? I thought I was supposed to pick you up from the airport."

As Mom circled around to the front of the couch, sat next to me, and covered us with a blanket I'd crocheted in fifth grade, I took in her clear eyes and concerned expression. She was lucid.

"I couldn't get ahold of you," I said, unsure of how much my mother knew about her own diagnosis. "You weren't answering your phone."

Her smile dropped slowly. "I wasn't around, was I?"

"No. You weren't around."

She traced the lines that had begun to deepen at the corners of my eyes. "Where did these come from?"

"I have a terrible tendency to lose every pair of sunglasses I own," I said. "It results in a lot of squinting at the sun."

Mom chuckled. "You get that from me. I used to buy them in bulk."

I offered her my mug of tea. "I missed you."

"I missed *you*." She tapped my nose like she used to do when I was small then inhaled the steam rising from the mug. "I miss myself a lot too."

I fixed the blanket to cover more of her lap. "You're still here, Mom."

SHE DOZED off a few minutes after the shark documentary ended. I gently woke her long enough to get her into bed, then tiptoed down the hall to my childhood bedroom. When I flipped the switch on the wall, the overhead light flickered feebly before gaining the strength to turn on. It cast a yellowish light over my past life.

Before I'd left Doveport, Mom promised I'd always have a place to come home to if I needed somewhere to land. She hadn't taken the Sum41 and Blink182 posters off the wall or gotten rid of my embroidered patch collection or donated the beat-up skate shoes in the closet. My high school diploma sat framed on the desk, alongside a stack of clipped, yellowing newspaper articles with headlines like *Police Stumped Over Missing Teenagers* and *Doveport Loses Another High Schooler.* I tipped the stack into the trash.

I flopped belly down on the twin-sized bed. My feet hung off the end. Someone had cleaned in here, either Mom or Melba, because the sheets smelled like fresh, lavender-scented laundry detergent, and not one speck of dust dared to float up my nose to make me sneeze. I rolled over and stared at the ceiling. When I was ten, I'd drawn a map of the stars and planets up there in various colors of permanent marker. Though Mom had scolded me for it, she never painted over my clumsy artwork. Ten-year-old me, however, wasn't particularly good at astronomy. Orion's belt had four stars and Pluto was closest to the sun.

The last time I was home, during some downtime between trips, I hadn't noticed the gaps forming in Mom's memory. Looking back on all the times she misplaced her keys or forgot someone's name, I wondered if I hadn't been paying enough attention. My thoughts spun faster and faster. Was it my fault for not being here?

I tumbled off the bed and to my feet. Jet lag danced like a court jester in the space behind my eyelids, keeping my brain and body far too awake for this time of evening. I checked on Mom to make sure she was asleep, then jogged downstairs, grabbed my jacket, and headed out.

IT WAS A COOL NIGHT, in the mid-fifties or so. The wind blowing in from the coast found its way beneath the seams of my coat and playfully tickled my skin. I walked with my head bowed and my hands in my pockets. Doveport had a way of sucking up light at night. The streets were dark except for the small circles beneath the overhead lamps.

The houses, too, were dark. This neighborhood was full of families with kids who had school in the morning. Like them, I should have gone to bed early, but I hadn't done anything to prepare for my career presentation tomorrow morning.

I walked all the way to the port. Boats rocked gently, moored to the docks. Water lapped at their sides like thirsty golden retrievers. The moonlight cast a silver sheen across the marina. I skipped a few stones, practicing the perfect flick of the wrist to get the most bounces. After my mind quieted, I headed to downtown Doveport.

Dove's Pub was not open twenty-four hours, but you couldn't tell that to the locals. No matter the time of day, the pub had customers. I arrived around midnight, and the place was bustling with older gentlemen with handlebar mustaches and corduroy pants and elderly women with faded tattoos and curled hair. You know, the locals.

"Is that Bex Lennon?" Arthur McKinnon, one of the aforementioned gentlemen who had a designated stool at the bar, clapped me on the back when I walked in. "How are you, sweetheart?"

"I'm hanging in there, Art," I said, climbing onto the stool next to his. "How about you?"

"Oh, much the same. What are you having?"

"Whatever's good."

Arthur waved at the bartender. "Two buddy brews!" He turned to me. "What brings you home, kiddo? We haven't seen you in a while. Done gallivanting around the world, are you?"

"Still gallivanting," I assured him. "Mr. Belford asked me to give a talk tomorrow at the high school for career day."

Arthur elbowed me excitedly. "Look at you go. What's your talk about?"

"I'm improvising," I admitted. "I guess I'll hit all the important points about being a social media influencer: how to brand yourself, gain and maintain a follower count, find your niche—"

Arthur waved his empty beer glass. "Whoa, lassie. I have

no idea what you're talking about. What do you do for your job?"

I showed him my Instagram page and scrolled through a few of my most popular posts. "People follow and engage with me. The more followers I have, the more successful I am."

He peered down his nose and tilted the phone to see it from a better angle. "But how do you make money?"

"I partner with advertisers to show off their products," I told him. "I also have a donation page. It's kind of weird to ask people for money, but you'd be surprised how many of my followers donate because they want to see me go more places."

"Why don't they go see the places for themselves?"

I lifted my shoulders. "Who knows? Lack of funds or motivation. Some of them are scared to travel or fly on planes. Some of them don't have time. Others *are* travelers who rely on me to scout places for them. It depends on the person."

The bartender returned with two beers. As he set them on the coasters, his eyes glanced between my open Instagram app and my face. "Hey, Bex! I didn't know you were back."

"Austin? Wow, I almost didn't recognize you with the beard."

Austin beamed and stroked his impressive amount of blond facial hair. Between that, his tattooed forearms, flannel shirt, and suspenders, he looked like every other hipster in Oregon. "It's good to see you. You missed our ten-year reunion."

"I think I was in Berlin during our ten-year reunion," I told him with an apologetic grimace. "How was it?"

"Pretty cool," Austin answered. "Most of the people who

showed up still live around here anyway. Only difference is they all have babies now. Except for me. No babies here."

"Me either."

He cleared his throat. "And we did a little moment of silence. You know... for the ones we lost. It was nice."

"Mm-hmm."

Austin nervously tapped his fingers on the counter. "Anyway, glad you're back. I should check on the other customers."

As Austin sidled off to the other end of the bar, Arthur chuckled low in his throat. "Funny, isn't it? How novel you are to everyone who never left."

I clinked my glass against his. "That's all I am, Art. A novelty."

"Hush your mouth."

We nursed our drinks in comfortable silence. Arthur's familiar scent of cigar smoke and brine might have bothered someone else, but I found it comfortable. He came from a generation of sailors and blue-collared workers. The evidence was in his callused palms and weathered, leathery skin. He was one of Davenport's protectors, a strong but gentle man who took pride in his hometown, no matter how he aged.

He nudged me in the side and pointed to the TV mounted above the bar. "Check this out. Some crazy man escaped from prison. Austin, turn up the volume."

As Austin did so, the reporter's voice filled the bar, but not many patrons cared enough to watch.

"—could be armed and dangerous," the reporter said. "Norman Beers was being held at Oregon State Penitentiary, a maximum security prison. Officials claim he could not have escaped without help from either an internal or external source."

A picture of Beers appeared adjacent to the reporter's feed. He didn't look like the average convict. In his mug shot, he wore a clean collared shirt. His hair was neat and tidy, and he didn't look particularly put out by his incarceration. The picture could have passed for his driver's license photo.

"Beers was incarcerated for attempted murder and is considered a highly violent individual. Police are warning individuals to steer clear of Beers if spotted and call the emergency hotline as soon as possible. Next, a big storm is moving up the coast—"

Arthur scoffed and rolled his eyes. "Unbelievable. How does a guy like that get out of a maximum security prison? Gotta have someone on the inside."

"Totally," Austin agreed without contributing anything deeper.

"We'll keep you updated on the storm as it develops," the reporter continued. She shuffled the papers on her desk and her expression grew stern. "In other news, the two missing girls from Doveport, Oregon still have not been located—"

My head jerked up, as did everyone else's in the bar. With rapt attention, we all stared at the newswoman as she spoke.

"Thirteen-year-old Carly Javier and fifteen-year-old Gemma Johnson both disappeared during or after football games at the local high school, two weeks apart," the reporter said. "Police have no leads on their whereabouts, and this isn't the first time Doveport has been hit with a series of disappearances. Five teenagers disappeared in 2004. Only one returned home safely, but the other four were never recovered. The police are asking locals to keep an eye out and to call this hotline if the girls are spotted."

A number in bright red showed up on the bottom of the

screen. As I typed it into my phone, my brain zapped over and over again. Text messages from an unknown number poured into my inbox, binging wildly. Arthur peered over my shoulder.

"You're popular," he said gruffly.

I clutched my head, hoping the pressure would make it stop zinging like oil on a hot frying pan. My ears filled with white noise as my phone buzzed over and over again. My stomach churned, threatening to dump the few sips of beer I'd had.

"Sorry, Art." I tumbled off the stool and wobbled away. "I gotta get out of here. I'll buy you a drink next time!"

I stumbled out of the pub, and the blast of cold air cooled my sizzling head. My nose stung as I took deep breaths to flood my lungs with the same refreshing feeling of jumping into a cold lake. My phone slowed its erratic beeping and my head cleared, leaving a dull ache behind.

H@pp3ning ag@in.

F1nd them?

n0rth3@st

I deleted all of the cryptic text messages and blocked the unknown number, though I knew from experience it wouldn't stop new messages from coming in. I sat on the curb to catch my breath. This was all too surreal. It was as if I'd been catapulted back to 2004, when the entire town of Doveport lived in fear of the inevitable.

The sound of shattered glass echoed in the alley behind Dove's Pub, followed by a series of frantic whispers. I pushed myself off the curb, stuck to the wall, and peeked into the dark alley. A bunch of teenagers—five or six all around the age of fifteen or sixteen—rifled through an open truck full of merchandise that had yet to be unloaded. The kids had managed to unbox a case of beer and were currently in the process of shoving as many bottles as they could hold under their shirts.

I shined my phone light down the dark alley and shouted, "Hey!"

"Shit! Let's get out of here!"

"Don't drop the beer!"

"Forget the beer!"

The teenagers scattered like cockroaches. Most of them escaped through the opposite end of the alley, but two were stupid enough to come my way. The first one—a boy in a hoodie—slipped past, but I caught the second thief by the arm and yanked them to a stop.

"It wasn't my idea!" the kid burst out breathlessly. "I don't drink. I didn't want to do this, I swear! I was just trying to fit in."

I swept the black knit cap off the thief's head, finding scared eyes and a hairstyle similar to my own beneath it. The kid was no older than fifteen, and if the chattering teeth were any indication, they were telling the truth about not wanting to be there.

"Please," the kid breathed. "I can't get in trouble for this. They'll send me to another home, and this is the best one I've had so far."

"You're a foster kid?"

"Yeah."

"Who are you staying with?"

"Edison Maxx," the kid replied. "I really like her. She's nice to me. Please don't tell on me. I promise I'll never do anything stupid like this again."

I let the kid's arm go but kept a firm grip on the hood of their puffy jacket. "Edison Maxx, huh? That's a name I haven't heard in a while. Does she still live on Apricot Avenue?"

"Yes."

"Come on then. I'll take you home."

Like a slippery snake, the kid whipped their arms out of the sleeves and danced out of reach, leaving me with an empty jacket. "You can't tell on me. I won't go back to the state."

"I promise I won't say anything." I folded the jacket and offered it to the kid. "Put it on. It's cold outside, and Edison will kill me if I'm the reason her kid gets a cough."

Tentatively, the kid took the jacket. "Who are you?"

"Bex Lennon. And you?"

"I'm nobody."

4

_E_dison Maxx's house hadn't changed in the last two years. As my teenaged charge led me up the front walk, a fresh wave of feelings washed over me. Like my mother's, Edison's house lay deep in the woods, but the nature surrounding it was less wild. No vines or weeds laced around my ankles as we followed the cobbled foot path. The yard was trimmed and neat. As the trees thinned, the house itself came into view, a historical building that Edison had redesigned with mid-century modern architecture in mind. The flat planes, clean lines, and big windows focused on bringing the outside in. Edison, like most people who lived in Doveport, valued the Pacific Northwest for its beautiful naturality.

"Are you sure you're not going to say anything?" the kid asked as we approached the front door. "Because this feels like you're going to say something."

"You want to sneak in the window or something?"

The kid squinted up at the second floor. The entire side of the house was basically made of glass. Unless you scaled a tree and hopped over to the balcony—which looked dangerous but possible—you weren't getting in.

"I'll pass."

"Guess you'll have to take my word for it then. You got a key?"

"Yeah, but you should knock," the kid said. "I don't know you, man. You could be an ex-con. I'm not letting you in without Edison's permission."

I rolled my eyes and rapped my knuckles against the door. We waited in awkward silence for a few minutes. The kid rocked back and forth on their feet, nervously kneading their hands. The curtain fluttered, and Edison peeked through the window to see who was on her front porch. She spotted the kid first and visibly sighed. Then her eyes wandered to me. My stomach buckled as I waved. Her eyebrows rose in what I hoped was pleasant surprise, and she threw the latch back to unlock the door.

"Bex Lennon," she said. "I'll be damned."

"Hi, Tommy."

She grabbed the sleeves of my coat to pull me across the threshold. "You know I hate that stupid nickname."

Edison's hugs were memorably aggressive. She yanked me in, thumped me on the back, and squeezed my arms with enough pressure to leave a mark.

"So... you two know each other?" the kid asked, pointing between us.

"We go way back," Edison said. She cast me aside to grab the kid's jacket strings. "But don't try to distract me from the real issue at hand. What are you doing out so late?"

The kid glanced at me for help. I shrugged.

"I promised not to rat you out," I said. "Not that you wouldn't have to tell her yourself."

The kid's shoulders slumped. "Mallory and Tank dared me to meet them outside Dove's to hang out. They said if I didn't go, they'd stop hanging out with me."

I cleared my throat. "And?"

"*And* they tried to steal some beer from a Dove's storage truck before Bex caught us," the kid admitted. "But I didn't join in! I don't even like beer. It tastes like crap."

Edison crossed her arms. "You know a kid named Tank?"

"It's not his real name."

"I sure as hell hope not."

The kid bowed their head and looked up through their eyelashes like a puppy begging for affection. "So I'm not in trouble?"

Edison pinched the kid's cheek. "Oh, you're definitely in trouble. Grounded for a week. You go to school and you come straight home. That's it."

The kid's face lit up, relieved Edison wasn't resorting to more extreme punishments, like contacting the foster system. "That's fine! I can hang out with Avery."

"If she lets you." Edison whacked the kid's butt. "Get upstairs. It's late, and you have school tomorrow. I'm not going to be the one to drag you out of bed."

The kid dodged out of range as Edison aimed another light smack. He saluted me and darted up to the second story, calling, "Avery, your mom didn't kill me!"

I jabbed my thumb toward the receding teenager. "I never caught her name. His name?"

"Their name," Edison corrected me. "That's Cade. They're non-binary. They prefer gender neutral pronouns, but they won't get too offended if you say she or her. They're pretty easy-going."

"They, their, they, their," I murmured, trying to stick the

kid's preferences in my head, knowing it was important. "I got it, I got it."

"It was a little confusing at first for me too," Edison said. "We've got a lot of kids who identify in ways I've never heard of. There are so many labels these days that I need a damn cheat sheet half the time."

She waved me into the kitchen, turned on the electric kettle, and patted the seat next to her in the breakfast nook. We settled against each other with familiar comfort.

"You look good," she said. "Tan and strong. Have you been doing a lot of yoga?"

"Pretty much every day. Don't you follow me on Instagram?"

She propped open the window behind her so the fresh scent of trees floated in to embrace us. "I'm having the kids do a social media detox. I'm trying to set a better example for them, so I haven't been on my phone as much. Last I saw, you were in Nepal? What are you doing home?"

I briefly explained my foray into high school motivational talks.

"Oh, that'll be good for the kids," Edison crooned as the kettle bubbled. "I've always thought you do such a good job balancing real life and social media. They need to see that's possible."

"I think so too," I agreed. "So is Cade one of the kids from Home Safe?"

"Yup. They came into the program about two months ago, but all our volunteers were at capacity." Edison rolled off the cushion in the breakfast nook, poured two mugs of hot water, and placed a tea bag in each. "I couldn't send Cade home. They'd been kicked out, had bruises all over their face. It was bad, so I took them in here."

I accepted the mug and dunked my tea bag up and down to better release the flavors. "I'm sure I've told you before, but what you do is amazing. I'm so proud of how big your program is now."

She cradled her mug on her chest and nodded. "We've expanded to five counties so far, but I eventually want to become a nationwide service. It's hard being a nonprofit though. We rely on donations, so until the money comes in, I can't move forward."

"How do you get donations?"

"We advertise on social media," she said, with a little shrug that seemed to say, *Of course.* "We post some of the kids' stories for people to read, as long as it doesn't put them in any danger. Some of them are from violent homes or have crappy guardians, and the last thing I want to do is put them at risk. But crowdfunding only works if you reach a big crowd. We have trouble with that. Maybe you could help out, huh?" She nudged me and wagged her eyebrows. "What do you say?"

"You don't have someone to run your social media accounts?"

"That's not what I meant, and you know it."

I sipped my tea a minute too soon, scalded the roof of my mouth, and let the liquid dribble back into the cup. "Sorry. I have no idea what you're talking about."

Edison peered at me over the lip of her mug. "Mm-hmm, sure. Get any weird text messages lately, or is that little aspect of your life taboo now too?"

As if to purposely betray me, my phone beeped and a new text from an unknown number popped up on the notification screen. Edison smirked as I winced with the brain zap. I flipped over the phone so she couldn't see it.

"No, read it," she said. "What's it say?"

I pretended to open the message. "It says Edison Maxx is an asshole."

"Oh, please. I rescue abandoned, at-risk youth and find them safe homes to stay," Edison bragged. "I'm so far from asshole, I practically don't have one. *You* on the other hand, have the tendency to bolt when things get tough."

"I like being on the move."

"Sometimes, it feels like you're running away."

I put my face in the path of the cool breeze as it drifted in. "At first, I think I was. After everything that happened—after you went to finish school somewhere else—I didn't have much to keep me here. Sure, I had my mom, but my best friend was gone, and I didn't want some dead-end career here in Doveport. Traveling seemed like the best option, and it turned out that I liked it."

Edison propped her legs on my knees. "I'm not trying to criticize you. You've done well for yourself. I guess I wish you were home more often for my sake. I miss you."

I tickled the top of her foot, and she involuntarily kicked to stop me. "You could have said that in the first place."

Upstairs, punk rock music blared, joined shortly by a louder set of drums, the beat of which was slightly rushed. I glanced up at the ceiling.

"You got Woodstock going on up there or something?" I asked.

"It's Avery," she replied. "She got a part-time job, saved up enough to buy a drum set, then quit the job. All she does is play that thing." She grabbed a broom, banged the handle against the ceiling, and shouted, "Hey! Go to bed, you slackers!"

The drumming continued, accompanied by faint shouts between Cade and Avery. I plugged my ears.

"Mind if I go up there?" I asked Edison.

"Be my guest."

I left my tea to cool on the breakfast table and climbed the stairs. The second level of Edison's house was half open concept, with yet another gigantic window with sweeping views of the woods, and half private bedrooms. Cade stood in the doorway of the first bedroom, plugging their ears as they shouted inside.

"Like, no offense, it sounds good, but I'm really tired, and we have school tomorrow!" Cade hollered. "Can't you practice in the morning?"

An intentionally intense cymbal crash split the air, making my teeth gnash together. I joined Cade in the doorway and said, "I got this. You can go to bed."

"Good luck," Cade muttered before taking off to their own room.

Avery, Edison's thirteen-year-old daughter, sat at a lightning blue drum set with her back to the door. Since the last time I'd seen her, she'd dyed her pretty brown hair to black and adopted an all-black attire. Even her pajamas were black. The punk rock music pumped from a set of old speakers with a fuzzy sound. Avery banged along with the beat, her entire body working to manipulate the drum set. I left her in peace as the song made its way into the bridge, and Avery gave it her all. Other than a couple missed beats and a few tempo issues, she managed to keep it together through to the end of the song.

As she finished with a final double cymbal crash, I pushed the pause button on her iPhone to keep it from playing the next song then clapped. Avery whirled around, her brow covered in sweat. She dropped her sticks in surprise.

"Bex?"

"What's up, kid?" I said, grinning. "That was impressive. Did you teach yourself how to play?"

She climbed off the drum throne and wiped her forehead with the back of her hand. "Yeah, for the most part. I watched a bunch of YouTube videos too."

I gestured to the speakers. "Old school pop punk used to be my favorite stuff. Early 2000s was the golden era. You ever learn any Sum 41?"

"I can play the entire All Killer, No Filler album," she replied with a note of pride. She breathed heavily. The way she played counted as a cardio workout. "And most of Does This Look Infected. You left your CD collection here, remember? I downloaded all the stuff I liked."

"Oh, right. I forgot I gave all that stuff to your mom." I gazed around her bedroom. Like mine, it was covered in posters of her favorite bands. "So are you still a hugger? Do I get a big, sweaty one?"

Avery took a step back. "I'm not really into hugs."

"No worries. How about a fist bump?"

She obliged, but the look on her face made it clear she was placating me. The dark hair didn't do any favors for her pale complexion. She looked like a Twilight character. Puberty had taken away her cute chunky cheeks and replaced them with sharp angles. She'd grown a good four inches but hadn't gained any weight. It left her lanky and long, with sharp elbows and knees, though she had impressively muscled arms from all the time she put in on the drum set.

"I met your new roommate," I said, gesturing to Cade's room next door.

It was the wrong thing to say. Avery let out a disgruntled scoff. "She's not my roommate. She's just staying here until Mom can find some other foster family to take her."

"You mean 'they?'"

"Whatever."

I plopped down on Avery's bed. "I thought your generation was supposed to be super understanding about this stuff. Do you have a problem with Cade or something?"

Avery crossed her arms and stared glumly at the empty space beside me, as if she wanted to sit down but preferred I left before she did so. This wasn't the happy-go-lucky kid I remembered from a few years ago. All body language signs pointed to wanting alone time.

"I don't have a problem with her—them," Avery mumbled. "But they showed up here and act like they've lived here forever. Like, stop talking to me, you know? I'm not their friend."

"The Avery I used to know was pretty good at making others feel comfortable," I told her gently. "She made friends with almost anyone. Did something change?"

"Mom says it's because I turned thirteen. Teenagers get moody."

"I'm not interested in what your mom says about you." Taking her cue, I got up from the bed and moved toward the doorway. "I'm interested in the way you feel and perceive yourself."

"Are you, like, a shrink now or something?" Avery sniped. "Just because you went to monk school in China or whatever doesn't mean you can analyze me and report back to my mom. Leave me alone."

I held up my hands in a gesture of innocence. "Whoa, take it down a notch, kid. I didn't come up here to shrink you."

"Then get out," Avery said. "And don't call me kid. It's condescending."

"Avery," I replied softly. "Why don't we talk about—?"

"I don't want to talk about anything." Her voice pitched into the next register, a warning sign of impending doom. "I want to go to sleep."

I nodded and backed out of her room. She reclaimed her bed like a piece of war territory.

"I guess I'll see you tomorrow then," I said.

"Tomorrow?" She narrowed her eyes. "What for? Are you staying here?"

"No, but I'm giving a talk at the high school for career day," I told her. "I'm sure I'll stop by one of your classes. Night, buddy. Get some rest."

I waved goodbye without allowing her to get the final word in. Though I didn't have kids of my own, I took my mother's approach to interacting with them. Sometimes, they needed discipline. Other times, they needed the rest of the world to back off for a second. With Avery, it was hard to tell *what* she needed, so I played it safe.

Edison waited for me at the foot of the stairs with a tight-lipped grimace. "Did she bite your head off?"

"She sure did," I said in a quiet tone, glancing up to make sure Avery wasn't listening in. "What's gotten into her?"

"She's been like this for the last year or so," she replied, slumped against the banister. "It's my fault. I put all my energy into helping other kids that I barely have time for my own."

"You should do something together," I suggested. "Just the two of you."

"I tried that," Edison said. "I convinced her to go mini golfing with me a few weeks ago. It rained, and she ditched me while I was in the bathroom."

"Ooh. Tough luck."

Her entire body sagged forward, her teenager troubles sapping all the strength required to stay upright. "I didn't think I'd be this kind of mom. When Avery was a toddler, I used to eavesdrop on older mothers bitching about how their teenagers don't love them anymore. I was convinced it was because moms couldn't leave their kids alone. My mom was on my back twenty-four hours a day, and look where it got me. I gave Avery space. I figured if she had room to grow, she'd come back to me when she wanted. Serves me right for acting superior to those other moms."

I hugged Edison and placed my head on the top of her chin. "You're doing fine. You both have a lot going on. Keep an eye on her, and I'm sure everything will be okay in the end."

"Hmm. I hope you're right."

I rubbed her back and let go of her. "Speaking of keeping an eye on things, have you seen the news lately? Two kids have disappeared."

She stiffened at the mention of it. "Yeah, I heard."

"Are you worried?"

Edison turned toward the front window and gazed absentmindedly away from me. "It could be a coincidence."

"What if it's not?"

"Then I'll deal with it."

When I placed a hand on her shoulder, she shrugged it off. "I'm fine, Bex," she said. "Listen, I'm throwing this huge charity event on Saturday. How long are you going to be in town?"

"Long enough. You want me to come?"

"It'd be nice to have you there, and…" She chewed on her bottom lip, deciding whether or not she wanted to say the other half of her sentence. "And it would be a huge help if you shared the event on your social media pages. We need as many people to show up as possible. Would you do that for me?"

"No question," I told her, walking myself to the door. "I should head out. I'll see you Saturday. And Edison?"

"Hmm?"

"Keep Avery and Cade safe."

5

I woke to the acrid smell of something burning, fell out of bed, and ran downstairs to find my mother cursing up a storm as she attempted to fry eggs, make bacon, and monitor a pan of canned biscuits in the oven all at the same time. Smoke poured from the oven as she donned a pair of silicone mitts and drew out the hot cookie tray. The biscuits were blackened.

"Damn!" Mom abandoned the tray, shook off the mitts, and hurriedly turned the bacon. When she saw me panting in the corner of the kitchen, she smiled brightly. "You're up! I was hoping to surprise you."

"Should you be cooking?" I took up the oven mitts and a spatula and got to work scraping the crusty biscuit massacre off the pan before it cooled and stuck forever. "In your current state, I mean."

"It's an electric stovetop," she countered, flipping the fried eggs with an expert's touch. She'd made me breakfast every morning growing up. "Less likely to go boom than a gas one if I forget to turn it off. Besides, we have smoke alarms."

As if in response, the alarm overhead went off. Maddening, earsplitting beeps echoed through the house. With one ear pressed to my shoulder to block out some of the noise, I wafted smoke away from the alarm with the mitts. Mom propped open the back door, and the dewy morning breeze swept in to clear the air. Coughing and sweating, I sat at the breakfast table to recover.

Mom ruffled my hair. "It's a bit short, don't you think?"

"It's more practical for traveling," I said. "I don't need shampoo or other hair products."

"I miss my baby's long blonde hair though."

"Ma, the bacon."

"Oh, crap!" She rushed back to the stove and pulled the meat off the burner. "Aw, well. You like it crispy, don't you?"

I helped set the table for two and toasted some freshly sliced bread since the biscuits had suffered a terrible death. Mom set out a plate of cubed pears and poured two glasses of orange juice. When her hand trembled, the bottle spat juice across the table. I dammed the flow with paper towels as it raced toward the edge and threatened to spill all over the floor. Mom lowered herself into her seat, her face flushed and sweating.

"Are you okay?" I dampened a paper towel with cool water and pressed it to her forehead. "Bad night's sleep or something?"

She waved off the cold compress. "I'm fine. We need salt and pepper for the eggs."

"I'll get it. You stay there."

Once we were settled, I watched Mom eat from the corner of my eye. She read the local newspaper on her tablet, concentrating more on the stories than her food. Her fork wobbled and lost a portion of its burden each time she lifted it. Crumbs littered the table around her plate, and it took her twice as long to eat as it did in the past.

I covered Mom's trembling hand with mine. "You would tell me, right?"

"Tell you what, honey?"

"If something was really wrong."

She set the tablet aside and cupped my cheek. "Yes, Bex. I would tell you."

"But you didn't," I said. "You could have called me when all of this started happening. I keep my phone on and available so you can reach me at any time."

Mom sipped her orange juice. "I didn't want to worry you."

"Mom, you need an in-home caretaker," I reminded her. "This is something to worry about. If I had known, I would have come home sooner."

"You're here now," she said. "That's all that matters."

The doorbell rang. Mom tried to slide out of the breakfast booth, but I beat her to it. "Finish your breakfast," I told her. "I'll get the door."

It was Melba, reporting for her daily duty. She sniffed the air as she stepped inside and hung her purse on the inside of the coat closet. "Is something burning?"

"Mom made breakfast, but don't worry," I added hastily. "She was lucid. Trying to juggle too many things at once though. You want some eggs?"

"I had breakfast already. Thanks, sweetheart."

Mom rushed out of the kitchen with a paper bag and a juice carton. "Bex, hurry! You're going to be late for school. Where's your backpack?"

As my heart fell into my stomach, Melba took Mom by her elbow and guided her away. "Good morning, Lydia.

Don't worry about Bex. She can get herself ready for school. Let's see if you've taken your medications today."

I WALKED to the high school, wearing a sherpa-lined jean jacket and a beanie. I'd thought about dressing professionally —it was career day after all—but it seemed deceiving to show up in slacks and a blouse when I never wore those things during the course of my travels. Instead, I wore the pair of jeans that had been to Rome, Paris, Athens, Beirut, and a ton of other international cities. I also brought my backpack with my twenty-five belongings.

As I approached Doveport High School, a lump of anxiety grew in my throat. I hadn't set foot in these halls since graduation day. The bright blue lockers and linoleum floors held secrets that no one wished to know. Sweat beaded on my neck, moistened the coat lining, and made me shiver.

Mrs. Dubire, the front office secretary, had not yet retired. Her gray hair was fixed into the same tight curls I remembered from ten years ago, and she wore a sunshine yellow dress with white lace, straight out of a vintage shop or her own closet.

"Bex Lennon!" she exclaimed as I walked inside. She stood up and hugged me over the front desk. "Goodness, it's been so long. I heard you were in Europe."

"Nepal," I corrected. "I can't believe you remember me."

"Oh, I remember all my favorite students." She thoughtfully tapped her chin with a pen. "If I recall, you always begged me to let you out of class early your senior year."

"All the classes I needed to graduate were over by fourth period," I reminded her. "There was no point staying an extra three hours for those electives. No one needs to learn wood-working anyway."

She handed me a visitor sign-in clipboard. "I imagine you used the time to go exploring instead. Are you back for career day?"

"I sure am." I scribbled my name on the sign-in sheet. "Is Mr. Belford around?"

"He and a few other volunteers are manning the fair in the gymnasium," Mrs. Dubire said. "I'm sure they could use an extra set of hands. In-class interviews don't start until after lunch."

She handed me a sticker with my name on it. I peeled off the back and slapped it onto the front of my jacket.

"How do I look?"

Mrs. Dubire smiled. "Like a hundred bucks."

THE GYM BUSTLED WITH KIDS, teachers, volunteers, and other members of the staff. Booths were set up in rows, like the merchandise tables at a fan convention, except Doveport High sold promising futures instead of comic books and autographs. Tables for video-game development and social media managing drew large, excited crowds of teenagers. The military and information technology tables were popular as well. Teaching, social work, and politics drew respectable crowds, while print reporting, logging, and sales booths rarely saw traffic at all.

Mr. Belford manned the teaching booth. He wore a blue shirt with the Doveport Sharks logo on the back and "I'm a teacher. What's your superpower?" printed on the front. As kids passed by, he brandished brochures at them. A lopsided banner hung on the front of the table: *Want to change the world? Become a teacher!* The booth also featured a tri-fold cardboard display outlining the steps to become a teacher and the benefits of working for public schools.

"I noticed you didn't put the salary up there," I said to Mr. Belford by way of hello. "What, you don't want the kids to know how little teachers make?"

Mr. Belford gave up as another group of students ducked under his brochures. He sighed gustily. "I didn't want to discourage them. Besides, you never know. By the time they finish college, we might have a new president who actually cares about education."

"Keep the dream alive."

He stepped out from behind the table and gave me an awkward one-armed hug. "Thanks for coming, Bex. I know it was a bit last minute. Where did you fly in from?"

"Nepal."

"Wow!" He clapped his hands to his cheeks. "Gosh, I've never been farther than California. You might be Doveport's most world-traveled graduate."

"I'll take it." I cleared my throat. "How does this work anyway? I didn't exactly prepare a speech, but I have a few talking points in mind."

Mr. Belford gestured for another teacher to take over his booth as he led me for a walk around the gym. "Don't worry. We want the career interviews to feel casual, not forced. Kids don't like practiced presentations. The looser you are, the better. Do you feel loose?"

I shook my arms out. "I think I'm good."

"Great!" He clapped me on the back. "When you're finished talking, we'll open the floor for questions. Are you comfortable with that?"

"Sure."

Two posters on the board behind Mr. Belford's head drew my attention, and I stopped short to read them. *Missing: Have you seen me?* Each one featured school pictures of the missing girls, Carly Javier and Gemma Johnson, along with a short bio and the dates when they were last seen.

"It's terrible," Mr. Belford muttered. "I'm doing everything I can to keep the students safe. Extra lockdown measures, new sign-out protocols, extended attendance checks. I can't believe this is happening again. I'm hardly over the disappearances from your time at Doveport."

"It's too much of a coincidence," I said under my breath. "Someone local must have taken them. It's the only explanation."

"Who?" he asked. "Everyone knows everyone else in this town. We leave our doors unlocked at night. Dove's lets customers leave their tabs open for days at a time and relies on the honesty system."

"Which is exactly why Doveport is the perfect place to kidnap kids," I replied. "We trust everyone too much."

"Did you ever see them? The kidnappers?"

My stomach plummeted as if I'd been kicked off the edge of a high cliff. "I wasn't taken, remember?"

"Yes, but your friend—"

"I never saw the kidnappers," I said. "If I had, I would have reported them to the FBI in seconds."

Mr. Belford caught wind of my sharpened tone and backed off. "Federal agents showed up two weeks ago when Gemma disappeared. With any luck, they'll get to the bottom of this."

"They didn't last time."

.   .   .

AFTER A FREE LUNCH in the cafeteria—the cheese pizza and chocolate milk tasted just as greasy and sweet as I remembered—Mr. Belford showed me to his old English classroom, which also happened to be my old English classroom. When the bell rang, freshmen filed in, chatting loudly as they took out their books and notes. The teacher, a woman with a high ponytail, looked straight out of graduate school.

"This is Bex Lennon," Mr. Belford introduced me to her. "Bex, this is Miss Scott. She took over my classes for me, including AP and honors."

Miss Scott smiled sweetly at me. "Pleasure to have you today, Bex. The kids are all yours as soon as I get them settled."

"I'll leave you to it," Mr. Belford said, backing out. "I have to help break down the fair."

More students sank into their seats. Cade bounced in on the balls of their feet, took a desk right up front, and tossed their backpack on the floor before they realized I was standing by the whiteboard at the front of the room.

"Bex!" Cade jumped to their feet and hugged me around the waist. "I didn't know you were giving a presentation today. Cool!"

"Back to your desk, Miss Christoph," Miss Scott chided. "We need to get started. Where's your friend?"

Cade wrinkled their nose at the misused prefix. "You mean Avery? I dunno. She wasn't at lunch."

Acid rose in my throat as I pictured Avery's face on one of those Missing Person posters. Right as the bell rang, signaling the end of passing period, Avery slumped into the classroom.

"Ah, there she is," Miss Scott said. "Cutting it close, aren't you, Miss Maxx?"

Avery beelined for the last empty desk in the back row. "I'm here, aren't I?"

Miss Scott cleared her throat. "How about you sit up front today?"

"No, thanks."

"It wasn't a request, Miss Maxx."

Avery backtracked and slid into the seat next to Cade's. She crossed her arms and scowled. With the black hair and heavy eyeliner, she was the picture of cliché teenaged rebellion. Though I stood three feet in front of her, she made no motion to acknowledge me.

"Thank you," Miss Scott said. She clapped her hands. "Afternoon, everyone! I hope you all had a productive morning at the career fair. Before we get started on today's lesson, Bex Lennon here is going to tell you a little bit about her job. Take it away, Bex."

I stepped to the center of the room and held up my backpack. "I'm going to tell you three things about myself. Based on those three things, you have to guess what items I might have in my backpack. Get one right and I'll give you a Pop-Tart."

The class tittered with excitement. If I remembered one thing about high school, it was that free junk food was a hot commodity. I brandished the box of cinnamon pastries, and everyone sat up a little straight.

"Number one," I began. "I travel the world without ever booking a hotel. Number two, I record almost all my adventures on social media. Number three, I keep everything I need to survive in this one backpack. Who wants to guess what's inside?"

Every hand went up except for Avery's. She feigned indifference. I called on a girl in the back row. "You in the pink shirt. What's your name?"

"Kiara," she said, bouncing in her seat. "You got a water bottle in there?"

I reached into my backpack, pulled out a metal canteen with a shoulder strap, and showed it to the class. "We have our first winner." I tossed a Pop-Tart all the way to the back of the class, where greedy eyes watched as Kiara unwrapped the foil. "My water bottle is one of the most important things I carry. It comes with a filter in case I need to get water from a stream or other natural source while I'm hiking. Next? You, in the hat."

A hulky boy in a JV letterman jacket leaned over his desk as if to get a better look at the shape of my backpack. "A phone? You gotta manage your social accounts somehow, right?"

I took my phone from the front pocket of the backpack, and the class groaned at how easy the jock got the answer right. I tossed another Pop-Tart into the crowd. "Without my phone, I can't make money. Without money, I can't travel the world. Who's next? Last one."

The students waved their hands, craning high to be seen over the others. To my surprise, Avery raised her hand. When I called on her, the room filled with dejected sighs.

"Avery?"

"Mace," she said shortly.

I tossed her a Pop-Tart. She immediately threw it onto Cade's desk, who tore off the wrapper and took off the whole corner in one bite.

"Avery's right," I said, pulling the can with the protective flip top out of my bag to show the class. "I always keep some kind of self-defense tool with me. Mostly mace, but I also have a Taser if things get dicey."

"Have you ever used them?" called a girl in a white T-shirt from a middle row.

"Many times," I said. "Sometime tried to mug me in Moscow. I got caught in a scuffle in an alleyway behind a Paris restaurant. You never know when someone might try to take advantage of you."

Miss Scott cleared her throat. Evidently, that was how she got your attention before scolding you. "Miss Lennon, why don't you put the mace away and tell the students more about your job?"

"Don't worry. This can is empty." I tucked the mace away anyway, along with the other items in my backpack. "If you haven't figured it out yet, I work as a social media influencer. Some people don't think it's a real job, but I make enough money to do what I want to be happy. To me, that's what a job should be. Who here has any kind of social media account?"

Every hand in the room went up. I pretended not to notice that Avery sat a little straighter in her seat, actually paying attention to what I was saying.

"That means you all have the opportunity to do what I do," I said, "but before you start posting random pictures of your lunch or whatever, I'm going to give you a few tips on how to become a successful influencer. Step one: find your niche. Everyone on Instagram has a shtick. Mine's travel. Others include fashion, food, surfing, music, video games, et cetera. What you pick doesn't matter, as long as you stick to it and build a brand around it."

To my surprise—and Miss Scott's—I kept the students' attention. I explained how to properly tag pictures, gather followers, and gain recognition from sponsoring companies. I let the kids take out their phones to create their own social media post then went around the room and gave them all advice on how to make the post more influential.

"If you want more people to like and comment on your picture, you have to post it at the right time of day," I announced to the room. "Around three or four o'clock, everyone is getting out of school or winding down at work. People are prone to check their phones more often in the afternoon. So what does that mean?"

Cade raised their hand. "We should post right after school?"

"You got it," I said. "Try it today. Save your post as a draft, then put it up at the final bell. See if you get more likes and follows than you usually do. That's about it. Any questions for—?"

A blaring alarm interrupted my sentence, accompanied by a bright, flashing light. Half the class clapped their hands over their ears. I joined them, the alarm beating on my eardrums through my flesh and bone.

"Let's go!" Miss Scott shouted, taking charge. "Leave your things! Quickly, quickly!"

The students got up and hurried out of the classroom, joining the crowd in the hallway. Miss Scott and I brought up the rear. I stood on my toes, looking for Avery. I caught a quick glimpse of her several feet ahead before she was swallowed by a group of hulking football players.

We evacuated to the football field, the entire school waiting as the alarm continued to go off in the distance. Students who had left their coats inside shivered between the yard lines. Others sat down and played cards. They all took the opportunity outside class to check their phones.

"There was no drill scheduled for today," Miss Scott said as she buttoned her cardigan. "I wonder what happened."

"Mm-hmm." I scanned the crowd for Avery, but she was nowhere in sight. My heart rate quickened. "Do you see Avery anywhere? She's my best friend's daughter."

Miss Scott shielded her eyes and looked across the field. "I'm sure she's around here somewhere."

Five minutes later, a firetruck pulled up to the school, causing a stir amongst the students. The firefighters filed inside, though there was no smoke to be seen. Another half hour passed before Mr. Belford climbed up the drum major's platform with a megaphone.

"Can I have everyone's attention please?" he called across the field. The crowd quieted. "The firefighters have cleared the school. There is no fire. It appears someone pulled the alarm in the library. This is a serious transgression. If anyone has any information on the culprit, please inform the nearest teacher immediately. Let's get back to class, please."

As we reversed our evacuation, I kept my eyes peeled for Avery. I made it all the way back to Miss Scott's classroom without spotting her. Slowly, the desks filled, but Avery's seat remained vacant. I pulled Cade aside when they came in.

"Did you see Avery out there?" I asked.

Cade shook their head. I scanned the classroom. Everyone was accounted for except Avery. I dodged Miss Scott and ran down the hallway.

"Avery?" I called, cupping my hands around my mouth. "Avery!"

My breath shortened and became shallow. My heart banged against my rib cage. I turned a corner into another empty hallway.

"*Avery!*"

"Why are you shouting?"

I whirled around to find Avery behind me, drying her hands with a brown paper towel outside the girls' restroom. I ran up to her and pulled her into a hug, breathing hard. She didn't pull away.

"Don't do that," I gasped. "Don't do that."

6

*A*fter my heart rate settled, the bell rang and Avery was off to her next class. I spent the rest of the day stumbling through the same career speech with half-hearted gusto. I kept waiting for the fire alarm to go off again or for Mr. Belford to slide in on his cheap loafers to tell me another kid had disappeared. When the final bell went off, signaling the end of the day, I collected my things and bolted from my old English room before the first eager freshman could reach the door.

"Hey, Bex!"

I turned on my heel to look for the voice's owner, but the bus loop was crowded with kids who were as keen to leave the school as I was. Finally, I spotted Cade waving at me from the low brick wall that, always and forever, had been dedicated as the official hangout for nerds. Avery sat next to Cade, her hood pulled over her hair, arms crossed tightly. I made my way through the throng to reach them.

"You heading home?" I asked them. "No after-school activities?"

Cade shook their head. "I got here too late in the school year to register for anything, but Avery's supposed to be in jazz band practice."

Avery threw Cade a dirty look. "Traitor."

"You don't want to go?" I asked Avery.

"No," she replied shortly.

"Then don't go."

Avery's brow lifted slightly in suspicious surprise. She had expected me to chide her for skipping practice. "Mom said to ask you if you're free for dinner tonight."

Cade elbowed Avery's side. "I was going to tell her!"

Avery shoved Cade back, and I stepped between them to end the scuffle. "Relax, you two. I got a text message from your mom earlier. Does pizza sound good?"

WE RECONVENED at Dal's Pizza later that night. Like Dove's Pub, the local pizza place had hardly changed. The spicy scent of oregano hit me as soon as I walked in. A handwritten sign near the register said "We don't have Coke. Order Pepsi or don't complain." Red and white checkered tiles covered the walls and the floors. The pattern circled upward and around, giving Dal's the look of a never-ending, life-size kaleidoscope. Thankfully, the bright red booths and tables broke up the monotony, but they were no less of a headache to look at.

I spotted my party at a table near the back. As soon as Cade saw me, they waved frantically to get my attention, leaning so far out of the booth that they were in danger of falling out. Across from Cade, Edison hooked her elbow over the back of the book and turned around. All of a sudden, I was in high school again, meeting my best friend at our favorite Friday night spot.

"Hi," I said to everyone, leaning into the booth to give Edison a quick hug before sitting down. Cade bounced in their seat, while Avery, as usual, slumped in the corner with her hood drawn over her head. "This place hasn't changed one bit, has it? Does the football team still trash it after Friday night games?"

"Yup," Cade declared. They checked their watch. "But we're early enough to avoid them. They don't usually stumble in until ten o'clock."

"We've got plenty of time." I picked up the menu and unfolded its sticky pages. "I don't know about you guys, but my favorite pizza from Dal's is the BBQ chicken. If you're down, we could share a big one. Your mom has to get a personal pan though. She's got terrible taste."

"I beg your pardon?" Edison bumped me with her shoulder. "Just because you don't like Hawaiian pizza doesn't mean no one else does either."

Cade wrinkled their nose. "No offense, Edison, but Hawaiian pizza is gross. I need my pineapples in a smoothie or as the garnish on a piña colada. That's about it."

"Oh, really?" Edison leaned across the table. "Where'd you get a piña colada?"

Cade's face went bright red. "Nowhere."

"Mm-hmm."

Avery muttered something from her shadowy corner.

"What was that?" I lowered the menu to bring the barriers down between our side of the table and Avery's. "A topping suggestion, Avery?"

Avery glared from beneath her hoodie. "I said she's not Cade's mom."

It took me a moment to process what she meant by the statement, then remembered I had directed my earlier sentence to both teenagers. "I didn't mean it like that, Avery."

"Whatever."

Cade attempted to rest a hand on Avery's shoulder, but the other teen pulled away. "Avery, I didn't think—"

"Shut up, Cade."

"Avery!" Edison hissed. "That is not how we treat other people. You do not tell Cade to shut up."

As soon as Edison spoke, Avery shut herself off. She yanked her hoodie over as much of her face as possible, turned toward the wall, and practically vanished. Edison's shoulders fell, and she pressed her lips together as if to keep herself from saying something else. Her eyes glassed over.

I put an arm around Edison and cleared my throat. "How about everyone gets their own personal pan pizza? It's on me."

That cleared up any further arguments about toppings. When the server came by, everyone ordered their favorite. Barbeque for me, of course, and a Hawaiian for Edison. Cade got the one with the most vegetables on top, a surprising choice for a teenager, and Avery ordered plain cheese.

A few bites in, Cade took their phone out.

"Excuse me?" Edison gently kicked Cade under the table. "You know the rules. No phones at dinner."

"Sorry, but look!" Cade angled the screen toward me to show me her Instagram page. "I posted my picture right when you said to, and I got a ton more likes than usual!"

Cade had taken a nice selfie of herself outside the school, used a filter that made the colors more vivid, and tagged it with things like #genderfluid, #lgbtq, and #nonbinary.

"Thirty-nine likes?"

They clutched the phone to their chest. "Hey, I don't have a lot of friends, okay? And I'm not the social media guru that you are."

I waved with my pizza. "I'm not trash talking you. That's a decent amount for just getting started. What about you, Avery? Did you try my tips?"

"No."

If I was honest with myself, I hadn't expected much else, but the old version of Avery was stuck in my head. A few years ago, she would have done anything and everything that I asked her to because she admired me so much.

I leaned across the table, giving Avery the illusion of more privacy between us. "You know, if you posted some videos of you drumming and tagged them properly, you'd have a huge following. You're really talented. You know that, right?"

Avery's eyes flickered upward to meet mine, and for the first time since I'd reunited with the Maxxes, I saw a glimmer of interest in her pupils. "You think so?"

"I know so," I assured her. "Let me see your phone."

"Do we have to do this at dinner?" Edison asked. "I hardly get to see you kids without your phones glued to your faces. We have rules for a reason."

As Avery handed me her phone from across the table, I said to Edison, "Don't worry. Today's the only exception."

Avery's home screen was a picture of her old cat, Marshmallow, who I hadn't seen since my visit to their house two years ago.

"She died," Avery announced, replying to my questioning glance. "She got out of the house because *someone* left the door open." She glowered at Cade first then her mother. "She probably got hit by a car or something."

Edison sighed heavily, as if they'd had this conversation a

few times before. "We don't know she's dead. She might come back."

"It's been a month and a half," Avery said.

I cleared my throat and tapped on the Instagram logo to get Marshmallow's picture out of sight and mind as quickly as possible. Avery's profile popped up. Though she'd been busy on her phone like the rest of the students during my career talk, she hadn't done the assignment I'd given out. She had no post drafts saved to work on.

Her profile was pretty sad already. It mainly featured pictures of Marshmallow in various sleeping positions, along with the occasional non-smiling selfie of Avery. In every one, her straggly black hair hung in front of her blank eyes, and she peered at the camera with absolute indifference. I clicked on the latest selfie to bring it to full size.

"Going for a little Kurt Cobain vibe here?" I asked Avery.

"Who?"

"The lead singer of Nirvana?"

"I only know one of their songs," Avery said. "It was too easy to play, so I stopped listening to them."

"Ah, I see. Do you have any drumming videos on here? We need something good to work with."

"In my photos."

I swiped out of Instagram and hovered over the photos icon. "There's nothing in here you wouldn't want me to see, right?"

Avery crossed her arms. "I know how to use a private album. I'm not stupid."

Edison raised an eyebrow. "What do you need a private album for?"

Avery pursed her lips and stayed quiet. I scrolled through her photo album until I came across a few drum videos. I selected the first one, hoping it would end the embarrassing conversation between Avery and her mom. A fuzzy recording of another Paramore song pumped through the phone's speakers as a low quality version of Avery hammered on her drum set. The audio was bad enough to make my teeth clench.

"Okay, not that one." I swiped to the next video, but the audio was just as bad. "Do you have any videos that you *didn't* record with a potato?"

"Mom won't let me get a new phone unless I save up half the money for it on my own," Avery reported. "That one doesn't have a good microphone on it."

I slid Avery's phone across the table to her. "I'll tell you what. I have an old external microphone in my room at my mom's house. How about I grab it after dinner and we can record a new video of you to post? We can use my phone to film."

"Do it!" Cade urged, shaking Avery's arm. "Everyone's gonna think you're so cool once they know you don't just play jazz music."

Avery glanced at her mother. Though she pretended otherwise, she sought Edison's validation and approval. Edison hesitated, but when I poked her knee under the table to egg her on, she smiled and nodded.

"Fine," Avery said. "I'll do it."

THE MAXXES GAVE me a ride to my old house to pick up the microphone. Melba's car was parked out front and the bath was running upstairs, so I didn't run into my mother or her caretaker as I jogged up to my room and unearthed the old microphone from a storage box in the closet.

At Edison's house, Avery and Cade dumped their coats on the sofa and raced each other upstairs.

"Hey!" Edison shouted wearily as Avery started banging on the drums. "Get back down here and put these in the closet where they belong!"

"I got it," I told her. "Go relax."

She almost argued but gave up at the last second, waved me away, and ambled into the kitchen to make herself a drink. I took the stairs two at a time and turned into Avery's bedroom. Cade sprang to their feet and made a grab for the microphone.

"Nope." I held the microphone out of reach. "No video until you two put your coats away like civilized human beings."

The teenagers groaned but ran downstairs to do my bidding. Hangers clanked noisily in the closet before their footsteps pounded upstairs again.

I plugged the external mic into my phone. "You ready, Avery?"

She sat on the drum throne and pounded on the snare. "Yeah."

"Wait a second. May I?" With Avery's approval, I swept her hair away from her face and tied half of it up. Without it swinging in her eyes, she looked much cleaner and more approachable. "That's good. Let's try this. What's your favorite song to play right now?"

She chewed on her lip as she though about it. "Ode to Sleep by Twenty One Pilots. There are a bunch of cool tempo changes that were hard to for me to nail, but now that I've got it, it's awesome."

"Well, we can only put one minute of it on Insta," I reminded her. "But let's record the whole thing. Then you can decide what's the best part to post. If you want, you can put the whole video on your YouTube channel and leave a link to it in your Instagram description. That way, people can get to know your skills even better."

"Can you show me how to do that?"

"I sure can."

Cade bounced eagerly on the bed, unable to contain their excitement. "Come on, Avery! I wanna hear you play."

I made sure the microphone was working then hit record. "Ready when you are, Avery."

Avery nodded and pushed play on her phone. The song pumped through the speakers, beginning with an alien synth introduction. When the beat started a few bars later, Avery did too. All her focus went into the syncopated rhythm. Her head and shoulders moved in time with the accented beats, her arms flying as the second half of the verse incorporated the toms into the main rhythm. When the tempo changed, Avery hit every beat perfectly, and the song soared into the chorus.

As Avery played, I panned around her to keep the video interesting. During particularly difficult sections of the song, I focused on her hands and arms as they flew across the kit. When sweat dropped off her brow and bounced off the snare drum, I filmed that too. It was like a cheap, one-shot production of a music video, and Avery was so into the music that she didn't pay a single ounce of attention to the camera.

A whole five minutes later, the drums faded to a simpler beat, and Avery sung the last few bars of the song in a beautiful, warbling voice.

"*You have no plans for me,*" she sang. "*I will set my soul on fire. What have I become? I'm sorry…*"

A beat of silence followed, during which no one dared

77

speak or move. A droplet of moisture fell from Avery's cheek, not sweat but a tear. She wiped it away and spun around on the drum throne, breaking the spell. Cade gazed at her with an admiring smile, but Avery peered hopefully at her mother. Edison had appeared in the doorway, holding a glass of champagne, to watch her daughter perform.

"That was great, honey," Edison said, clapping her free hand against her forearm. "I didn't know you could sing."

"I can't really," Avery said. She looked up at me. "Did you get it?"

"Yeah, you wanna watch it?"

Avery tossed aside her drumsticks and sat next to me on the bed. With her on one side and Cade on the other, I pushed play on the video. The teenagers watched over my shoulder.

"This looks *so cool*," Cade said, the last two words vibrating deep in their throat like a growl. "Damn, I'm jealous."

"What do you think, Avery?" I asked her. "Do you want to post it?"

Avery bit the inside of her cheek then nodded. "Yeah. Let's do it."

"Bex?" Edison called. "Meet me downstairs when you're done, okay?"

"Sure. Okay, Avery. Let me send you the video, and I'll tell you what to do with it."

For the next twenty minutes, I helped Avery pick a section of the video to post on Instagram and taught her how to link it to YouTube. Cade gleefully contributed ideas for tags like #girldrummer and #TøP, which was how the band

Avery liked stylized their name in shorthand. Once it was finished, I hovered over the button to post the video.

"Are you ready?" I asked Avery.

"Let me do it." She reached over and pressed *Post* then let out a big sigh as the video uploaded. "There it goes. Hopefully, no one thinks I'm a loser."

As soon as the confirmation popped up to notify us that the video had successfully uploaded, I reached into the same part of my brain that zapped with electricity whenever I received those daunting text messages. I didn't often access it intentionally, but in this scenario, it felt like something I needed to do. It was for Avery.

A few seconds later, Avery's phone chimed once, then again, then over and over as notifications for likes, new followers, and messages poured in. Avery's eyes widened.

"Fifty likes already!" she gasped.

Cade leaned over her shoulder. "Sixty now!"

The teenagers squealed with excitement as they watched Avery's popularity soar right before their eyes. Avery leapt up from the bed.

"I gotta tell Mom!" she shouted and raced downstairs. I followed with less exuberance in my step. The years of traveling kept me humble and slow during my downtimes.

"That's amazing, honey!" Edison was saying as Avery showed her the post. "See, I knew you could do it."

Avery jumped on the balls of her feet as she scrolled through her new followers. "Half the popular kids at school are following me now!" She squealed again and ran back upstairs. "Cade, look! That girl you like from art class just followed me!"

As the teenagers enclosed themselves in the bedroom,

Edison's smile faded. "You know, this is the first time she hasn't pushed Cade away."

I sat next to her at the dining table and sipped from her full champagne glass. She'd refilled it recently. "That's good, right?"

"I guess." She eyed me suspiciously. "You had something to do with this, didn't you? All of Avery's new followers?"

I lifted my shoulders and raised my palms. "All I did was show her how to shoot a decent video and use hashtags."

"Bullshit. You know what I mean."

"Fine. So what if I did?" I challenged. "Avery's talented, and she feels invisible right now. She deserves for people to recognize her. Everyone does. Why does it matter if I gave her a little boost?"

"Because weird things happen when you use your power," Edison bit back.

"Don't call it that."

"I don't know what else to call it when someone uses their mind to control technology."

I shuffled uneasily in my seat. "That's not what it is. You know that."

"I don't, actually," she replied. "Because you won't tell me. You never would. Not even back then."

I drained the rest of the champagne. "You still want my help to get as much people at the fundraiser as possible tomorrow, right?"

"Of course."

"Then do me a favor and get off my back about this." I placed the empty champagne glass in front of her. "I wouldn't drink any more of that if I were you. You've got a big day ahead of you tomorrow."

oday's the day, everyone! I'm back home in Doveport, Oregon to support Edison Maxx's Home Safe fundraiser event. Edison happens to be one of my best friends, and she's doing a lot of great work for homeless and at-risk youth in our area. There will be games, good food, and plenty of local color to enjoy at the fundraiser. If you're nearby, come say hi and leave a donation! Don't forget to tag all your posts and pictures #Home-Safe. #charity #fundraiser #nonprofitorganization

I added a few more hashtags to the description then posted it with two pictures of me and Edison, one from when we were thirteen and a more recent one from Edison's last fundraiser two years ago. I also posted Home Safe's logo and tagged the linked Instagram page so people could check out Edison's organization for themselves. As the post went public, I did the same thing I'd done for Avery yesterday, reaching into the Internet's internal universe with my brain to push my content as far as possible.

I didn't know how it worked, this thing Edison called my

"power." I only knew that I had a slight hold over anything electronic: phones, tablets, TVs, computers. You name it. If it ran off some kind of technological advancement, I could interfere with it. It was how I'd made a name for myself as The Wanderer so quickly. Yes, I had the content that people wanted to see, but most of getting big in social media had to do with how many people actually looked at your posts. With my power—ability, whatever you wanted to call it—I could look into the enormous, branching web of the Internet and push my content into the correct channels, and it only took a couple seconds for me to do it.

I hadn't been struck by lightning. I wasn't dipped in a vat of unknown chemicals or bitten by a radioactive spider. I didn't suffer any sort of near-death experience that forced doctors to shock me back to life, thereby imbuing me with this strange ability. For as long as I could remember, I had a weird connection to technology, but it wasn't until I was a teenager that I intentionally honed the skill and used it.

In my experience, there were a few things wrong with this power. I had reasons for not using it all the time. For one, the brain zaps were a huge issue. It happened every time I accessed my ability, in varying intensities. For the social media pushes, the little pulse of electricity lasted no longer than a second. That I could handle, and the advantages outweighed the pain. Long ago, I'd dug into the far reaches of my head and ended up passing out from waves of agony. Since then, I learned not to push myself too far.

The unknown prevented me from experimenting. For instance, I knew my own head generated the cryptic text messages from blocked numbers, but it never happened intentionally. It was like my anxiety manifested through the phone. I couldn't stop them from coming, and the messages never clarified themselves. What good was my supposed ability if all it did was send me useless worries? To prove my point, my phone buzzed and my brain zapped.

c0w@rd.

"Sure, I'm a coward," I muttered and tossed the phone across the room. I rubbed the soreness from my temples and the knots from my neck. The twin-sized mattress wasn't the most comfortable after all these years, and the only extra pillows my mom had in her house weren't as supportive as they needed to be for ultimate neck comfort. You'd think years of sleeping on the floor in various countries would have prepared me for this, but in the couple days I'd spent back in Doveport, I'd been more uncomfortable than at hostels and strangers' homes.

It wasn't long before the notifications poured in, responding to my post about Home Safe's fundraiser, sending my phone a-buzzing. I put it on Do Not Disturb so I could get dressed in peace. It was nine o'clock, and all I desperately wanted was to keep sleeping, but I couldn't break my promise to Edison to help set everything up. Thankfully, the fundraiser didn't start until noon.

"Morning, everyone," I said to Mom and Melba as I stumbled bleary-eyed into the kitchen and groped through the cabinets for a coffee mug. "How'd you sleep?"

"Great!" Mom replied cheerfully. "I moved the mugs, honey. They're by the fridge now."

I opened the correct cabinet. "How about you, Melba?"

"Oh, you know." Melba had her nose in the morning paper. "Sleep gets more difficult with age. Personally, I find I have to get up to pee every thirty seconds."

"Sorry to hear that." I eyed the front of the newspaper. The headline focused on some political strife, as always. "Any news about the missing kids?"

Melba turned the page and flapped the paper to get it to stand up straight. "Nope. The cops are as clueless as ever."

Mom pursed her lips and shook her head. "Isn't it terrible?" A tear trembled at the corner of her eye. "I can't imagine what I'd do if I lost you, Bex."

"I'm right here, Mom. I'm safe." I poured myself coffee and put a frozen waffle in the toaster oven. "Today's Edison's fundraiser. Are you two going to stop by?"

"What do you think, Lydia?" Melba asked my mother. "Would you like to go?"

Mom's brows knit together. "Bex, I don't like the idea of you out and about by yourself all day long. We don't know when these kidnappers are going to strike next."

I glanced at Melba, who gave a small shrug. Mom's lucidity was as fickle as a house cat's affection for humans. One moment, it was there. The next moment gone.

The toaster pinged. I hastily grabbed the waffle and frosted it with peanut butter as quickly as possible. "I'll be okay, Mom. Gotta go. Edison needs me to help set up."

"Wait just a minute, young lady."

I froze in the doorway of the kitchen. Nothing good ever followed "young lady."

Mom got to her feet. When I was a teenager, she towered over me, but shortly after my fourteenth birthday, a late growth spurt sent me soaring over her head. Nevertheless, what I called her disciplinary posture had not changed. The square shoulders, lifted chin, and narrowed eyes still invoked fear in me to this day.

"You will not go to that fundraiser without supervision," Mom said, her voice low and menacing. "I refuse to be one of those stupid parents who thinks nothing bad will ever happen to their children. I'm coming with you."

Melba cleared her throat. "Lydia, you have an appointment this morning."

Mom paused, puzzled. "On a Saturday?"

"It's Monday," Melba lied easily. "You have a check-up with Dr. Herndon. Bex is going to school. They have security to watch the campus. She'll be fine."

"Oh." My mother's nose wrinkled as her brain caught up with the new information. "I suppose that's okay then. Be careful, Bex. I can't stand the thought of losing you."

I gave her a brief hug, pulling away before she saw through Melba's false story. "I'll see you this afternoon, Mom. Love you."

"Love you too, honey."

THE HOME SAFE fundraiser was being held on the marching band's practice field at Doveport High. The real football field was off-limits because the coach didn't want a bunch of people wrecking the turf. Not to mention, Edison had ordered several of those enormous inflatables that had to be pounded into the dirt to keep them secure. These included a moon bounce, a Velcro climbing wall, and a game where you were strapped to a bungee cord with the goal of running farther than your opponent before you got snapped back to the starting line.

Since my mother's car wouldn't start, I'd ridden my bike there. As I locked it to the chain-link fence, Avery and Cade tested out the bungee inflatable. I watched as they readied themselves, each with a beanbag in hand. When the game referee said so, they both raced forward, pulling against the bungee cord. At the farthest point, they each planted their beanbag on the Velcro strip in between their racing lanes. Then the bungee cords yanked them back, and they both fell on their butts, breathless and laughing. The referee checked the placement of the beanbags—they were quite close together—and decreed Avery the winner.

Avery whooped and jeered in Cade's face, but Cade rolled their eyes and smiled, a good loser opposite Avery's win. As I jumped over the fence and headed toward them, Avery spotted me. She hurriedly pulled the bungee belt off her waist, jumped off the inflatable, and ran toward me.

"Look, look, look!" She shoved her phone in my face, open to the video we'd posted last night. "I have over five hundred views and two hundred new followers! It's crazy. What should I post next? That was part of your speech, right? You have to post consistently or people will lose interest, right?"

"Slow down, kid," I said. "Is there coffee here? I had to abandon my cup earlier, and I'm about to collapse from lack of caffeine."

"Mom ordered boxed coffee from Maxine's."

I groaned with delight. "Tell me she got donuts too. I miss Maxine's donuts."

"Original, vanilla-dipped, chocolate, and blueberry bites."

"Take me to your leader."

As Cade practiced her bungee running skills, Avery led me to a white tent near the back corner of the field. Inside, a few folding chairs and card tables had been set up as a break room for the fundraiser volunteers. One space heater kept the morning chill at bay. The five volunteers who had already arrived nursed coffee and donuts as they went over everyone's duties. Edison, however, stood alone in a corner, her phone pressed to her ear.

"Mom's in a mood," Avery informed me. "So this is where I leave you."

As Avery ducked out of the tent, I made my way to Edison.

"What about this don't you understand?" she was saying. "The fundraiser starts at noon. *Lunchtime.* I specifically asked the caterers to be here a half hour early to set up. If everyone gets here and there's no food for them, they'll leave. I can't have that." There was a brief pause as the person on the other end of the line replied. "No, I don't want a discount! I want you to get here on time. If you're not here by 11:45, *at the latest*, I want a full refund. *And* I'll tell everyone I know never to use your services again. I know a lot of people!" Another brief pause. "Thank you. Goodbye."

Edison huffed as she hung up the phone. When she spotted me, she sighed with relief and gave me a quick hug. "Thank God you're here. I need you to take back the social media thing you put out this morning. The caterers aren't going to show up on time, no matter what they say, so we have to stall. Can you get people to come at one o'clock instead?"

I clicked my tongue. "It doesn't really work that way. Once I post something, everyone sees it. I can't take it back. It would mess with my brand."

"Your brand?" She scoffed. "Is that all you care about?"

"It's literally my career, but I'll let that one go because I know you're stressed." I beelined for the refreshments, filled a Styrofoam cup with coffee, and bit into a vanilla-dipped donut with a moan. "God, I forgot how good Maxine's donuts are."

Edison snapped repeatedly in front of my face. "Hello? I'm in crisis mode!"

I smacked her hand away. "Yeah, I can tell. Lucky for you, I have a solution."

Her eyes widened. "Don't play with me, Lennon."

I wiped vanilla frosting from my mouth, balled up the napkin, and tossed it at Edison. "I'm not playing. Dove's has a food truck now. I saw it parked behind the pub on my way here, which probably means it's available for hire today. Call them up and see."

She squeezed my shoulders in thanks. "You're a genius!"

"I know."

Edison ran off, dialing Dove's number from memory. I joined the other volunteers.

"Let's get this show on the road, shall we?"

THE CATERERS *WERE* LATE, but Dove's truck showed up on time. As much as Edison wanted to, she didn't have the option of telling the caterers to stuff it. Edison had planned for a certain number of people to show up to the fundraiser, but because of my social media bump, a few hundred more made appearances. It wasn't just locals either. People from all over the state drove in to support Edison's cause, simply because I'd told them to. We needed the extra food to feed the additional mouths.

Live bands played on the center stage. Carnival rides whirled around in neon lights. The lines for the inflatables wrapped around the primary-colored monstrosities of durable plastic. Kids begged their parents to buy them another round of tickets for Whack-a-Mole, skee ball, and other games. Selling tickets for entertainment was the perfect way to raise money. One hundred percent of the profits went to the funding for Home Safe. Edison held a raffle as well. The more money you donated, the better chance you had of winning one of the top prizes.

At Edison's request, I supervised the booth where donators could meet some of the kids and teenagers that participated in the Home Safe project. In the hours behind that table, I understood more about Edison's mission than I ever had before. These kids needed help for a slew of reasons. Most of them had been kicked out of their homes for one terrible reason or another. Two of them, Jessica and Monica, had gotten pregnant at early ages, due to a lack of sex education at home and in school. They both came from religious parents who neither believed in abortion or birth control. Jessica had given birth to a beautiful baby girl with nowhere to raise her, but with Edison's help, they both had a home in town with one of the locals. Monica was six months pregnant and lived with the Blackthorns, who had four children of their own and were well-practiced with newborns.

Other teenagers, like Cade, were part of the LGBTQ community and had parents or family that disapproved of the so-called "lifestyle." Still others came from abusive or violent homes. Jett had run away from a juvenile correctional facility, with scars across his wrists as proof of what he'd put up with there. Lily had escaped a stepfather with ill intentions. Cade, I discovered, had been subject to traumatic "corrective therapy," where they were forced to pick a gender from the two approved choices *and* to identify as straight. Every kid had a horror story and unending gratitude for Edison and the Home Safe program.

"Edison saved my life."

I heard it from every kid in the program, and every time one of them said it, tears sprang to my eyes. I hugged the ones who were okay with physical affection and praised the strength of the ones who weren't. The more time I spent with those kids, the more I realized how lucky I was to have made it to adulthood with less struggles.

As my duty to Edison, I played my part as the social media influencer throughout the day. A lot of the out-of-towners had shown up because they knew I would be there, so I shook a lot of hands, gave a ton of high fives, and posed for hundreds of pictures. Each time I met a new follower, I encouraged them to donate to the cause. Many of them dropped dollar bills into our collection bowl on the Home Safe Teenagers table right away. I hoped they stuck around to buy more tickets and enjoy the rest of the carnival.

Around four-thirty, toward the end of the fundraiser, Edison stopped by our table for the third time that hour. "Everyone okay?" she asked the teenagers. "Does anyone need anything? Water or a snack? You guys need a break? You don't have to be talking about your trauma all day. It's all right to call it in early."

"Relax, Edison," Jett called, his long legs crossed as he lounged in a folding chair. "We don't mind. We're here to promote the program."

"Yeah, we're good," Cade agreed. "When's your victory speech anyway? It's about that time, right?"

Edison checked her watch. "We're getting there. The volunteers are counting how much money we made in donations today so I can announce it."

"And?" Jett prompted. "Are we loaded now?"

Edison grinned. "You'll have to wait and see like everyone else."

AT FIVE O'CLOCK, the festivities officially came to an end. The final band struck the last chord of their closing song as everyone crowded around the stage. Most everyone had stuck around for Edison's final speech, eager to know how much money they had raised. Not to mention, the winner of the raffle was to be announced as well. The band's lead singer, a twenty-year-old boy with a green Mohawk, took the microphone.

"Attention, humans!" he roared across the crowd. The noise and chatter settled. "It's been a pleasure playing for you today. Our band, Attack Back, is a huge supporter of Home Safe for one big reason. Eight years ago, Edison picked me up off the streets and gave me a place to call home. That was right at the beginning of her journey with Home Safe, and I'm so proud of how far she's come. I wouldn't be where I am without Edison. I owe her my life."

Edison, standing near the stage, placed her hand over her heart and held back tears as the lead singer continued.

"You're the one person who always cared about me no matter what crap I pulled," the lead singer said, his eyes on Edison. "You're the closest thing I have to a mom, and I can't thank you enough for that." He turned back to the crowd, pointing at Edison. "This woman is the strongest person I know! She never let her childhood trauma get to her. Instead, she transformed it into something bigger than all of us. She is the woman of the hour, of the day, and in my opinion, of the past eight years. Without further ado, here's Edison Maxx!"

The crowd stomped and cheered with approval as the green-haired boy held out his hand to help Edison onto the stage. She wiped away tears as she and the lead singer hugged. Then he passed her the microphone, kissed her cheek, and let her have the stage.

"Wow," Edison said, clutching the mic with both hands as she beamed at the lead singer. "Thank you, Derek, for that lovely introduction. I'm blessed to have watched you grow from that scrawny little kid to the man you are now." Derek bowed his head, and I suspected he was also hiding tears as Edison addressed the crowd. "As you all probably know, Home Safe was born out of my own experiences as a teenager. When I got older, I wanted to do something for the next generation of teenagers who were unlucky, underprivileged, or simply misunderstood. Sometimes, all you need is for someone to listen to you, and I think Home Safe provides our kids with this and more."

The kids from the program, all gathered near the front of the stage, whooped and cheered, slinging rolled-up T-shirts and neon light-up necklaces above their heads as if they were all at a rave instead of a fundraising event.

"I know you're all waiting for the raffle prizes to be awarded," Edison went on, "but before we get to that, I wanted to share with all of you how effective today's fundraiser was. With your help, we raised over *twice* the amount I expected to, a grand total of twenty-two thousand dollars!"

A shiver ran up my spine as the crowd erupted, and the Home Safe kids cheered louder than ever. Edison could do so much with that money. She deserved it, and so did all the teenagers that she took care of.

"This wouldn't have been possible without one person,"

Edison said, crying freely now. "She stepped up and spread the word when we needed it most. Thank you to my best friend, Bex Lennon, who has been there for me in the best of times and the worst of times. You are my rock, Bex, even when you're out roaming the world. Without you, I wouldn't be alive."

I started crying too.

8

*I*t took a solid three hours to break down the fundraiser. The inflatables deflated. The carnival rides screeched in protest as they were pulled apart. The Whack-a-Mole and other games were dismantled. The volunteers cleaned up trash, folded and returned chairs to the storage room in the school gymnasium, and broke down booths and tables. As night fell and the sun no longer volunteered to warm us, a chill swept in. It crept underneath the hem of my jacket to tickle and taunt my skin. Shivering, I carried the final stack of folding chairs into the gym, savoring the warmer air inside, though it smelled strongly of dirty socks, sweat, and basketballs. On my way out, I surveyed the practice field to make sure nothing had been left out or forgotten. The marching band deserved a decent place to call home as much as the football team.

Edison found me combing the field with a small handful of nuts, bolts, nails, and other items that might pierce through the bottom of a trombone player's sneaker. I'd also gathered a fair amount of dropped quarters and the occasional dollar bill. I dropped the money into Edison's palm.

"There you go," I said. "That's a whole five dollars and sixty-two cents to add to your twenty-two thousand."

She pocketed the cash with a chuckle. "Your contribution, huh?"

"Hey, I helped all day long," I reminded her. "Besides, I'm broke."

"How do you manage to travel so much then?"

"When you fly as much as I do, you can practically do it for free with airline points." I held out the bolts and nails. "What should I do with these? Donate them to the hardware store?"

"Is that what you've been doing out here for the past half hour?" she asked, incredulous. "Everyone else has gone home."

"I didn't want one of the band kids to step on anything."

She fished a plastic grocery bag out of her big tote and spread the sides open. "Put them in here. I'll give them to Cade. They're always noodling around with stuff."

I dumped the handful of hardware into the bag and dusted my palms of dirt. "Where'd all the kids go anyway? It's pretty early for a Saturday night."

"I rented out Bounce House for the night," Edison said. "The place with all the trampolines? I figured the kids deserved something nice after working all day. I practically pimped them out to get more money out of people, so this was the least I could do."

"You mean getting them to tell their stories?"

She nodded and tucked the bag of hardware safely in her tote. "If someone had asked me to share my trauma with a bunch of strangers, I would have told them to screw all the way off."

I folded her small form beneath one of my arms and tucked her closely to my side as she shivered. Together, we walked to the parking lot. "There's one major difference between the way you handled your trauma and the way these kids handle theirs."

"What?"

"You, dummy." I gave her a big smile. "Derek—the kid with the green hair, right? He said it best. They wouldn't be where they are today without you. You made a huge difference in their lives by giving them a chance when no one else did. If you had had someone like that in your life, maybe the past fifteen years wouldn't have been so hard for you."

She reached up and ruffled my hair. "When did you cut all of this off?"

"You don't like it?"

"Actually, I love it," she said. "It suits you."

The compliment warmed my soul, but I realized what Edison was doing. "Don't try to distract me with sweet talk. You're avoiding a heart-to-heart."

She rolled her eyes. "Of course I am. Your heart-to-hearts aren't heartwarming at all. It always feels like I'm seeing a therapist."

"I'm just checking in on you."

"I know." She wrapped an arm around my waist. "But I don't need you to. I'm fine. Really."

I cleared my throat. "Speaking of therapists, are you still seeing one?"

"You're pushing."

"It's a simple question. You don't have to answer if you

don't want to. But," I added hastily, "in the name of friend-ship, I'd appreciate if you did."

She heaved a dramatic sigh to make sure I knew how much effort went in to replying. "No, I'm not seeing a thera-pist anymore. First of all, there's only one in Doveport, and she's nuts."

"Who?"

"Ava Duhaney."

Ava Duhaney was an older woman who spent the majority of her time talking to the birds in the park and feeding them seeds from the palm of her hand. And if there weren't any birds around, she spoke to herself.

"She is nuts," I conceded.

"Yeah, so I'd have to drive out of town to see someone," Edison said. "Which I don't want to do. Besides, I've gone the therapy route, and I'm tired of hashing the same story out over and over again. I'm level. I can cope. It's my kids I'm worried about."

"Avery?"

Edison tied her scarf more tightly as a gust of wind swept her long brown hair around her face. "Avery, Cade, all of them."

"Because of the disappearances?"

Her lips all but vanished as she pressed them together. "I don't want to talk about it. Do you want to go to the bank with me?"

The sudden change of subject gave me whiplash. The recent cases of disappearing teenagers had to be dredging up old memories for Edison, but I couldn't make her talk about it if she didn't want to. "What do you need to go to the bank for?"

She lifted a large lock box from her tote bag. "It's the cash we made today. I can't leave twenty-two thousand dollars at my house. Barley said he'd stay late so I could deposit it."

For as long as I could remember, Barley had been the manager and head teller at the town's one and only bank. Like Ava and a lot of other Doveport locals, he'd been here for his entire life.

"Sure, I'll tag along." I got the feeling that Edison didn't want to be alone anyway, especially in the dark with so much money on her person. "I don't suppose you have room for my bike in your car."

"That's yours?" She eyed the rusty one-speed cabled to the fence. "Wow, you need an upgrade. But if you must keep it, I've got a bike rack on the back."

After hitching the bike to the back of the car, I got into the passenger seat. Edison had already turned the heat up to stave off the chill. She pulled out of the school's gravel parking lot and turned toward the main road.

"Tell me about your travels," she said. "The real stuff. Not the stuff you post on social media. Give me the dirty details."

"I post almost everything," I replied, cracking the window when the air got too stuffy. "Didn't you see the one where I drank bad water in Mexico? Not pretty."

Edison wrinkled her nose in disgust. "That was a little too much information for me."

"It's educational for other travelers."

"Whatever. I'm talking about the juicy stuff. Any hook-ups?"

"We are not sorority girls at a frat party."

She steered with one hand so she could shove me gently. "Come on. Give me something! Two teenagers in the house is like having a giant neon marquee across my head that says don't date me, I'm a single mom."

"I thought you didn't date much by choice."

"I do," she insisted. "I mean, I don't. I don't know. Either way, I need to live vicariously through someone else. Give me the dirty deets, Bex."

I held on to the bar above the window as she took a corner a little too quickly. "I hate to break it to you, but international hook-ups aren't really my thing. It's safer not to engage."

"Wow, that's boring."

"Sorry, kid."

She drummed absentmindedly on the steering wheel. "What about that guy you travel with? He's on your blog all the time. The one that looks like Aquaman?"

"Taj?"

"Yeah! You can't tell me you guys were never a thing."

I grimaced at the thought of doing anything with Taj. His beard alone was a huge turn-off for me. "No way. He might as well be my brother."

"You do realize he's the most attractive man many of us have ever seen?" Edison turned into the parking lot for the bank and pulled into the spot closest to the door. "And you are lucky to be in his presence?"

"I mostly keep him around because he pulls in so many likes from the moms who follow me, all desperate for an adventure with a hunky man." I nudged her playfully across the center console. "Just like you."

"Har, har." She offered me the lock box. "Can you carry this? I feel like people are way less likely to attack you."

"What's that supposed to mean?"

"That you're built like a dump truck."

"I'm sorry, was that a compliment?"

"Just take the box. I'm right behind you."

I tucked the lock box under my arm and stepped out of the car. Edison rushed around the front to join me and linked her arm with my free one. Her eyes darted here and there, looking for prowlers in the dark, but Doveport was as quiet and innocent as it had always been.

Barley was asleep behind the front desk. When I rapped on the glass door, he jolted awake. A slight panic stirred his pupils as he spotted me—tall, muscled, and militaristic—first. Then he spotted Edison, relaxed, and came to open the door.

"You gave me a fright, Bex," Barley said in his gravelly voice as he beckoned us inside. "I didn't recognize you."

"I could tell." I passed the lock box to him. "Let's get this squared away, shall we?"

It took Barley several minutes to run all the money through the automatic counting machine. Thousands of dollars in ones and fives turned out to be quite a few bills. With each stack of hundred that Barley put away, Edison's smile grew wider. At last, Barley straightened out the last pile of cash and loaded it into the machine.

"That's the lot of it," he said, checking the number. "Twenty-two thousand, two hundred, and nineteen dollars, all to the Home Safe account. I'm so happy for you, Edison."

Edison's tears were on a roll tonight. She beamed with pride as Barley printed her receipt. "I have plans for that money. First and foremost, I want to expand the program as much as possible."

Barley patted her hand. "I remember when you first came back to Doveport after all of that nonsense that happened to you. You were a different person then, so young with a tiny little baby to take care of all on your own. I think I can speak for the whole town when I say how proud we are of what you've done with your life."

Edison flipped her long hair over her shoulder and let out a great sniff. "Don't make me cry, Barley. I'm getting dried out."

Barley chuckled. "Go get a drink, sweetheart. You deserve it."

WE ENDED up in a booth at Dove's Pub, way back in the corner of the restaurant. Despite our hidden placement, people kept spotting us on their way to or from the bathroom and stopped by to offer congratulations to Edison for the success of the fundraiser.

"Thank you, Joyce. Really, it means so much to me," Edison said to the most recent local to drop by. As Joyce waved and made her way back to her own table, Edison's smile dropped off her face. "I think my cheeks are cracking. Look at me. Do I look older? Are my lines deeper?"

"Relax. You look fine."

She signaled the bartender—Austin again—for another beer. "I appreciate their enthusiasm. I really do. But damn, I just want to relax and drink without playing the part anymore."

"I have an idea."

I shuffled around to the other side of the round booth, forcing Edison into the shadowy area beneath the TV. Without any light to illuminate her face, she was almost unrecognizable. She tensed up as another familiar local approached us, but his eyes slid right past Edison's face as he walked back to the bathrooms. Edison relaxed.

"Have I mentioned you're a genius?" she asked.

"Once or twice."

Austin approached and set a Guinness in front of Edison. "Anything else I can get you ladies?"

"Hot truffle fries," Edison said. "I'm starving."

"Coming right up."

Edison tapped her glass of fresh beer against mine. "Cheers to us for having accomplished more than our parents expected of us."

"I'll drink to that, but I'm giving my mom a pass," I said.

"Why?" Edison wiped white froth from her upper lip. "Your mom berated you non-stop for never going to college. Don't you remember what you said when you told her you were going to become an influencer?"

"Vividly," I replied. "But I won't hold it against her."

"New outlook, huh?"

I lifted my glass with a shrug. "She was a single mom. She wanted me to have the best life possible, and in her book, going to college would give me the chance to do that. She was protecting me."

Edison peered at me over the lip of her glass. "Last time you were in town, you couldn't stop bitching about her."

I drew patterns in the condensation dripping from my glass. "Things change, I guess."

She studied me for a long minute. "Something's wrong."

"What? No. What are you talking about?"

"You're a good liar, Bex, but you're not that good. What's going on?"

I pressed my cold fingers against my eyelids, savoring the cooling sensation. My head felt like a baked potato sitting in the microwave for too long. At some point, it was going to explode.

"Mom has some kind of early onset dementia," I told Edison. "I didn't know about it until I got home. It's erratic.

Half the time, she thinks I'm fifteen. It's like going back in time."

Edison didn't make any attempt to comfort me physically. She was one of the few people that understood how affection made me jumpy when I wasn't in the mood for it. Instead, she kept her hands to herself and her voice soft. "I'm sorry, Edison. I didn't know. I guess that's why I haven't seen her out in town as often?"

"Probably."

"What are you going to do?" she asked. "I didn't think you were planning to stick around Doveport much longer."

I took a long swig of beer, letting the bitterness flow across my tongue and wash the emotions away. "I wasn't at first, but like I said, things change. I don't want to jet off across the world then come back in a year to find Mom's completely out of it."

"So you're sticking around?"

I set the empty glass on the table with a note of finality. "For a while, at least. I gotta suss out this situation with Mom. Put things in order. Maybe see a doctor with her. Besides, I know you miss me too."

Edison fixed me with a wry smile. "I won't deny it. It'll be nice to have you around. I think you have a good effect on Avery too. She won't stop talking about her new followers. I'm not sure if I like it though."

"I'll teach her how to balance social media and real life," I promised. "It doesn't have to be one or the other."

"Good to know—" The television overhead caught Edison's attention, and she craned her neck to look at the news report. "Oh, these idiots again."

"We have an update on Norman Beers, the escaped prisoner from Oregon State Penitentiary," the newscaster was saying. "Investigators have linked Beers to the infamous Whale Watchers organization, a radical group of environmentalists that claims to fight for animal rights. Beers was incarcerated for attacking David Brickston, the owner of Brickston farms, on behalf of the Whale Watchers. Shortly after the attack, Brickston Farms—a supposedly humane operation for organic beef and chicken—was exposed for abusing its animals. Police have released a clip of Beers speaking on the subject following his arrest."

A grainy video replaced the live feed of the newscaster's face. It showed Norman Beers, still in his pressed collared shirt with his hands cuffed behind his back, speaking to at least a dozen microphones from surrounding reporters as the cops led him into the booking station.

"Brickston lies about his animal practices," Beers declared, calm and steady despite the rough manner in which the cops handled him. "He's a vile human being who claims to treat animals fairly. Slaughtering animals for food is inhumane to begin with, but to lie about your entire company's motto is another level of disgusting. I didn't attack him. He attacked *me* when I threatened to unveil the abhorrent acts his company is performing. All I did was defend myself—"

A burly cop shook Beers roughly. "Enough!"

The clip ended as Beers's escorts forced him through the doors of the penitentiary, and the reporters were cut off from recording anything else.

"The Whale Watchers, huh?" I asked Edison. "You've heard of them before?"

"Every once in a while, the news reports some stupid stunt they've pulled," Edison replied. "Violent protests and whatnot. For animal welfare activists, they sure don't care about harming humans."

"Vegans can be pretty intense," I agreed. "But I get where they're coming from."

Edison's lip curled as another picture of Norman Beers popped up on screen. "It doesn't matter what they're fighting for. It doesn't excuse behavior like his."

"Of course it doesn't." I checked the time. "It's getting late. Do you mind giving me a ride home? I'm not about to bike through this wind."

WHEN EDISON DROPPED ME OFF, Melba's car was already gone. I expected the house to be dark, but a single lamp was on in the front room. My stomach dropped. Something about that single lamp drew bad memories from the depths of my mind. The pressure that had been building in my head since Dove's finally released. My brain buzzed over and over, each zap accompanied by an incoming text message. I left my phone in my pocket. I didn't need enigmatic texts to know what was waiting for me inside.

The door squeaked when I pushed it open. The floorboards creaked under my booted foot. The hangers clanked loudly as I hung up my coat. Every noise sounded like an explosion when you were trying your best to stay quiet.

But there was no escaping the inevitable. When the lamp was on, it meant one thing: Mom was still up, sitting in the leather armchair and watching the front walk for me to come home. It was past my ten o'clock curfew. If I got lucky, she'd fallen asleep, and her wrath would fade by morning. Not today though.

"Where do you think you're going, young lady?"

I froze with one foot on the bottom step of the stairs,

braced myself, and moved into the living room. "Hey, Mom. What are you doing up so late?"

Mom's usually kind face transformed into something monstrous when she was angry or scared. Her lips turned upward in a nasty sneer and her eyes went frighteningly blank.

"What am *I* doing up so late?" she demanded, getting to her feet. "What are *you* doing out so late? Do you realize what time it is?"

I held my hands out to keep some distance between us. "Mom, you're confused. I'm thirty years old, remember? I don't have a curfew anymore."

"Don't talk back to me!"

I didn't see her hand as it came out of the shadows. I only felt it as it landed with a hard smack to my cheek. I clapped my palm to my face and stumbled backward, staring open-mouthed at my mother.

The harsh sound seemed to jolt Mom back to her senses. Her lips relaxed, and her eyes regained some emotion. As she examined the red welt on my cheek, she covered her mouth with both hands.

"Oh, Bex," she said softly. "I'm so sorry."

When she reached for me, I stepped quickly away. "It's fine, Mom. You weren't thinking straight. Get up to bed, okay?"

Before she had the chance to reply, I bounded upstairs, taking the steps two at a time, and locked myself in my old room. I fell onto the bed, my cheek still stinging, and stared at the ceiling. Stale memories bombarded me from every direction. I pushed my face into a pillow and let out a muffled yell.

9

*I*t was difficult to adjust to a life I'd already left so many years ago. Doveport, for the most part, remained unchanged, which was exactly why I never cared for it. The locals were perfectly happy to visit the same places, eat the same food, and do the same things over and over again. In the days following the fundraiser, I did my best to find joy and excitement in the little things, but life turned stale quickly.

"Third day in a row!" Maxine announced as I wandered into her café one morning, bleary-eyed. "Does this mean you're one of my new regulars?"

I clambered onto one of the wood stools at the counter and propped my feet on the iron rung. Maxine's café had been remodeled to fit in better with the expectations the rest of the nation had of the Pacific Northwest. It now boasted high ceilings, white walls, exposed brick, industrial influences, and a lot of greenery. Whether you wanted a cozy corner to do homework or a big table to catch up with friends, Maxine's could give it to you. In fact, it wasn't even called Maxine's anymore. The sign over the door read Aero-latte Café.

"I'm one of your old regulars," I reminded Maxine. "What's with the rebranding anyway?"

"Oh." Maxine sighed as she gathered the ingredients for my mocha cappuccino. "Business died down a couple years ago, so I hired an advisor to help me keep the place up and running. He suggested the remodel and the new name, and I suppose he was right. Ever since we became Aerolatte, we've had a ton of new customers. Did you know there are some people who travel the world looking just for coffee shops?"

"I did," I replied. "I follow quite a few of them on Instagram. They're good people to know when you're somewhere you've never been before and dying for a cup of caffeine."

Maxine shook her hair out. For as long as I could remember, she sported bright red hair that traveled all the way to her waist. She never wore a hair net, and by some miracle, no one had ever found a single strand in their food or coffee. When I was younger, I persuaded Edison that Maxine was a magical nymph with enchanted hair.

Maxine poured a foam heart into my cappuccino, set the mug in front of me, and topped it off with a sprinkling of cacao powder. "There you go, hun. Want some breakfast? I came up with a new sandwich." She ticked the ingredients off on her fingers. "Smoked salmon, cream cheese, arugula, and avocado on a whole wheat bagel. Interested?"

"Sounds great."

"Coming up."

When the café first opened, back when I was nine or ten years old, Maxine was a twenty-year-old with no college education and no business sense. Her journey had been the opposite of mine. She'd moved from a crappy neighborhood in New York, all the way across the country to Doveport, in the hopes of finding the perfect nook to try her hand at coffee roasting.

"I've always admired you," I told Maxine as I watched her assemble my sandwich. "Have I ever told you that?"

She snorted, hopefully not onto my bagel. "What are you talking about?"

"When you first showed up in Doveport, I thought you were the coolest person I'd ever seen," I said. "With your hair and that nose piercing, remember? I started drinking coffee when I was ten because I wanted to be like you."

Maxine chortled and popped the bagel into the toaster. "Yeah, I served you half cups because I thought your mother would kill me if she knew how much caffeine I was giving you. I also recall you dumping a ton of sugar in my perfectly brewed coffee."

"What can I say? My taste buds weren't as refined back then." I sipped the cappuccino and let out a satisfied sigh. "God, I can appreciate your skills a lot better now."

Maxine wiped steamed milk from the tip of my nose as she passed by my seat at the counter. "I'll get you a napkin, cutie."

"Can I ask you something?" I blotted my nose with my sleeve to make sure all the milk was gone. "What did you see in Doveport? What made you want to stay here?"

She pulled my bagel from the toaster and frosted it with cream cheese. "Hmm. I guess I loved the small-town feel of it. Everyone here was so welcoming. I was a stranger, but they treated me like family. New York's not like that. It's dirty and fast-paced, and if you don't get out of someone's way quickly enough, they'll run you over. I hated it."

"But why Doveport?" I asked, wrinkling my nose.

She finished building the sandwich and set it in front of me. "Because it felt like home as soon as I drove past the welcome sign. I liked the natural feel of things. I liked the people. And you know what?"

Three bites deep in the bagel, I mumbled, "Huh?"

Maxine smiled fondly. "On my first day in town, I was looking at an empty storefront, wondering if I could turn it into a coffee shop without any experience. All of a sudden this little kid ran up to me. Short blonde hair, scabs on her knees, some of her adult teeth still growing in. She tugged on my shirt, looked up at me, and said, 'I'm not supposed to talk to strangers—'"

"But my name's Bex," I finished. "So we're not strangers anymore."

Maxine nodded her confirmation. "And then you told me you loved my hair and that I should stay in town forever. It felt like a sign. I leased that storefront the next day."

"Glad to provide some much-needed perspective," I joked.

She dumped ground espresso beans from the portafilter, refilled the basket, and inserted the filter into the espresso machine with a practiced turn of her wrist. "What's with the questions anyway? You turning on us?"

"Of course not," I said, though I shifted nervously in my seat. "I guess I need a different perspective for myself."

As the espresso machine rumbled and spat dark liquid into a small cup, Maxine smiled at me. "We're always here for you, Bex, no matter how long you've been gone. This town knows what you've gone through *and* what you're going through."

"You heard about my mom then?"

"She's wandered in once or twice, thinking it's 2004," she admitted. "It was a blast from the past, I'll tell you that."

"Yeah." Absentmindedly, I twirled my mug in its saucer. "A total blast."

The bell over the door rung, and Edison strolled in from outside, her cheeks pink from the wind. She shook off her coat with a shrug, slung it over the back of the stool next to mine, and collapsed in the seat.

"Coffee," she gasped at Maxine. "Please."

Maxine hurriedly poured a cup. "There you go, sweetheart. Thaw out, would you?"

Edison warmed her hands around the mug and inhaled the steam. "God, why is it so cold already? It's not even October yet!"

"Climate change," I answered dryly.

"How's your mom?" she asked. "No other incidents?"

Edison was the only person I'd told about my mother's slip the other night. "Nope. Though I have to say, I've been avoiding her."

"Are you okay?"

"Fine. Why?"

Edison shot me a knowing look. "Don't play that game with me. I know your damage as well as you know mine."

I couldn't deny that. After my dad passed away and my mother's temper grew shorter, Edison was the person I told all my woes to.

"I'm stuck," I admitted. "When she's lucid, it's great. It's nice to spend time with her after being away for so long, but when she loses it…"

"It's hard," Edison finished for me. "Life would be a lot easier if we didn't have to deal with our parents, huh?"

I took another bite of my bagel to avoid answering. After chewing, I asked, "What about your parents? Do you talk to them?"

She grimaced. "Not much. They send a card for Avery's birthday every year."

I scoffed and rolled my eyes. "I hate that. They shouldn't get to claim Avery as their grandkid considering they kicked you out of the house when you got pregnant."

Edison blew across her steaming coffee. "If they hadn't, I never would have started Home Safe. Beside, I'm glad Avery gets to know at least *one* pair of her grandparents."

I hesitated, chewing on my lower lip. "So her dad—"

"Bex, don't."

I shut up. For thirteen years plus nine months and counting, I didn't know who Avery's father was. Edison wouldn't tell me, and as far as I knew, she hadn't told anyone else either. I'd gone as far as to sneak a peek at Avery's birth certificate when she was a baby, but her father's name was not printed on it.

"Sorry."

"Whatever," Edison said, waving it off. "Can we talk about something else?"

THE DAY WORE ON. Eventually, Edison and I journeyed to the leather armchairs in the corner of the café for better comfort. Edison worked on her laptop, chewing on her nails as she decided what her next steps for Home Safe should be. I took *Existentialism is a Humanism* from Maxine's free library, read the entire essay in an hour, then promptly searched for a literary analysis of the piece to better understand it. Maxine didn't bother us except to refill our drinks, offer us water, and use us as guinea pigs for new menu items she was thinking of selling. Other customers came and went. Some spent an hour or two, some only stopped in for a quick coffee, but no one camped out for as long as we did.

The sun traveled to the other side of the building and shone through the glass storefront as lunchtime faded into the afternoon. The bright orange glare bounced off the shiny coffee machines and reflected into my eyes. Wiping tears away, I rearranged myself to avoid the blinding light, then caught sight of Avery and Cade outside. The bell chimed again as they shoved their way inside.

"Move!"

"You move!"

"I got here first."

Pushing against one another, the teenagers approached the counter. In one's haste to beat the other, they knocked over a small pitcher, sending creamer across the bar top.

Maxine planted her hands on her hips. "People, if you're going to behave like this in my establishment, I'm going to have to ask you to leave."

"Don't bother," Edison called, looking over the top of her laptop. "They don't need coffee anyway. Like I want them bouncing off the walls for the rest of the night."

Avery and Cade stepped apart, halting their scuffle at once. Edison's tired and annoyed expression said it all: the teenagers were driving her nuts.

"I wanted hot chocolate," Cade said. "Not coffee. I have my own money. *Avery* is the one who wanted coffee."

Avery raised her hands like the cops were after her. "I have no idea what Cade's talking about. I came in here for a donut."

"Quiet," Edison ordered. "Get what you want and sit over *there*." She nodded to the corner at the farthest end of the café. "If I hear even a *whisper* of you two bickering, you're both going home. Do some homework or something. Got it?"

The teenagers nodded and ordered from Maxine with the utmost politeness. Then they sat at a table, opened their backpacks, and drew out their notebooks, but every once in a while, one kicked the other beneath the table.

"What's going on with that?" I asked Edison. "I thought they were getting along."

"That lasted for about an hour," she replied wearily. "Avery's new social media fame got her in with the cool kids at school, but she intentionally left Cade out. So Cade does their best to get Avery's attention, which ends up annoying Avery, and I'm left to deal with the fallout."

"Why are teenagers such jerks?"

"Hormones?" Edison shut her laptop, groaned, and rubbed her eyes. "I can't look at spreadsheets anymore. I'm going blind. What are you doing for dinner? You want to take the kids off my hands? I could use a quiet night at home."

I pretended to consider it. "That depends. What's in it for me?"

"Fun times with the kiddos," she prompted. "You said you wanted to spend more time with Avery."

"Not when she's being a jerk."

"Maybe you can un-jerk-ify her."

"It didn't work with you."

Edison kicked me under the table, taking after her daughter. "Please? I'll pay you. I'm rich now, remember?"

"Your charity's rich," I amended. "And you need that money."

"Stop being right," she whined.

Across the café, Cade and Avery exploded in a fight, drawing every customer's eyes.

"You're just jealous!" Avery spat, yanking her phone from Cade's hand.

"Of what?" Cade challenged. "The fact that you're friends with stupid Chad now? Guess what, Avery? Stupid Chad is *stupid!* I don't want to be friends with him, and I don't think you should do some dumb talent show just because he said so."

"You're afraid everyone's gonna think I'm cooler than you," Avery replied. "That's why you don't want me to do it."

"I don't care *who* thinks I'm cool."

"Psh! Yeah, right! You've been hanging off of me for the past week!"

"Hey!" Edison shouted across the cafe. The teenagers immediately shut up, their faces draining of color as they looked our way. Edison beckoned them over with one finger. Avery visibly swallowed as she pushed her chair away from the table and crossed the room. Edison leaned toward them and said in a deadly quiet voice, "Is this the way I expect you to behave in public?"

Avery and Cade shook their heads.

"Then why are you shouting at each other?" Edison asked.

"I want to do the talent show," Avery said at once, "but Cade wouldn't let me sign up for it."

"Cade?" Edison prompted. "Is this true?"

"Everyone knows Avery has stage fright," Cade said. "It's the only reason Chad told her she should do it in the first place. He wants to see her fail. I'm trying to protect her!"

"Let's dial it back," Edison said. "When's the talent show?"

"Tonight," Avery replied.

"Is it too late to sign up for it?"

"No." Avery crossed her arms and glared at Cade. "There are still a few open spots left. Mrs. Hall said to call the school if I wanted to do it."

Edison uncrossed Avery's arms for her and took her hands. "Honey, are you sure you want to do this? Don't you remember what happened a few years ago at your dance recital?"

Avery shook off her mother's touch. "That was different. I hated dance. I don't have stage fright when I play the drums."

"If you're sure," Edison said, "you can sign up for it."

Avery whooped and pumped her fists. As she ran off to phone the school, Cade stared glumly at the floor. I playfully stepped on their toes.

"Don't sweat it," I told Cade. "You can hang out with me."

Cade's expression brightened. "Really?"

"Yeah, no worries."

EDISON TOOK Avery home to pick an outfit for the talent show. I volunteered to take Cade with me, thinking the teenagers would benefit from a little time apart. We dropped by my house to waste some time. Thankfully, Mom was lucid and welcoming. She helped me light the fire pit in the backyard so me and Cade could hang out on the back porch. I shared my Instagram adventures with Cade as Melba and Mom cooked dinner together, then the four of us ate in the dining room like a family of strangers. Cade and I ducked out shortly after that and made our way to the school early for the talent show.

"Thanks for letting me tag along with you," Cade said as we walked to the gymnasium together. "You didn't have to do that."

"I got the sense that you and Avery were driving each other insane," I replied. "Thought you could use a break."

Cade hung their head as we joined the small crowd filing into the gym. "I'm stupid. Avery was never gonna like me. She thinks I stole her mom."

I put my arm around Cade's shoulders. "Edison and Avery's relationship was complicated before you showed up. You don't have anything to do with that."

"I hate myself," Cade muttered.

"Don't say that," I said sharply. "Don't let anyone make you feel that way, not even Avery. Come on, there are a couple of seats over there by the stage."

I distracted Cade with a dumb game on my phone as the seats filled in the gym and the lights dimmed. As the curtain opened, Edison walked in late and waved from the aisle.

"Excuse me," she said, making her way along the row. "Pardon me. Ooh, sorry about your shoes. They look great though!" She plunked into the seat we'd saved for her, balled up her coat, and shoved it beside her. "Is it hot in here or is it just me?"

"It's just you," Cade and I chorused.

Someone hushed us as the MC, Mrs. Hall, came out on stage. According to Cade, Mrs. Hall was Doveport's new music teacher. She tapped the microphone to make sure it was on and cleared her throat.

"Good evening, everyone!" she said, gazing out at the crowd. "Welcome to Doveport High's annual talent show. We've got some amazing performances for you tonight from our truly talented students, so let's get things moving. First up, we have Carmen Ruiz and Dickie Mellon with their comedy sketch entitled 'Friday Night Live!'"

I dozed through the first half of the show as kids sang,

danced, played instruments, performed stand-up comedy, recited poetry, and treated the stage like an open mic night in downtown Portland. Cade elbowed me more than once to let me know I was snoring, saving me from the other parents' dirty looks. Edison looked bored too. Her elbow kept slipping off the armrest, jolting her into the next seat, much to her neighbor's dismay.

At long last, Mrs. Hall reappeared on the stage and said, "Thank you, Tommy, for that wonderful piece of prose. Up next is Avery Maxx, playing Ode to Sleep by Twenty One Pilots on the drums!"

Edison wiped drool from her mouth and sat up a little straighter at the mention of her daughter's name. Mrs. Hall looked left and right, but Avery didn't appear on the stage.

"Avery?" Mrs. Hall called. "Avery Maxx, are you ready to perform?"

"Told you," Cade muttered in my ear. "Stage fright."

I shushed Cade. As Mrs. Hall peered into the shadows behind the thick red curtain, a zap cut through my brain like a bee sting. I hastily pulled my phone out of my pocket and checked the messages.

G0n3.

"Mrs. Hall?" A student had appeared from the wings of the stage. "Avery's not here. We can't find her anywhere."

"*D*on't panic," I murmured to Edison as my own heart rate skyrocketed. "She's probably getting some air out back or something. No need to—"

Edison shot to her feet and ruthlessly wormed her way out of the row, not apologizing this time when she stomped on someone's foot or kicked a purse out from under a chair.

"Go," I hissed to Cade, gently pushing the teenager out of their seat. I grabbed the coat that Edison had left behind. "Follow her."

"What? Oh, jeez." Cade, bent over so as to not block the view of the stage, stumbled through the row too. "Sorry, guys. I swear this isn't my fault. She made me do it."

To the audience's confusion, Edison clambered onto the stage and disappeared into the wings. People muttered in the crowd, some of them worried and others indifferent.

"Edison Maxx's kid? Makes sense, doesn't it."

"Yeah, but did she run away or get kidnapped?"

The words drew acid into my throat. I swallowed it as I ushered Cade along.

"Don't make me do it," Cade muttered as we approached the stage. "You're going to make me do it, aren't you?"

"Stop being a baby."

We crawled onto the stage as well. Mrs. Hall gestured with the microphone as if to say, *What the hell are you all doing?* Cade took a mocking bow in front of the crowd before I grabbed them by the arm and led them into the dark wings backstage. The remaining students who had not performed yet waited there, watching us with confused expressions.

Mrs. Hall cleared her throat. "All right. Sorry, everyone, for that short delay. Looks like Avery Maxx won't be performing, so up next is Gal Miller. Come on out, Gal!"

A girl with a contrabass bugle lifted the enormous instrument onto her tiny shoulder and hurried out from behind the corner. A short moment later, the short low tones of her performance resonated through the backstage area.

"Edison!" I whisper-called into the darkness. When no answer came, I addressed the nearest teenager, a skinny boy holding a single triangle. "Hey, did you see Avery's mom go through here? She's got long brown hair, looks a little like a hippie?"

He jabbed his thumb over his shoulder. "Thataway. Toward the emergency exit."

I patted the kid's shoulder. "Thanks, man. Let's go, Cade."

At the back of the gym was a single door with a red exit sign over the top. A warning label on the handle read *Do not open unless in case of emergency. Alarm will sound.*

Cade pushed through it without hesitation. I braced myself for the alarm, but it never came.

"Someone disabled it," Cade said, stepping into the poorly-lit school yard. "People sneak out this way to smoke during gym class." She conspicuously cleared her throat. "Not that I would know or anything. I'm a perfect student."

"Sure, sure." I let the door close behind us. A single light mounted to the side of the building cast a yellow glow across the faded green grass and the asphalt of the nearby basketball court. Beyond its reach, the yard was black except for the streetlights in the distance. "Edison! Avery! Where are you?"

"Over there."

Cade pointed to the far end of the basketball court, where all I could see was the dark outline of Edison's shadow.

"Wait here," I told Cade.

As I came up behind Edison, she shivered. I draped her coat across her shoulders. Together, we gazed into the shadows of Doveport. Avery was nowhere to be seen.

"She's gone, isn't she?" Edison murmured. "I saw you check your phone."

"My phone—my head—isn't always right."

Edison sniffled. Tears rolled freely down her cheeks, glistening in the moonlight. "She was long gone before I got out here."

"We should phone the cops," I said softly. "As soon as possible. There's a chance she's still in the area."

"They'll say she ran away."

"Not with everything that's already happened."

"Yes, with everything that's happened!" Edison snapped, swiping the moisture away from her face. "What have the authorities done to recover Carly and Gemma? Nothing! I've spoken to the girls' parents, trying to offer them some comfort. Neither of those girls came from broken homes. They had no reason to run away. It's a repeat of what happened to me. Nobody came looking for me. Nobody cared. They all though I was just another teenage rebel, and they'll think the exact same thing about Avery."

"I came looking for you," I reminded her.

"Yeah, a fifteen-year-old with superpowers," she scoffed, as if she'd never believed in my abilities in the first place. "Didn't do me much good in the long run, did it?"

I pulled out my phone. "This isn't helping. We need to call." I dialed 911. "Hi, yes. I'm at Doveport High School. Another girl has gone missing. Her name is Avery Maxx. We're afraid she's been kidnapped like Carly Javier and Gemma Johnson."

"How long has she been gone?" the operator asked in a nasally voice. "Where was the last place you saw her?"

I checked the time. "It's been about two hours. She was supposed to perform at the high school talent show tonight."

"I'm going to transfer you to our missing persons department," the operator said. "Please hold."

An annoyingly cheerful tune played in my ear. Edison hugged herself, gazing absentmindedly into the distance. She'd stopped crying, but her eyes had gone blank, like she wasn't feeling anything at all anymore.

"Doveport Police," a gruff voice came on. "This is Officer Greer."

"Hi," I said hurriedly. "I need to report—"

"A missing person," Greer finished. "I know. Name, age, physical description, please."

"Avery Maxx. She's thirteen," I answered. "She's about five foot three, with a pale, heart-shaped face and dyed black hair."

I spoke to Officer Greer for a solid fifteen minutes, telling him everything I could remember about Avery. Every so often, he asked a question I couldn't answer, so I looked to

Edison for help then repeated her muttered reply into the phone.

"Okay, we'll put out a BOLO and report it to the FBI right away," Greer said once he was finished questioning me. For his brusque manner, he was thorough and attentive. "Are you Avery's mom?"

"No, I'm a close family friend, but I have her mom with me."

"Tell her not to touch anything at her house or in Avery's room," Greer ordered. "I'll get an investigator out there tomorrow to have a look around. It's best if everything's left the way it is so we can get a clearer picture of where Avery might have went."

"I'll let her know."

When I finally hung up, Edison had sank to the ground to sit on the cold asphalt. I took her by the elbow to help her up, but she was all dead weight. With a defeated sigh, I sat next to her. The cold permeated the butt of my jeans right away. For a few minutes, we regarded the school yard in silence. In that time, Edison's shock wore off and she dissolved into full-on hysteria.

"It's my fault," she sobbed, bowing her head into my lap. "I pushed her away. I didn't pay her enough attention. I took Cade in even when I knew Avery didn't want me to. I've been too caught up with the nonprofit to bother with my own daughter."

I glanced over my shoulder to make sure Cade wasn't within earshot. They were sitting on the step outside the emergency exit door, the hood of their coat pulled tight around their neck and face.

"It's not your fault." I rubbed Edison's shoulders. "You know what happened. Someone took her. But we've done this before. We know how kidnappers operate. We'll find her. I promise."

Before I could supply more support, my phone rang. Thankfully, it wasn't accompanied by a brain zap.

"Hello?" I answered right away.

"Hi, honey. It's Melba—"

"Where is she? She's going to be in deep shit when she gets home!" My mother's yell pierced my ear, and I held the phone farther away in an attempt to defend my hearing. *"Out this late! Who the hell does she think she is?"*

"I think you should come home," Melba shouted over my mother's tirade. "I was supposed to leave here at six o'clock, but Lydia has been upset that you're not around."

"Can you stay a little longer?" I pleaded, rubbing circles on Edison's back as she continued to cry all over my pants. "Avery's missing. I'm dealing with a crisis."

"Well, we have a crisis here too. Ow! Lydia, do not throw things!"

Glass shattered on the other end of the line.

"Melba, I'll be there as soon as possible, but I have some things to take care of. If it gets too bad, call the police."

"The police?" Melba said, shocked.

"Yeah, have her sedated for all I care."

"I don't think—"

"See you soon." I hung up, breathing hard through my nose. "Edison, I hate to do this to you."

She lifted herself from my lap and saw how hard I was working to keep all the stress in my head from exploding outward. "Go," she said. "I'm going to drive around town and look for Avery. Maybe you're right. Maybe she got scared and walked off. I'll keep you posted."

We helped each other stand. I kissed the top of her head.

"Everything's going to be okay," I said to her. "I promise."

EDISON DROVE me home in silence. Cade asked a million questions about Avery from the back seat, but neither one of us felt like answering. When we pulled up to my house, I almost didn't get out. Melba's car idled in the driveway, the headlights reflecting against the garage door. Her silhouette became visible as we pulled in behind her. She was hiding from my mother's wrath but didn't feel comfortable leaving her alone either.

I bid goodnight and good luck to Edison, sincerely hoping they might drive around the next corner and happen upon Avery. Then I approached Melba's driver's side and tapped on the window. She rolled it down. Apparently, it was a night for crying. Melba's eyes were bloodshot and teary.

"I'm sorry," she said, dabbing her cheeks with a handkerchief. "I couldn't take it anymore. She started throwing plates. Look." She turned her face to show me her opposite cheek. A thin cut, already cleaned and dressed, drew a red line across her skin. "Be careful when you go in there. There's glass everywhere."

I cupped my forehead as if to hold the pressure in. "God, why are you apologizing? *I'm* sorry. I should have been here sooner."

Melba shook her head and took my hand through the window. "It's okay, Bex. It's no one's fault. I shouldn't have gotten upset. I've dealt with rougher patients than Lydia, but it's different when you're caring for your best friend and she suddenly forgets who you are."

"I won't blame you if you want to send a replacement."

"No, no." She squeezed my hand harder, holding on for

dear life. "Listen to me, honey. I want to spend as much time with your mom as possible, and you should too. She's deteriorating faster than I expected her to. Soon enough, she won't recognize you anymore. Cherish her lucidity while she still has a little left."

I gulped, swallowing back all the feelings that threatened to spill out of my stomach like bad oysters. The way Mom treated me after Dad died, our hot and cold relationship, and the guilt I felt for leaving her behind while I traveled the world welled up inside me.

"I'll call you later," I promised Melba. "Take care of yourself."

She finally let go of my hand and put the car in reverse. "Wait! What happened to Avery? Did you find her?"

My shoulders fell. "Not yet. We reported her missing, and Edison's out looking for her. We're hoping for the best."

"I'll keep my eyes peeled." Melba blew her nose in her handkerchief. "This town doesn't need a little more tragedy."

I watched Melba's car as she reversed out of the driveway and disappeared down the street, but once her taillights were gone, I couldn't put off going inside any longer. My feet heavy with dread, I trudged up the front steps.

ONCE AGAIN, the single lamp in the living room was on. I braced myself for the onslaught of screaming, but Mom wasn't in her usual post. As I shed my coat and stepped forward, broken glass crunched under my feet. Not only had Mom thrown several plates, but she'd also taken her temper out on her crystal collectibles.

"Mom?" I called tentatively through the house. "It's me, Bex."

"Out back, honey."

I tiptoed through the demolished kitchen and out the back door to find Mom sitting in her chair on the porch, one blanket across her lap and another over her shoulders. She cradled a cup of tea that had long gone cold. Three of her fingers sported Band-Aids. She took in my nervous look and hesitant stance.

"My adult kid is afraid of me," she stated matter-of-factly. "I never thought I'd be that type of mother."

"I'm not afr—" I stopped myself from completing the sentence, lest a lie come out of my mouth. "That sentiment is going around a lot lately."

"I scared Melba off."

"She doesn't like to see you like this." Slowly, I lowered myself into the chair next to hers. "It's like watching her friend disappear right in front of her."

My mother's lower lip wobbled. "Is that why you left? Because of me?"

"No, Mom." Despite the direct question, I couldn't clarify any further. I'd left Doveport for a whole list of reasons. Mom might have been included on it, but she wasn't the sole reason I felt the need to ditch town as soon as possible. Besides, lying was a kindness sometimes. "It wasn't you."

She recovered quickly. "How much of a mess did I make inside?"

"A pretty big one." I opened the outdoor fridge, took out a beer, and popped the cap off using the arm of the chair. "Let's just say you'll probably have to buy some plastic plates."

She massaged her forehead in the same way I did when stress got the better of me. "Why is this happening to me?"

I took a swig of beer, taking comfort in the refreshing

taste of lager as it flowed to the back of my throat. "Poor genetics?"

That got a laugh out of her. "That's good. Blame your grandma. She was nuts too."

The night had taken all the chuckles out of me. I didn't have any humor left to spare. I leaned forward and dangled the beer bottle between my knees. "Look, Mom. I think we should start talking about what to do when" —I nervously cleared my throat— "when you can't make decisions for yourself anymore. It's getting to a point where—"

She pulled the beer out of my grasp and downed a third of it in a few gulps. "Not now," she said, wiping her mouth. "Please. Give me one more night not to think about it. We can talk tomorrow."

I swiped the beverage back from her. "Fine. We'll talk tomorrow."

"Good. How was your day?"

"Awful."

"Well, we are a pair."

FIRST THING IN THE MORNING, I called Edison to see if she had any updates on Avery. She didn't answer her cell phone or her own phone, nor did she reply to any of my text messages. I got the same treatment when I texted and called Cade. Brimming with discomfort, I jogged downstairs and toward the front door.

"Hey!" Mom shouted from the kitchen. "Where are you going?"

"Edison's!" I hollered back. "We'll talk tonight!"

With that, I slid my arms into my coat, rolled my bike off the front porch, and started pedaling up the street. Every day, the air grew a little chillier. My eyes watered as the wind swept by. I pulled a beanie from my pocket, riding one-handed, and yanked it on over my head so my scalp wouldn't be so cold. If I loved one thing about Doveport, it was the way it smelled during the turn of the season. The crisp scent of drying leaves always made me feel more alive.

By the time I made it to Edison's, I was frozen to the bike. A nondescript car was parked outside her house, the windows tinted too dark to see inside. I leaned my bike against the garage door and let myself in. Edison and I were familiar enough with each other not to use keys.

"Avery?" The hope in Edison's voice nearly broke my heart when she heard the door open. "Is that you?"

"It's Bex!" I called. "Who's that parked out front?"

In the living room, Edison leaned on the back of her sofa, arms crossed and cheeks tearstained. A man was with her, one arm propped so casually on the stair rail that he might have been in his own home. He was tall and handsome with pointed cheekbones and dark hair slicked back against his scalp. He wore a tailored white shirt, unbuttoned a little too far down to be professional, slacks, and a jacket that might have matched if it weren't a different shade of black than his pants. He glanced up from the notebook he was jotting in as I walked into the room.

"Who's this?" he asked Edison. "Potential suspect?"

"Bex Lennon," I answered for myself. "And no. Avery's basically my niece. Who the hell are you?"

The man smiled without his eyes and held out his hand for me to shake. "Sorry about that. I'm Agent Rocco Marioni. I'm with the FBI."

"That was quick," I muttered.

"We've been following these disappearances for a while,"

Marioni said. When he spoke, he looked at Edison. Never at me. "It's too coincidental that all these teenage girls are going missing at once."

"But you're not doing anything about it?" I questioned. "Do you have any leads?"

He flipped his notebook shut. "That's for us to worry about. You were close to Avery?"

"I *am* close to Avery," I corrected.

"Then I'll need to have a lengthy conversation with you," Marioni replied. He glanced at Edison. "Somewhere private."

"Not right now," I said. "Edison needs me."

Marioni left his post at the bottom of the staircase to approach Edison. He stood a little too closely to her, in my opinion, under the guise of creating privacy. When he touched her arm, she didn't pull away. "Ms. Maxx, my number one priority is returning Avery to you safe and sound, but I can't do that if you don't open up to me. What do you say we do this in a different setting? Sometimes, it can be difficult to get out of your head when you're at home. It's too emotional here. How about that Italian restaurant on 4th Avenue, tonight at six? I hear it gets good reviews from the locals."

"Did you swipe right on her or something?" I grumbled, stepping between the agent and my friend. "Doesn't seem professional for you to ask her on a date when you're supposed to be looking for her missing kid."

Marioni didn't miss a beat. His annoying smirk returned. "I can see how you might be confused, but it's not a date. I know from experience it's better to have discussions like these in a place unrelated to the missing person."

"Nowhere in Doveport is unrelated to Avery," I shot back. "She grew up here. She's been everywhere."

Edison poked me in the back. "Stand down, Bex. He's just doing his job."

Marioni tapped my nose with his pen, a weird and condescending gesture. "She's right. I'm doing my best." He collected his long black coat from the sofa and squeezed Edison's knee. "See you tonight then?"

"Mm-hmm."

I waited until I heard Marioni drive away. Then I said to Edison, "That guy's a scumbag. I could smell it before I walked into the house."

Edison flopped over the back of the sofa so her feet were straight up in the air. "He's the one who's been assigned to Avery's case, and he's been working in Doveport since the first disappearance. He's our best bet at finding her."

"You didn't hear from her at all?" I asked desperately. "Or see her last night while you were driving around? Did you call her? What about her friends? Maybe they know something we don't."

Edison put a throw pillow over her face and let out a muffled groan. "What do you think, Bex? If I'd seen her last night, I would have brought her home! I tried her phone. It goes straight to voicemail, and I made Cade text all of her friends last night. We got nothing."

I plopped onto the couch next to her. She put the throw pillow on my lap and rested her head on it.

"I was up all night," Edison murmured as she played with a small ripped seam in my pants. "Wondering where she could have gone. If she ran away or if she was taken. I kept thinking she'd never run away, but when I think about what our relationship has been like lately, I have to take everything into consideration."

"You're handling this well," I said. "I'm more of a wreck

than you are."

"I doubt that," she said. "I'm keeping all of my wreckage inside. You heard Marioni. I couldn't answer any of his questions. My throat kept closing up every time I tried."

"We'll find Avery," I told her. "We have to."

She sat up, straightened her posture, and folded her hands in her lap. It was something I'd only seen her do in high school, usually when she was in trouble with her parents or a teacher, the posture of faux innocence.

"What if *you* found Avery?" she questioned.

"What do you mean?"

She rolled her eyes. "Come on. I know you don't like to talk about it, but you have a damn gift."

"Edison, I told you—"

"Shut up!" She exploded off the couch, the fuse to her temper finally running out. "Don't give me that crap, Bex. Don't act like you can't do it. You said it yourself last night. You found *me* with nothing more than a flip phone in the middle of the woods with no damn service. You could sure as hell find Avery!"

"Are we doing this?" I asked. "Are we finally talking about this? Because if you want to deep dive into my shit, I want some damn answers."

"I can't give them to you!" she shouted. "I can't tell you what you want to know, Bex. I can't say who kidnapped me all those years ago or who Avery's father is or whatever else you want to stick your nose in."

"Why not?"

"Because I'll fucking explode!" she bellowed. "Don't you get that? I've been burying this shit for thirteen years. Hell, I've been *living* with it for that long. Why can't you see that? Why don't you understand that I *can't* do this? It doesn't matter who you are. I don't have the strength to tell you what you want to know."

With that, she collapsed onto the sofa and dissolved into a crying fit that made her whole body vibrate. I placed a cautious hand on her back, and when she didn't move away, I hugged her closer.

"I'm sorry," I muttered. "I didn't know you were still struggling with all of this so much."

She pushed her phone into my hand. "Please? Please try. I know you can do it."

I swallowed hard. "Edison, it's not what you think. If I'm being honest, I have no idea how this stuff works."

"Can you at least try to explain it?"

"It's like—" I struggled to find the words. "It's like there's a part of my brain that operates on a different level as everyone else's. In that level, I can go into cyberspace and manipulate shit like social media. I can send texts and voice-mails to people without ever touching my phone."

She sniffled and unapologetically wiped her nose on my shirt. "But how did that help you find me?"

"My brain generates messages for me too." I pulled out my phone and showed her the unknown numbers. "It's like I have more knowledge than I'm conscious of, so it has to travel through the phone for me to access it. The night I found you, I got compass directions in a bunch of texts from an unknown number. I didn't know it was my own brain doing it."

"B-but why won't you try to find Avery?"

"You don't remember because you were in the hospital for so long," I told her, putting my phone away. "But after EMS got you into that ambulance, they had to call another one for me. I had a grand mal seizure."

he events of so long ago—from when Edison and I attended Doveport High—were buried deep in the back of my brain. For years, I hadn't touched them. I hadn't allowed them to surface to a place where they would disrupt my thoughts. It wasn't the most effective way to deal with trauma, but we all had our own coping mechanisms. Edison, like me, shoved her problems deep down too, deciding to focus on the present issues instead. For the most part, it worked. I'd been able to travel without fear of being abducted and nourish my social media accounts despite the judgmental nature of the Internet scaring me. Edison, likewise, transformed her trauma into empowerment. It motivated her to start Home Safe and save kids from poor versions of childhood that they didn't deserve. Unfortunately, like most trauma, the past had a bad habit of resurfacing.

"Mom?" I called through the house as I arrived home. The leftover scent of bacon lingered, a little less appetizing now than it was when it was fresh. "I'm home!"

Edison had requested some alone time, and though I was hesitant to give it to her, I respected it all the while. After an indulgent bike ride through the middle of town, I decided I couldn't put off talking to my mother any longer. Besides, I had other things to do at home that might help us find Avery.

Melba popped her head out of the kitchen. "She's outside, dear."

"Is she... herself?"

"For now."

I zipped my coat back up and inspected the cut on Melba's face. She'd done an impeccable job of cleaning it. All that was left was a thin red scab. It probably wouldn't scar. "How are you doing?" I asked her. "Better than last night? You could have taken today off, you know."

"Oh, I wouldn't have done that." She affectionately patted my cheek. Her palms smelled like bacon and moisturizer. "It's my job to not let these things faze me. Besides, I can't hold grudges against people who don't know any better. You left early this morning. Good news?"

"I wish," I said. "Avery's still missing. The FBI are officially involved now."

Melba poured a cup of hot water from the kettle, scooped fresh tea into an infuser, and dunked the infuser in the mug. "This must be difficult for you."

"I'm more worried about Edison," I muttered, staring blankly at the flashing blue light that indicated the kettle was ready to shut off. "She already went through this once herself. She doesn't need to do it again with Avery."

"Do you think—no, never mind." Melba pressed her lips together, tending to the steeping tea. "It couldn't be."

"What?" I prompted. "What were you going to say?"

"Well," Melba said slowly. "There are quite a few similarities between what happened all those years ago and what's happening now. For instance, more than one girl has disappeared. Back then, it was five. Today, it's three."

"Only one of them came back," I muttered, dread creeping through me. "Edison."

"Because you brought her home," Melba reminded me. "Don't look at me like that. Everyone in Doveport has heard the stories. It seems no small coincidence that Edison was captured in 2004, and her child is kidnapped now."

"What are you saying?" I asked. "That the same people are kidnapping kids from Doveport again?"

"They're kidnapping young girls," Melba clarified. "Which means they're using them. Something terrible is afoot, if you ask me. Why doesn't Edison shed some light on the situation?"

"She won't," I said. "She locked up all the stuff that happened to her so she doesn't have to think about it anymore."

Melba removed the tea infuser, dropped it into the sink, and offered me the mug. "If she wants to find her daughter, she might consider a different tactic. Take this. I find a fresh cup of tea soothes all worries, no matter their intensity. Go talk to your mother. She's waiting for you."

I accepted the tea, made sure my coat was zipped up, and went out to the porch. Just like last night, Mom sat in her chair, swathed in blankets. Only her hands and feet stuck out. She played a game on her tablet.

"There you are," she said as I sat next to her. "I see Melba gave you the ol' herbal tea treatment too. Whatever happened to a good cup of coffee?"

"Caffeine makes me crazy sometimes," I replied. "What are you playing?"

She showed me the tablet screen. "Word Rush. It gives you six letters, and you have to find all the words you can make with those letters. I downloaded it this morning. Thought it might keep me from losing my mind so quickly." She chuckled at her own joke but let the attempted humor go when I didn't join in. "Any luck with Edison?"

"None."

"You should check the basement."

"For what?"

She readjusted her blankets so the tablet rested more securely on her lap. "Don't you remember? When Edison disappeared, you kept every scrap of news that mentioned anything about the missing girls. It's all still down there."

I remembered the few newspaper clippings that I'd found in my old room when I first arrived home. "You kept that stuff?"

"More like I didn't feel like putting in the effort to get rid of it," Mom admitted. "But I also figured it was your decision whether to trash it or keep it."

"So you think it's related too," I guessed. "Edison's kidnapping and Avery's disappearance."

"I think it would be naive of us not to consider the possibility," Mom replied. "You might want to mention that to whatever investigators are covering this."

I sneered as the image of Rocco Marioni's slick face and greasy hair popped up in my head. "I'll deal with it in a little bit. Have you thought any more about our talk last night?"

Mom's hand trembled, missing the letters on the screen. A red flash popped up to indicate a misspelled word. "Yes and no. It kept me up all last night, and I've been avoiding it all morning."

"We shouldn't put it off."

She swiped across the tablet, ending her game early. "I know. Let's keep this short and easy. I'd like to stay in my own house as long as possible. I know Melba can't take care of me twenty-four seven, and I don't have money in my retirement account to afford a round-the-clock aide."

"Then who's going to take care of you?" I asked. "Especially when it gets worse?"

She gave me a pointed look.

"*Me?*" My pulse quickened. "Mom, how am I supposed to do that? I'm never here."

"I know that," she said, "which is why I'm asking you to stay for a few years at least. Let me enjoy the time I have left with my daughter."

My heart seemed to have relocated to my throat. I swallowed, but the tightness there didn't release. "I'm not sure I can do that."

"It would kill you, wouldn't it? Taking care of me."

"Taking care of you isn't the problem," I said hotly. "It's staying in Doveport. I can't make money here, Mom. My career depends on my travels."

She tossed her hands in frustration, upending the tablet and sending it across the deck. "Pick a different career, Bex! One that you can do locally. God, I'm not asking for much!"

"You're asking for me to change my entire life," I pointed out in a shaky voice. "To give up everything I've worked so hard for in the last decade."

Her upper lip curled. "So you care more about your watered-down version of fame than your own mother, is that it?"

I stood up and clenched my fists to keep them from shaking. "I will do my best to make sure that you're taken care of, but I won't upend my happiness for you. Not with the way you treated me while I was growing up. You can act like it never happened, but I can't forget it. Excuse me."

As I stomped through the kitchen, Melba asked, "Everything all right, love?"

"Ask her," I snapped.

I ducked into the dark corner of the house that no one ever entered unless they needed something from the pantry. In the shadows, I found the door to the basement. The handle always stuck, so I gave it a good yank to get it open and stomped downstairs.

Melba peered down from above. "I'll make some lunch!"

I flicked the switch, and the canned lights in the ceiling came on after a few flickers. When I was a kid, the furnished basement was my favorite place to hang out. The carpet was a ridiculous color of mint green, a garish leftover from the nineties. The paneled wood walls were the perfect soundboards for the pop punk I blared in the early two thousands. Back then, this was where Edison and I had spent most of our time after school. It was far away from her strict, demanding parents and my mother's bottled wrath. Down here, it felt like we could do anything we wanted. It helped that there was a back door that led outside. I lost count of how many times we'd slipped in and out of the house without Mom knowing.

Over time, our basement hangout went by the wayside. When Edison disappeared, I avoided it. I felt her presence everywhere, something I couldn't tolerate when the real person was gone, and the possibility of her return seemed slim. Two years later, when Edison got pregnant with Avery, she disappeared again, this time at the behest of her parents. As "good Christians," they decided the best thing for a teenaged girl who got pregnant out of wedlock was to send her to a special high school out of state for "girls like that." I missed Edison for our entire senior year, and the constraints at her new school kept us from talking regularly. Not long after graduation, Edison moved back to Doveport with baby Avery. Her parents had long since left the area, and Edison liked it that way.

By that time, I was already gone. As soon as I turned eighteen, I gathered the money from Christmas presents past and bought a plane ticket to Mexico. Often, the only reason I returned to Doveport was to spend time with Edison and Avery. It was a relief to maintain our friendship despite the distance between us. In a way, we were using the rest of our lives to make up for the time that was stolen from us in high school.

When I left, Mom began to store odd bits and bobs in the basement. One corner was completely full of junk, including a broken exercise bike, leftover tiles and other supplies from the kitchen remodel, and cardboard boxes full of the candles that Melba had hidden. I waded through the mess until I found a dusty stack of Vans and Converse. One by one, I pulled the evidence of my childhood free from the confines of the past. Then I sat in the middle of the ugly carpet to go through it all.

I dumped the boxes. Out came old pictures, random mementos, magazine clippings, newspaper articles, homework assignments I'd been particularly proud of, diary entries, and a collection of MP3 players and flip phones from before the smartphone era. I untangled the cords and played a game of "match the charger to the phone." Miraculously, all four phones booted up when I plugged them in. While the batteries gained strength, I sifted through the newspaper articles.

The headlines mimicked the ones from my room. *Dove-port's Missing Girls, No Leads in Missing Children Case,* and *FBI Gets Involved in Local Case.* I organized the newspapers by the date they were published and scanned through the articles to refresh my memory. Five girls had disappeared without a trace that year. Edison was the last one to vanish and the only one to return. The others were high school acquaintances of ours. I remembered Cherie Miller, a junior varsity cheerleader with a brain like a steel trap. She sat next to me in Geometry class, and when she stopped showing up, I assumed she'd been bumped up to Algebra II because geometry bored her so much. Then there was Gretchen MacMann, the drum major for the marching band. She vanished right after halftime, during the band's third quarter break, at a Friday night football game. For the entire fourth quarter, the band had no one to direct them.

I was less familiar with the two other girls. They were both members of the drama club and disappeared on the same night. It was a particularly devastating blow to the Doveport community. The kidnappers seemed to be rubbing their success in the locals' faces. *Ha ha, we got two in one this time. What are you going to do about it?* Everyone in Doveport, especially the parents of teenaged girls, was scared shitless. Curfews grew shorter, rules became stricter, and people actually locked their doors at night. My own mother was too frazzled to restrict my comings and goings, but that was probably for the best.

When Edison disappeared, it was like the bottom had dropped out of my entire world. Worst still, I was there when it happened. It was a Friday afternoon, broad daylight. We'd just gotten out of school for the week. Halloween was around the corner, but the idea of trick or treating didn't hold as much excitement as it usually did.

"I'm not allowed to go," Edison pouted as we walked to Maxine's Café. We had exactly one hour after the final bell to hang out before Edison's parents demanded her presence at home. "Mom and Dad are freaking out. What about you?"

"Mom hasn't said anything," I answered, hiking my backpack higher on my shoulders. "But she's been in her own little world since Dad died. Not sure she'd notice if I went missing."

"Yeah, but I would."

I grasped her arm and held it prisoner. "Sneak out! Say you're going to bed early and leave a couple pillows under your comforter. I hear Miss Montgomery is handing out king-sized chocolate bars at her house this year."

Edison tugged on my hair. Back then, it was about chin-length. "You know how much trouble I'd get in if I snuck out? You wouldn't see me for years."

"That's why it's called sneaking," I said. "So you don't get caught."

A rainstorm sent us running into Maxine's for shelter. With coffee in hand, we took up our favorite booth and got to chatting. More than once, someone shushed us for being too loud.

"It's not a library," I retorted.

"Don't you two ever do homework here?" Maxine asked as she came by with two muffins. Blueberry for Edison, banana nut for me.

"No, we save homework for prison," Edison joked. She checked her watch. "Speaking of which, I've gotta take that muffin to go. Mom'll kill me if I'm late getting home again."

As Maxine packed Edison's muffin in a paper bag, Edison hugged me goodbye. "Thanks, Maxine. See you later."

I watched as Edison disappeared through the back door of the *café, as she always did. A moment later, I realized she'd left her coat on her chair. I grabbed it and jogged out.*

"Hey, Edison!" I called from the back door.

Behind the café was a small parking lot for deliveries and the entry to a shortcut through the woods that led to Edison's neighborhood. In the few seconds since I'd last seen her, she shouldn't have gotten far, but she was nowhere to be seen.

"Edison?" I shouted again, confused.

Her coat dangled limply from my grasp. She'd be cold without it.

MY THROAT TIGHTENED as I recalled that day. Later, Edison told me her kidnappers had been waiting in the delivery lot. As soon as she came out of the café, they threw a hood over her face, tossed her into a van, and drove off. They knew we went to the café every day. They knew Edison took the back way out, by herself, to go home. They'd planned the whole thing. It was the first and last piece of information Edison had ever shared with me about her ordeal.

She was gone for five and a half months. In that time, I developed depression and started skipping school on a regular basis, unable to sit next to my best friend's empty desk day after day. My grades dropped, and I stopped attending extracurricular activities. I skipped the practice SAT then skipped the real one, blowing any chance I had at college out of the water.

For Christmas, Mom bought me a new phone, the one I'd been begging for before Edison disappeared. A few days later, I got my first brain zap. Of course, it came with a text: *find h3r?* I had no idea what had happened, so I ignored it. Except the texts kept coming, soon with more and more information. At first, I thought someone was pranking me. I demanded to know who it was, but no answer ever came. Then I noticed the texts were linked to the brain zaps. For three months, I followed up on every clue that came through to my phone. Most of them were dead ends, but one rainy night in April, I had a breakthrough.

I didn't wince when the zap hit. They were coming so often that Mom was starting to get suspicious, and the last thing I needed was her to take me to a doctor. She didn't notice anyway. She was too busy watching a baking show on TV while I pretended to do my homework at the kitchen table. Quietly, so she wouldn't hear, I took out my phone and flipped it open.

NOrth.

I swallowed the nerves rising in my throat and checked the clock. Nine o'clock at night already. I had school tomorrow, if I decided to go. There was no way Mom would let me leave the house now.

"All done," I announced, closing a textbook over an unfinished outline for an essay that was due tomorrow. "I'm gonna watch TV in the basement."

"Sure, honey," Mom replied absentmindedly.

Downstairs, I switched the TV on and turned up the volume. Then I put on my raincoat and snuck out, making sure the door to the basement didn't slam. Once outside, with the phone in hand, I jogged north.

I passed Doveport High. Another zap, another message. E@st. Toward the creek. I changed directions. My white sneakers squelched in the mud as I got closer to the water. The creek had overflowed with all the rain. There was no bridge to cross it, but I had to keep going. I plunged in and waded across, waist-deep in muddy water, then clambered out on the other side.

NOrthEAst.

I corrected my path again and ran through the woods, crunching dead leaves and snapping twigs beneath my heavy footfalls. My heart pounded faster and faster. My legs began to ache, but I didn't slow down. Something told me to keep moving, no matter what.

I ran for minutes or hours, past the county line and out of Doveport. I caught a glimpse of the highway through the trees and a green road sign with the mileage to Portland. I was soaked from head to toe and chafing between the thighs. A blister bled freely on the back of my right heel, staining my sneakers red. I kept going.

As I pounded onward, my breath wheezed in and out of my chest. I was at the end of my rope, far from home, and lost in the woods. Maybe I was wrong. Maybe the text messages were just that —text messages. But one last zap—a big one—surged through my head.

Str@1ght @h3ad.

I ran smack into Edison.

We both screamed when we collided, neither of us recognizing the other. She was covered in dirt, and like me, she dripped from the rain. A fresh cut oozed blood on her forehead.

"Bex?" she gasped hoarsely, eyes widening as if she couldn't believe what she was seeing.

"Edison!" I threw myself into her arms and dumped my phone, the battery nearly drained, in her lap. "Here. Call 911."

Then I fainted.

A jingly version of the Power Rangers theme song jolted me back to present day. One of the old flip phones was finished charging, and the tune was to let me know I had unheard voicemails...from high school. I flipped it open and pushed the stiff buttons, trying to refamiliarize myself with the ancient technology. The phone was so old that it only stored a certain amount of data before it was automatically deleted, but I managed to access my old text messages. They were all from Edison and unknown numbers. This was the one that I'd been carrying through the woods the night I'd found her. I wondered if it had any magic left in it.

With a nervous gulp, I held the phone in both hands and let my focus rest on it. Over years of practice, I'd discovered a distinct difference between pushing my ability into cyber-space and simply touching on it. The first resulted in more pronounced electrical pulses in my head and a profound adrenaline rush if I pushed it too far. The second allowed me to gauge how much risk a certain activity might be should I complete it.

It took a little more prodding to get past the phone's clunky hardware and into its memory. My fingers twitched spasmodically, as if the extra action in my brain needed a way to express itself physically. I honed in on my focus and tried again. The tiny screen on the front of the phone lit up neon blue. Then the phone lifted itself from my palm and floated an inch above my skin, revolving in a slow circle. If I kept up my rhythmic breathing, I could hold it there forever. Theoretically, at least.

"What the hell, Matilda?"

At the startling sound of Cade's voice, my focus went wild. The phone flung itself across the room and hit the old stereo system. My brain zapped as the stereo turned itself on and blared "Great Balls of Fire" at top volume. As Cade clapped their hands over their ears, I waved at the stereo, and it shut itself off.

Cade slowly lowered their hands as their jaw dropped. They pointed at the stereo. "Did you just do that with your mind?"

"Shhh!" I yanked Cade into the dim basement and checked that the door at the top of the stairs was shut firmly. "Keep your voice down. What are you doing here?"

"I asked Edison where you lived," Cade said in a normal tone. "Your mom's friend let me in. Are they, like, an old gay couple? Because that would be super cute."

"No, she's my Mom's aide," I answered. "You didn't answer my question."

"You didn't answer mine," they retorted. "I'm not crazy. You turned the stereo on and off without touching it."

"It's remote-controlled."

They scoffed and patted the closest speaker. "This dinosaur from the nineties has a remote? Yeah, right. If you weren't using telekinesis, explain how your phone was floating."

I stammered, struggling to come up with an answer that made sense, but Cade wasn't having it. They leaned against the stereo and watched with raised eyebrows as I babbled.

"Cut the crap," they finally said. They picked up the flip phone from where it had landed on the carpet. "Gosh, this thing's a relic. It should be in a museum."

"I'm not that old."

They tossed the phone at me. "Whatever. So it's true then? What Edison said about you?"

"She told you about me?"

"Not exactly." Cade flopped onto the sofa and put their feet up on the coffee table. "I was upstairs when you two were talking about it, and I overheard some snippets."

"Snippets?"

"Yeah, snippets."

"Look, Cade," I said. "I don't know what you *think* you heard or saw just now, but I don't have any special powers, okay? It's a coincidence."

Cade stared me down. "What's your problem? We both know you're lying. Why won't you help find Avery? Because you're afraid you'll have another seizure?"

"Wow, you really did hear everything."

"Yeah." They kept staring at me, waiting expectantly for an answer. "Well?"

I groaned and lay down on the floor amongst the abandoned cell phones and old newspaper clippings. I rubbed my eyes, watching a rainbow of fireworks pop up in the darkness behind my eyelids. I didn't want to talk about this with a kid I barely knew.

"Fine, I'll go first," Cade said. "You want to know what I'm doing here? I came to help you find Avery. I think if we team up, we might be able to track her down."

I peeked at them from the spaces between my fingers. "What makes you think that?"

"Because you're not the only one with weird abilities."

That caught my attention. I sat up. "Don't mess with me."

"I'm not," Cade said. "You wanna know why my parents locked me up in a mental institution? It wasn't just because of the whole lack of a gender thing. I told them I hear voices in my head. I knew I wasn't crazy, but they weren't convinced."

I studied Cade's face, looking for a crack in their facade. "This isn't some elaborate prank you cooked up with your friends, is it?"

Cade made a point to sigh as heavily as possible. They dug into their pocket and tossed something into my lap. Another phone. This one had a huge crack across the screen. "That's Avery's. I found it in the parking lot outside the school this morning. She must've dropped it before she disappeared. It's been talking to me all damn day."

"What do you mean?"

"I told you," Cade said, exasperated. "I hear voices, but I don't have a personality disorder. From what I can figure out, the voices are people reaching out for help through their subconscious. Half the time, they're not even aware that they're doing it. One time, when I was twelve, I accidentally bumped into a lady on the street. It was a one-second interaction, but it was enough. I heard her—in my head. She told me her husband was abusing her, that she was afraid he might hurt her for real soon. I didn't do anything about it. I didn't tell anyone. The next morning, her face was all over the news. He'd killed her."

"God, Cade. I'm so sorry that happened to you."

"Don't be sorry for me." They rifled through my collection of newspaper articles, eyes dashing across the headlines. "Feel sorry for that woman. Anyway, I started paying more attention to the voices after that. If I heard someone having a terrible day, I'd find a way to approach them to ask if they were going to be okay. I can't do any superhero shit, but I like to think I helped a few people. Do you know many times I've heard someone wish they were dead? This country has a mental health issue."

I clapped my hand over the newspapers to stop the rustling. "Are *you* okay?"

"I'm fine now," Cade declared. "Once I got away from my parents and that institution, I figured out how to control the voices. I don't have to listen if I don't want to, but if someone's really desperate, their voice breaks through."

"Like Avery's."

"Yeah," Cade said. "And it's weird because I usually need to be close to someone to hear them, like within a few feet, but Avery clearly isn't around. I think I'm hearing her through the phone. That's why I was hoping you could help me. I can't unlock it. It's charged though."

I clicked the phone on, and with no effort at all, completely bypassed the password screen. Cade's eyes widened as they grabbed it from me.

"What the heck?" they exclaimed. "I spent three hours trying to guess her password. I tried everything. How'd you do that?"

I wiggled my fingers like a witch. "Techno magic."

Cade swiped through Avery's stuff. "So that doesn't initiate a seizure?"

"No," I replied curtly.

"Then I don't see why we can't make this work," the teenager said in a tone similar to a mafia boss laying down the rules of a tough negotiation.

"First of all, you're a kid," I pointed out. "Second, I'm not a cop. Agent What's-His-Face has better resources to find Avery."

Cade wrinkled their nose. "You really believe that? Dude, that guy's a slug. He was hitting on Edison the entire time he was there."

"That's what I said!" I blurted out before realizing that my exclamation was more ammo for Cade. I cleared my throat. "I mean, I'm sure he's got his own way of handling things, even if they are a bit less professional than I would prefer."

"From what I understand about Edison's past, the last thing she needs is some random dude taking advantage of her while she's vulnerable." Cade experimentally flipped open my old Sidekick. "Whoa! Aww, look at all the buttons."

I snapped my fingers in Cade's face. "Focus, kid."

"Right." They closed the Sidekick and boldly slid it into their pocket right in front of me. "What was I saying? Oh, yeah. Agent Marioni's a creepy dork. I don't want him to find Avery if it means hurting Edison."

"Well, he's not going anywhere." Absentmindedly, I searched the Internet for more recent stories on the missing girls of Doveport. "We're going to have to deal with him. Better yet, maybe we can tap into his resources to help us."

Cade sat up a little straighter, their eyes brightening. "Does this mean you're in? Are you going to help me find Avery?"

I eyeballed Cade over the top of my touchscreen. *"We're* not doing anything. Like I said, you're a kid. I won't purposely drag you into the line of fire."

"But—"

"Ah!" I cut them off with the same sound I'd use on a misbehaving dog. "You like deals, right? I'll make you one. You can help me on my terms. That means you stay put and behave yourself. I don't need Edison freaking out on me."

Cade crossed their arms and sank into the couch. "What kind of deal is that? You won't let me do anything."

"You'll be an informant," I told them. "Every time you hear Avery's voice, report it to me. I'm going to need all the help I can get, and if she happens to tell you where she is, then we're home free. What did she say to you anyway?"

Cade chewed on the inside of their cheek, lost in thought. "It's not like how it usually is. Her voice was garbled. Muffled."

"Like she was gagged?"

The teenager's eyes watered as the impact of my statement hit her. "Oh my God, do you think they gagged her?"

"It's likely," I said frankly. "They have to keep her quiet somehow. Did you understand anything she said?"

Cade extracted a small moleskin notebook from her back pocket and flipped through it. Each page was covered in cramped cursive writing. "I write everything down now," they said, answering my silent question. "When I hear people, it kinda feels like a dream. If I don't write it down, I forget what they say to me. Here we go—" They paused on a particularly saturated page. "It's a bunch of gibberish. Hotel, echo, Lima, papa, Mike, echo. It goes on like that for a while."

"It's not gibberish," I said. "It's the NATO phonetic alphabet. Don't they teach you anything at that school anymore?"

"I tend to fall asleep a lot."

I grabbed a pen out of a cup balanced on the edge of the TV stand, shuffled over to Cade on my knees, and circled the first letter of every word.

"Help me," Cade muttered. Tears sprang to their eyes. They reached for the pen. "Can I borrow that?"

I handed it over and sat quietly as Cade marked up the journal. At least five pages were dedicated to Avery's subconscious messages. Several minutes later, Cade finished decoding it and sat back to read it.

"Not much of it is helpful," they reported, dabbing the tears on their cheeks with the back of their sleeve. "She apologizes a lot, to her mom, for being a brat and stuff. She said when she thought about running away, this wasn't what she had in mind. Be careful what you wish for, right?" They gulped back nerves. "She thinks she's gonna die."

"She won't," I said forcibly. My words didn't match my thoughts though. The four other girls from my high school were never found. They'd never made it back to the land of the living, and there was a large possibility that Avery wouldn't either. "Avery's strong. She learned from the best. Did she say anything else? Maybe a clue that would help us find her?"

Cade circled a section of the notebook and handed it to me. "Looks like she caught a glimpse of a road sign before the kidnappers realized she could see through the blindfold. She only got a few letters off it though."

I studied the phonetic letters. India, papa, echo, Romeo, Oscar. Cade peered over my shoulder, breathing heavily in my ear as I visualized a map of Oregon in my head. An image from my memories jumped to the front of my mind.

"San Junipero Park!" I exclaimed. "I've driven past that

sign a hundred times. That's where they had to be heading, right?"

"Isn't that a state park?" Cade asked. "Would a bunch of kidnappers risk camping on government land, especially with a victim in tow?"

"It's genius," I said. "They're hiding in plain sight, and San Junipero is a lot less populated than most of the other parks because it's such a wooded area. It's a perfect place to hold someone hostage without the cops finding out."

"No park rangers?"

"It'd be easy to throw them off the trail," I explained. "They don't go into people's vehicles. As long as the kidnappers keep Avery quiet, they won't get caught."

Cade bounced excitedly out of their seat. "So we have a lead! What are we waiting for? Let's check it out."

I yanked Cade to a stop as they passed me on the way to the back door. "Where do you think you're going? What did I just say to you five minutes ago? You've done your part. You gave me the information I needed, but *I'm* the one who decides what to do with it."

Cade's brow furrowed. "So you're going to go alone?"

"I'm not going at all," I told them. "I'm going to tip off the local cops and Agent Marioni. They can check it out for themselves."

The teenager stomped their boots. "Are you kidding me? Haven't we already established that the cops and the FBI are useless? They won't find her!"

"It's the way things are done, Cade."

They snatched the notebook out of my hands. "Fine. If you're too scared to do it, I'll go by myself. I know how to hotwire a car. I can make it to San Junipero in a few hours."

They hopped out of my reach and made a break for the

back door. I scrambled up from my seat on the floor and ran after them. Cade's legs flew as they bolted across the front yard and vaulted over the fence with ease. With no hope of catching them on foot, I mounted my bike like it was a horse and pumped the pedals. When I caught up with Cade, I skidded to a halt in front of them, forcing them to put the brakes on.

"Christ," I gasped, heart pounding. "You should run track."

"You know I can get around you," Cade said, dodging left and right. It made me think of that night outside Dove's Pub, when I caught them by the arm as they made a break from the alley. Did they want to be caught? "I've got skills, man. Mad skills."

"I'm sure you do," I panted. "Listen, kid. You have to understand where I'm coming from. If we go after whoever took Avery, I'm putting both of us in harm's way. It's irrational."

Cade planted their hands on my bike handles and caught my eyes in an intense stare. It seemed to be their specialty. "We have superpowers, Bex. We're meant to be the heroes of this story. If we don't use our abilities for good, we're just as bad as the villains."

"I think you've watched one too many Marvel movies."

They smirked and saluted. "Higher, further, faster, baby." They stomped their feet like a two-year-old having a temper tantrum. "Come on," they whined. "I have a good feeling about us teaming up. Think about it. If we follow this lead, we have a chance of bringing Avery and those other girls home tonight."

A particularly gusty breeze tickled my scalp. I thought about Avery, alone and terrified in the dark woods of San Junipero State Park. I remembered what Edison looked like when I'd found her after so long. I didn't want Avery to go through that.

"Okay," I finally agreed.

"Yes!" Cade jumped up and pumped their fist.

I grabbed their jacket to keep them still. "Take it down a notch. We have to lay some ground rules. First of all, Edison can't know what we're doing. She'll kill me if she finds out I took you on a road trip to track down Avery's kidnappers."

"Call her up and tell her you're taking me to a concert out of town," Cade suggested. "That I'm really upset over Avery's disappearance and you thought this would be a good way to cheer me up."

"You want me to lie?"

"It's not hard."

"Fine," I said. "We have our cover story. Next order of business. If we find these people—the kidnappers or whoever took Avery—I don't want you to go anywhere near them. They're probably armed, and we know they're dangerous. I refuse to put you in the line of fire. Promise you'll leave the heavy lifting up to me."

Cade flicked my bicep, the swell of it visible through my long-sleeved shirt. "I'm okay with that. You seem capable enough."

"Meet me back here at five o'clock. I'll call Edison and get us a car." I began pedaling away then called over my shoulder. "And keep this on the down low!"

"No one says that anymore!" Cade hollered back.

CHAPTER **Thirteen 1714**

. . .

I SPENT the rest of the afternoon trying to get my mother's car in working order. It needed gas, oil, and a tune-up. Since I was running low on cash, I bought the stuff I needed from the local auto shop and did the work myself. Before he died, Dad taught me the basics of cars. In his free time, he bought old antiques that didn't work anymore, fixed them up, and sold them. The process fascinated me, and Dad liked having his "little helper" around to hand him tools when he needed them. When I got a little older, he showed me how to do the work myself. We spent most summers in the garage, sweating through our coveralls as we covered ourselves in grease from head to toe. I was happiest there.

When Dad died, a 1965 Shelby Cobra sat abandoned in the garage for the next year, swathed in a gray car cover like the ghost that it was. Out of sight, out of mind might have worked for Mom, but for that entire year, I swore I could hear Dad in the garage, working on that damn car. Every morning, I'd check on the car to see if anything had changed. Of course nothing had. Then one day I woke up and the car was gone. Mom had sold it to some out-of-towner who'd collected it in the middle of the night, taking the last memory I had of my dad with it.

With my supplies from the auto shop in hand, I yanked the rusted handle of the garage out of the locking position and pushed the door up. The faded smells of cigar smoke, motor oil, and musk hit me like a prized fighter's finishing hook in a championship match. I half-expected Dad to rise from the spare fridge in the back corner with a cold beer for himself and a frosty Coke for me.

Throat and chest tight, I pushed Mom's car into the garage and lined it up in Dad's homemade lift machine. It wasn't like the fancy ones you saw in the Costco tire center that took the whole car up ten feet. With Dad's, we were lucky to get two feet out of it. It worked though, and that was all that mattered. I greased the hinges and cranked it up, jacking the car into place.

With a deep breath, I pried open Dad's red tool box. It looked smaller than I remembered it. Or perhaps I was bigger now. I gathered the things I needed, laid back on Dad's old creeper, and rolled smoothly underneath the car.

I lost myself in the work. Most of the work was muscle memory, a good thing considering I'd forgotten a good deal about mechanics. My current problems vanished from my mind as I concentrated on the task at hand. For the first time in years, I felt comfortable in my home. This was where I belonged. With Dad.

After a few hours, I got the car to turn on. I whooped happily, slid out of the driver's seat, and checked the fridge. Surprisingly, it still worked, but a six-pack of Dad's favorite summer lager had exploded inside. One can had survived. Did beer expire? I popped the lid and, for the purpose of ceremony, took a sip. It tasted awful, but I lifted the can to a picture of me and Dad, both of us covered in grease, that was framed next to the fridge.

"I'll get you fresh ones," I promised his spirit before chucking the lager into the trash.

"Bex?" My mother peeked into the garage from outside. The rumble of the car engine must have drawn her from the comfort of the back porch. "What are you doing out here?"

I wiped my hands on my pants, smearing oil across them. "Thought I'd get your car up and running. You don't mind if I borrow it, do you?"

"No, I don't use it anymore." Mom shuffled toward the

back of the garage, gazing around. "I haven't been in here in years."

"I can tell."

She took a deep breath in through her nose. "God, it smells exactly the same. Like grease and body odor."

I let out a laugh. "You hated when Dad and I would come into the house after working out here. Remember when you started making us shower outside?"

Mom's gentle smile faded when she caught sight of the photo beside the fridge. She traced the outline of my father's face. "What a good man."

"The best," I agreed.

Mom shook her head as if to dislodge a pesky fly, turned away from the photo, and clasped her arms tightly across her chest. "Don't come into the house like that. I don't want grease everywhere. Dinner's ready, by the way. Melba made Caesar salad with salmon. That's your favorite, right?"

Though her tone was cold and distant, there was something in the way she asked the question that made me take pause. Was she trying to make up for that morning's spat by cooking my favorite meal?

"Uh, yeah."

"Mm. See you inside."

As I heard the front door to the house close, Cade appeared from the overgrown bushes that lined the left side of the driveway. They brushed twigs and dirt from their sleeves. They were dressed in all black from head to toe.

"What the hell are you wearing?" I asked as I rinsed my hands in the big metal basin sink at the back of the garage. "We are not Charlie's Angels."

"We're going on a caper, aren't we?" they countered. They fished a black ski mask out of their jacket pocket and pulled it over their head. "Eh? What do you think? Can you tell who I am?"

I flicked cold water at Cade's face. "I can tell you're a giant dork. How long were you hiding in the bushes out there?"

They pulled off the ski mask, hair sticking up in all directions. "A few minutes. Was that your mom? She seems nice."

"It's complicated."

"Oh, you got baggage," Cade noted, shrugging. "That's okay. Who doesn't?" Their eyes drifted to a spot over my shoulder. "You look like your dad."

I studied Dad's pale hair and blue eyes. His family was Finnish, and I'd inherited most of the trademarks of the people there. The only difference between me and my dad were the eyebrows. His were so light and thin that they were barely visible. Mine were thick like Mom's.

"Yeah," I said. I clapped Cade on the back. "Come on, let's get inside. Mom's not going to let me leave the house without eating."

To avoid questions, I told my mother and Melba that Cade was part of an experimental mentor-mentee project that Edison wanted to try out for Home Safe. The lie explained why I was suddenly best friends with a fifteen-year-old as well as our absence for the night. We fed Mom the same story that Cade had told Edison: we were heading to a concert two hours away. With any luck, we'd be back with Avery before anyone realized we weren't telling the truth.

After dinner, Cade and I climbed into Mom's newly-restored car. Cade thumped a fist against the dashboard as if to test its durability.

"How old is this thing?" they asked. "It's not gonna break down on us, is it?"

"It was brand new," I answered. "In 2004."

Cade rolled their eyes as I programmed San Junipero State Park into my phone's navigation app. "You called Edison, right? I'm not sure she bought my concert story."

I gritted my teeth. "Actually, I forgot."

Cade tapped on my phone, pulled up Edison's number, and hit the call button. As it rang, they said, "Be convincing. I can't do *everything* for you."

I smacked the back of their hand away from my phone.

"Hello?" Edison answered in a nasally voice. She'd been crying again.

"Hey, Ed," I said. "Just calling to make sure you're okay with me taking Cade for the night. They said you gave them permission, but I don't trust the little sucker."

Cade pointedly put on an unamused expression.

Edison sniffed into the phone. "Yes, I said it was okay. Pretty whimsical, isn't it though? What's this concert you're going to?"

"Uh—"

Cade whispered, "King Princess."

"King Princess," I reported back to Edison. "He's one of Cade's favorite artists."

"King Princess is a girl!" Cade hissed.

"I mean, *she's* one of Cade's favorites," I corrected hastily, slinging my arm over Cade's chair to back the car out of the garage. "We're on our way out, and you know cell service gets shoddy around here. I'll call you when we're heading home. We'll probably be late."

"All right," Edison said. "Take care of each other."

"Will do. See ya, Ed."

I hung up before she could ask any more questions. Cade bounced excitedly in her seat as I drove out of the neighborhood and approached the highway. The clunky car chugged along, rattling slightly. According to the map, San Junipero State Park was an hour and fifty minutes from our position. Unfortunately, that gave Cade a lot of time to pester me with questions.

"So, like, how does it work?" they said. "Your power, I mean. Because, like, I don't really get mine. Do you get yours?"

"No," I growled, doing my best to check my temper. "Not really. I get electric pulses through my head. They mess with the technology around me, usually cell phones."

"Electric pulses?" Cade muttered. "That makes sense. You're having miniature seizures every time you use your powers. You get that, right?"

I'd never made the connection until that very moment, but I sure as hell wasn't going to admit that to Cade. "Of course. That's why I can't afford to use my ability as often as you'd like. I might have a huge seizure and die."

"Ehh." Cade tilted their head back and forth. "Seizures don't mean death, even big ones. Your head might be a little screwy though."

"You're telling me," I murmured.

"One of my friends from back home went into this crazy rage after she had a seizure," the teenager went on. "You know, like postictal shit? Anyway, she went nuts and totally trashed her room and her parents had her committed because they were afraid she'd hurt herself. We ended up at the same mental ward. Crazy, right?"

Empathy closed like a fist around my heart. From Cade's

easy-going, can-do attitude, you'd never know about all the crappy stuff that had happened to them in the past.

"Crazy," I agreed.

Cade opened the glove compartment and rifled through my mom's old crap. "Ooh, Virginia Slims. So your mom was *that* kind of lady back in the day, huh?"

I slapped the cigarettes out of Cade's grasp. "*What* kind of lady?"

"I dunno." Cade kept digging and unearthed a Rubik's Cube with only one level solved. "The kind of lady who smoked Virginia Slims."

As Cade slid the puzzle pieces around, I softened. "She was the kind of lady who kept cigarettes in her car because she didn't want her husband to know she smoked at the same time she kept bothering him to quit."

Cade chortled. "I like your mom."

"Mm."

"Tell me about the baggage."

"What baggage?"

Cade maneuvered the cube's pieces at lightning speed. Either they worked at random or they actually knew what they were doing with the puzzle. "Whatever shit's going on between you and your parents."

"My dad's dead."

"That'll do it."

"And my mom's losing her marbles," I added.

"And in between?" Cade asked. "I've never sat at a more awkward dinner table. You still argue with your mom, don't you?"

I bit on a piece of dry skin on my lip, working it away from my mouth with my teeth. I ripped it too far, and my lip stung with the familiar bite of an open wound. I blotted the tiny spot of blood with a fast-food napkin stored in the door pocket.

"Like I said, it's complicated," I told Cade. "After Dad died, Mom kind of went nuts. You know the five stages of grieving, right? Mom hit depression first and took a vacation there for a good six months. Then she skipped right to anger and never made it to acceptance. It's hard to be a kid when your mother is *always* angry."

"I know what that feels like," Cade said quietly. "How did your dad die?"

"He had a brain aneurysm," I answered. "According to the doctors, it had been there for years. Anyway, it ruptured one day. He was dead before he made it to the hospital."

"You never saw it coming."

"Nope," I said. "Neither did Mom. She thinks he knew about it and didn't tell her."

Cade's fingers kept working on the Rubik's cube. She'd solved another level of it. "How come your mom was so mean to you? It's not like it was your fault."

"Like you said, I look like my Dad." My throat tightened. I coughed to clear it, but it did no good. "She saw him in every part of me. It was like a constant reminder that he was gone. After she died, she stopped looking at me. When she needed a way to vent, she screamed at me or hit me. I spent a lot of time avoiding home."

"The two of you seem on better terms now," Cade noted.

"When I left Doveport, I started doing therapy online while I traveled," I explained. "It helped me understand why my mom acted the way she did toward me."

"So you forgave her?"

My grip tightened on the steering wheel. "I'm not sure if I'll ever be able to forgive her, but I'm at peace with the things that happened to me. There's a subtle difference. I promised myself I'd be the bigger person. That's why we're civil to each other. If she gets cranky, I get out of Dodge. She only gets to interact with me if she's nice."

Cade was quiet for a few minutes. "Wish I could do that with my mom."

"You still could," I assured them. "But wait until you're a little older. Edison has your back. That's all you need for now."

Cade plunked the completed Rubik's Cube on the dashboard. "I guess you're right."

CADE DOZED off into the second hour of our road trip. The sun set, and the roads grew darker as we drove toward the middle of the state. Once you got past all the cities and towns, the streetlights disappeared. I turned on the high beams and kept my eyes peeled for deer or rabbits on the road. One of my biggest fears of driving was hitting an animal.

When I spotted a familiar sign up the road, I nudged Cade awake.

"Wha—?" They wiped drool from the corner of their mouth. "What'd you do that for?"

"Look."

They caught a glimpse right as we passed it. San Junipero State Park, five miles.

Cade's talkative streak ended. They were silent for the rest of the ride, and when I pulled up to the park ranger's small house at the entrance to San Junipero, Cade's hands shook visibly.

"Stay cool," I muttered to them as I rolled my window down.

The park ranger, who'd been snoozing in his chair, shook himself awake and slid open the door to talk to me. "Hi there, folks. You guys camping overnight?" He peered into the empty back seat, mustache bristling. "Doesn't look like you've got enough to keep you warm."

"We're meeting our group," I lied easily. "They have our stuff." I hit my forehead with the palm of my hand. "I'm such an idiot though. I totally forgot what number their campground is. I don't suppose you could tell me where they are?"

The park ranger rifled through a few papers in a file folder. "Easy enough. We've only got a few groups staying here tonight, and I'm guessing you're not joining the couple on their honeymoon."

"No, sir."

"Last name?"

I froze.

Cade leaned across the center console. "Maxx. Two Xs."

The ranger's brow furrowed as he checked the papers. "Ah, yep. Maxx. Gotcha. Campground twenty-six. Take the road all the way to the back. Take a left then a right at the forks. Have fun, ladies."

I pulled the car forward. "How did you know it would be under Avery's name?" I asked Cade.

They shrugged. "It seems like the sick kind of thing kidnappers would do."

"Stupid though. Easy to track."

"Who said kidnappers were smart?"

We followed the park ranger's directions, slowly rolling through the woods. The farther we drove, the further from humanity we seemed to be. The trees grew so close together that they formed a solid wall along the road. There was nowhere to go but forward.

Each campground was marked by a wooden sign at the entrance, the number painted in bright yellow paint so campers could easily find their assigned location. I pulled the car into the entry to campground twenty-five.

"It's the next one," Cade said.

"I know, but I'm not about to drive my car right into a kidnapper's campsite." I zipped up my coat and stole Cade's ski mask, but I wore it like a beanie rather than over my face. "Stay here," I told them. "I'll go check it out."

I got out of the car. It was colder in the woods than it was in Doveport. I picked my way through the trees, heading toward the next campground over, rather than sticking to the road. Though I might get a few ticks, it was worth the camouflage.

The crackle of fire embers caught my eye. I hunched behind a thick bush and peered into the kidnappers' campground. Parked opposite each other were two RVs, one bigger than the other. The smaller one had a sliding door, easy to open and close when pulling a victim inside. Three tents had been set up too.

"Hey," a voice whispered behind me.

I jumped, but it was only Cade. "What are you doing? I told you to stay in the car!"

"I got freaked out." They squinted through the bushes. "Is she there?"

"I don't know."

"It's empty. Where is everyone?"

There were no signs of any humans at the campsite. The windows of the RVs were dark.

"Asleep?" I guessed.

Cade stepped over the bush and passed the last tree concealing us, totally visible to anyone who might be lingering in the campground.

"What are you doing?" I hissed.

The teenager darted around the edge of the campground, giving me no choice but to run after them. I caught up with Cade as they unzipped the top of a tent and glanced inside.

"Are you crazy?" I whisper-yelled.

"No one here," they whispered back. "I think they're all gone. Check the next one."

"No! Let's get out of here."

"I'm not leaving until I find Avery."

Cade moved on to the next tent, leaving me to tend to my heart palpitations. If I wanted to leave, I'd have to go along with Cade's insane plan. With clenched teeth, I checked the third tent for myself. Like the others, it was empty, but something on the floor caught my attention.

"Cade! Get over here."

As Cade jogged toward me, I ducked into the tent and pulled a few items out. A pair of drumsticks and a practice pad.

"These are hers," Cade muttered, turning the sticks to show me Avery's initials carved messily into the wood. "She's here somewhere."

A truck engine roared into the clearing, and the two of us were bathed in the bright LEDS of the truck's high beams. Whoever was sitting in the passenger seat rolled down the window and leaned out. All I saw through the lights was the barrel of a shotgun.

"Move!" I tackled Cade to the ground right as the gun went off. The bullets went way over our heads. It was a warning shot, not meant to hurt us, but it was terrifying all the same. I yanked Cade to their feet and pushed them out of the truck's path.

"Hey!" a deep voice shouted from the truck. "Get back here, you pieces of shit! You wanna snoop in our camp? We got a present for you!"

"Run, run, run," I chanted at Cade as we dashed across the campground and into the safety of the woods. Another shot went off. This time, the pellets smacked into a tree a few feet to the left, showering us with bark. I repositioned Cade so they were directly in front of me. If the idiots fired again, they'd hit me instead of the teenager. "Go, Cade!"

We stumbled through the trees and found the car. I pushed Cade into the passenger seat first and glanced behind me. Three flashlight beams flickered through the woods. They were coming after us.

I turned the key in the ignition. The car whined.

"Come on, you old piece of crap," I pleaded. "Come on."

The engine turned over just as the flashlights landed on the windshield. I slammed my foot on the gas pedal, spraying dirt into the eyes of our assailants as I pulled a wide U-turn and escaped from the campground.

"You okay?" I asked Cade. Their eyes were wide with shock and fear. "Hey, snap out of it! Are you okay?"

"I think I got shot."

13

I hit the gas and barreled through the wilderness until I found a particularly dark patch of trees to pull into. With the car under cover, I reached over to the passenger seat to tend to Cade.

"Let me see," I ordered. Cade covered the wound with both hands, as if trying to keep all the blood inside their body. Their face was sheet white. I pried at their fingers, grasped around their shin. "Cade, let go. I have to look at it."

Trickles of blood ran down Cade's leg as I inspected the wound. One tiny BB pellet had lodged itself in the skin, probably after bouncing off a tree trunk. It wasn't enough to do any permanent damage, but it was definitely enough to scare a fifteen-year-old out of their wits. I grabbed an old bottle of rubbing alcohol from my mom's backseat and doused my hands in it. With bare fingers, I plucked the BB out of Cade's leg and tossed it out the window. To their credit, they didn't flinch.

"It's not bad," I told Cade, now saturating a stack of fast

food napkins with alcohol. "Believe me, cleaning it is going to hurt a lot worse. Don't think about it."

Without warning, I pressed the napkins against the small hole in Cade's skin. They writhed in pain, mouth dropped in a silent scream as I wiped away the blood and made sure the wound was clean.

"All done." I covered the wound with a wad of unused napkins. "Hold that there. We gotta get out of here."

A flash of light reflected in the rearview mirror right as I reached for the parking brake. I turned off the car and pushed Cade's head below the dashboard.

"What are you doing?" they whispered, mustering weak contempt. "Shouldn't we be getting out of here before they find us?"

"We're covered." I kept an eye on the headlights as they inched toward our position. "I don't want to show them where we are. That's why I killed the engine. Once they pass, we'll get out of here."

The nearby vehicle moved at a snail's pace, crawling up the dirt road. My eyes watered. I was so focused on keeping watch that I'd forgotten to blink. The headlights drew closer. My teeth chattered, but not from the chill gradually creeping into the car. Could they see us through the thick branches?"

"She was there," Cade whispered, voice shaking. "Why else would they have her things?"

My heart plummeted into my stomach at the thought of Avery's initialed drumsticks. I'd seen her play with them only a few nights before. We were so close, but we couldn't rescue Avery if the two of us fell victim to the attackers in the truck.

The truck ambled up to our section of trees. For one heart-stopping moment, the glare of the headlights shone right through our back windshield. Then the truck moved on, driving slowly past us. Once it was farther up the road, I turned the car on, wincing as the noisy engine started. Slowly, I maneuvered us out of the trees and took the first fork in the road. There had to be another way out of the park that didn't involve following our attackers.

We drove in a roundabout way, circling past the outer campgrounds, before we made it back to the park ranger's outhouse. It was closed for the night, and the ranger had gone home. He was completely oblivious to the crimes happening on the land he was supposed to watch over. As I pulled onto the asphalt and headed home, Cade sniffled in the passenger seat.

"We failed," they said, pressing their forehead to the window and staring glumly into the darkness. "It's all our fault."

Anger rose in me. It had nothing to do with Cade's statement and everything to do with what we'd discovered at the camp, but the rage all came down on Cade anyway. "Shut up," I snapped. "Avery *wasn't* there. Just because they had her things doesn't mean they still have Avery. For all we know, we could already be too late."

My harsh words cracked the last level of control of Cade's emotions. They burst into tears, sobbing freely into the front of their shirt. The anger that had welled so quickly in me dissipated just as fast.

"Hey." I reached over to comfort Cade, but with my eyes on the road, I could only find the knee of their undamaged leg. "I'm sorry. That was out of line." My throat tightened, as it was prone to do when I had to talk about something that I didn't want to talk about. "I'm scared, okay? That was one of the scariest things that's happened to me, and I got mugged in Beirut once. Let's focus on the positive things, right? First of all, we made it out of there alive. Secondly, we have a dropped pin on Avery's location. We can tell the FBI what we know. It's a huge lead."

Cade took an uncontrollable, shuddering breath and wiped their nose. "Yeah, but there's one terrible thing we won't be able to avoid."

"What?"

"Edison."

CADE WAS RIGHT. When we pulled into the driveway of Edison's house, the lights were still on despite the late hour, and Agent Marioni's ugly car was parked outside. We'd called the FBI on our way back, hoping they'd get out to San Junipero as soon as possible.

"Oh, boy." Cade unlatched their seatbelt and let it snap into place. "Are you ready for this?"

"Not one bit," I replied.

"Stick together," Cade advised. "We have a better chance at surviving if we don't pin the blame on each other."

"Cade, this is not the principal's office."

I stepped out of my mother's car and squared my shoulders as we approached the front door. I kept an arm around Cade in a display of togetherness. Before we reached the doorstep, the front door flew open. Edison stood framed there, with golden light pouring around her like an avenging angel.

"Where have you been?" she demanded. "I looked up King Princess's concert dates. You know where she is right now?

173

Florida! *Florida!* At least research your lies before you act them out!" She glanced at Cade's leg. Their pants were rolled up to expose the small wound. Edison's jaw dropped. "What the hell happened?"

"It hurts so much," Cade wailed. They limped over the threshold and fell into Edison's arms. "Can you help me?"

"Overkill," I muttered into Cade's ear as I passed them. Once we'd gotten the bleeding to stop, the teenager was fine, though I appreciated the attempt to ward off Edison's wrath.

Agent Marioni stood by the fireplace. He wore the exact same outfit as the other day, his hair slicked back in the same way. Today, he didn't carry his notebook. Rather, he turned his phone over and over as if contemplating tossing it into the fire.

"Don't you ever sit down?" I grumbled at him.

"I prefer to stand," Marioni replied. He pocketed his phone and clapped his hands, perhaps to promote blood flow. I clenched my teeth at the sharp sound. "Let's get right to it, shall we?" He beckoned Cade and Edison into the living room. "I have an update from my team at the campsite."

Edison and Cade sat down. Cade propped their leg on the coffee table so everyone could see the little hole the BB pellet had made in their skin. Ever the martyr. Edison perched on the armchair, as far away from me as possible. When she looked at me, it was with a glare. When she looked at Agent Marioni, it was with hope and admiration. Gross.

Agent Marioni, like before, only spoke to Edison. "I'll give it to you straight. By the time my team reached San Junipero State Park and searched campground twenty-six, there was no evidence that Avery Maxx or her kidnappers had been there."

Edison let out a heartbreaking gasp of deflated hope and buried her face in the crocheted throw blanket on the armchair. To my shock, Marioni actually looked like he felt bad.

"I'm sorry," he said, keeping his voice firm and professional. "Clearly, *someone* had been at the camp, and they left quickly. The fire pit was hot, and there were holes in the ground from tent pegs. We do have some good news. The kidnappers left three sets of tire tracks. That'll help us identify their vehicles, and we can go from there."

"One of them was a huge truck," I said. "A Dodge maybe?"

"Why don't you leave the investigation to us, Miss Lennon?" Marioni said coldly. "If you'd done that to begin with, Miss Christoph here wouldn't have a hole in her leg."

"I'm not a Miss," Cade spat. "And I'm fine."

"Rocco's right," Edison cut in. She turned to me. "What the hell were you thinking?"

"You're on a first name basis with Agent Marioni?"

"Don't change the subject," she said. "How did you figure out where the kidnappers were going to be anyway? And why would you take Cade with you? You put a child in harm's way, Bex."

"This was what you wanted me to do!" I replied, my volume rising out of aggravation. "*You* asked me to find Avery!"

When Edison's lips pressed together, I realized I'd given away too much of the plot. After all, Agent Marioni didn't know about Cade's ability or mine, and he didn't need to. His gaze bounced between me and Edison.

"Let me be frank," he said, all business. "Whatever plan the three of you hatched? It ends now. If you hadn't driven out to the campground and alerted the kidnappers to your presence, we might have found Avery by now."

I laughed with derision. "You're kidding, right? The only reason you guys have a lead on Avery's whereabouts is because *we* tipped you off."

"And where has that gotten us, Miss Lennon?" Agent Marioni fumed, his nostrils flaring. "Now, the kidnappers know we're on their trail. Do you know what that means? It means they might kill Avery faster rather than risk traveling with her."

Edison abruptly stood up and left the room, unable to stand the thought of her daughter's possible fate. Agent Marioni and I glared at each other.

"This is how things are going to go from here on out," Marioni said in a deadly whisper. "You will not interfere with my investigation. You will not collude with Edison or *children*, for Pete's sake, then go off on some harebrained mission to rescue Avery. If you have any information on Avery's whereabouts—God help whoever it comes from—you will immediately report that information to me. Do I make myself clear?"

"As clear as you can be with all that gel in your hair," I answered. "Aren't you afraid a bug might fly in and get stuck?"

Marioni's lip curled. "Tell Edison I'll be in touch."

He stomped outside, slamming the door in his wake. Cade raised a hand.

"Yes, Cade?"

"Can I have a Band-Aid?"

. . .

EDISON GAVE me the silent treatment for a week. Every time I attempted to point out that I'd been following *her* orders by going to the campground, it tacked on another hour of surliness from her. She couldn't avoid me forever though. In an attempt to win her back, I started giving Cade rides home from school in the afternoon. Not only did it give me more chances to talk to Edison, but it afforded me peace of mind as well. At least Cade wouldn't be kidnapped on her walk home.

But I couldn't talk to Edison with Agent Marioni watching my every move. I saw him everywhere. I ran into him at Maxine's cafe, where he was picking up coffee and donuts for Edison. I spotted his ugly gray car on the corner of Mom's street. Maybe he thought I wouldn't notice he was watching me or maybe he didn't care. Either way, I flicked off his tinted windows as I rode past his car on my bike. He showed up at Edison's house most often. Every time I dropped Cade off at home, his car was parked outside. I stopped walking Cade in after a while. Watching Edison play house with Marioni made my stomach turn.

They grew annoyingly close. To me, Marioni clearly took advantage of his position. Edison was a beautiful, vulnerable woman, and Marioni had no problem acting as her hero. Under the guise of supporting her in her time of need, he attempted to woo her in underhanded ways. More than once, I saw them at one of the nicer restaurants in town, talking quietly over a candlelit meal. If those conversations were about Avery, I'd bite my tongue.

"He's taking advantage of you," I said, exasperated, to Edison on a rare Marioni-free morning. By coincidence, I'd run into Edison at Maxine's. As she ordered her coffee to go, I cornered her by the counter. "Can't you see? Has he made any progress on Avery's case at all? All he cares about is winning you over!"

Edison accepted two to-go coffees from Maxine. She filled one with cream and sugar. She never used cream and sugar. "Let it go, Bex."

"That's for him, isn't it?" I gestured to the sugary coffee. "You're running coffee for him? Edison, please—"

"I said let it go," she barked with such ferocity that I took a step away from her. Her hands shook as she picked up the coffee cups. "I'm doing my best to deal with this the way I see fit. If that displeases you—well, that's your problem."

As more time passed, everything fell apart. With Edison's approval to look for Avery taken from me, I became listless and useless. I spent hours at a time in my old bedroom, either staring at the ceiling or napping the day away so I wouldn't have to face the harsh truth of Avery's continued disappearance. The brain zaps stopped coming, and so did the text messages. Days passed, then weeks, without word of Avery's whereabouts. Despite Marioni's supposed dedication to the case, he hadn't made any progress. Cade—who eaves-dropped on almost every conversation between Edison and the FBI agent—told me that the tire tracks hadn't turned up any new information. The FBI found the make and model of the vehicles involved but had no way of identifying who drove them. All they could do was put out a BOLO and follow up on whatever tips from the public came in.

Cade wasn't doing too hot either. Picking them up from school was the one thing I dragged myself out of bed for. One afternoon, about a month after Avery's disappearance, Cade didn't meet me in the pick-up loop after the final bell. Automatically, I panicked. I waited in the parking lot until the very last kid had left and then for another fifteen minutes after that. Finally, I entered the front office.

"Mrs. Dubire?" I said, fighting to keep my tone light and even though my blood pumped through my veins at an alarming rate.

Mrs. Dubire looked up from her computer. "Hi, honey! I didn't know you were still in town. What can I do for you?"

"I'm looking for Cade Christoph," I replied. "I'm supposed to be picking them up from school, but I didn't see them in the parking lot."

"Let me see what I can do." She pulled up the attendance records from that day. "Looks like Cade wasn't in school today. They never showed up to first period. Were they out sick today?"

"That's a good question," I muttered. "Thanks, Mrs. Dubire."

I drove to Edison's with a heavy heart, hoping against hope that Cade *was* sick and had forgotten to text me. Halfway there, I passed the park and spotted a familiar form lying flat on the weird iron carousels, spinning the platform around with one foot on the ground. I hit the brakes and parked on the curb.

"Hey!" I called to Cade. "What are you doing out here? It's freezing!"

Cade dragged their foot on the ground to stop the carousel. "Hi."

"That's it? Hi?" I grabbed the handles of the playground device. "What happened today? I went to the school to pick you up, but they said you never showed."

"I didn't go," Cade answered glumly.

"Why not?"

179

"Because Avery's loudest at school. Are you gonna get on or what?"

I stepped on to the carousel and crouched down to stay balanced. Cade pushed off with their foot to set up spinning again. "Are you still hearing Avery's voice?"

"Nonstop," Cade reported. Dark circles decorated the underside of their eyes. "It's like she's standing next to me yelling in my ear. The only time I don't hear her is when I'm asleep, and then I have nightmares about her anyway."

"Well, what is she saying?" I held tighter to the iron bars as the carousel spun a little faster. "Anything helpful?"

"I can't understand her," Cade replied. "It's like her thoughts are all jumbled up, like her mind is constantly running around in circles. It overlaps, and I can't make anything concrete out of it. What about you?"

"Nothing," I said. "It's been radio silent for weeks. I've never gone this long without a zap before."

"Trauma'll do that to you."

My stomach turned as the carousel made another loop. I took a chance and leapt off, stumbling across the rubber mulch. "Come on, kid. When was the last time you ate?"

"I can't remember."

I grabbed the handle of the carousel and pulled it to a stop. Then I helped Cade off. "Let's get you some sustenance."

WE ENDED up at Dove's Pub because the specialty rosemary truffle fries were one of Cade's favorite things to eat. I let them order as many as they wanted, along with the pub burger. As they wolfed down the meal, I nursed a pint of Dad's favorite lager. It was much better fresh.

"It wasn't the first time," Cade said between bites. "Skipping school, I mean. A few weeks ago, I started showing up for first period to get counted for attendance. Then I left during passing period. After school, I met you in the parking lot and pretended I'd been there the whole day."

As a guardian-like figure, I was probably supposed to give Cade a firm talking-to about the hazards of skipping school, but I couldn't muster the energy. I knew how they were feeling. It was hard to keep up appearances when your friend was gone.

"You gotta go to school," I told them. "Take it from someone who's been there. When Edison disappeared, I did the same thing. The only reason I managed to graduate was because I took a shitload of summer classes. Couldn't get into any good colleges either."

"Yeah, but you still made something of yourself," Cade pointed out. "You have a ton of followers. People love you."

I let out a sigh. In the last few weeks, my follower count had dropped dramatically. I hadn't posted any new content since the Home Safe fundraiser. Without content to keep my followers interested, they abandoned me. It was that simple.

"Finish school," I implored Cade. "I know it's hard with Avery gone, but you have to take care of yourself too."

Cade pushed cold fries around the plate. "It's hard to concentrate when someone's screaming in your ear." Their eyes flickered up to gauge my reaction but caught sight of something behind me instead. "Oh my God! Look!"

I whirled around. On the TV above the bar, a news show played silently. The headline *Whale Watchers Strike Again!* rolled across the bottom while a security video playing on a loop showed a white van screech into the parking lot of a butcher's shop. Five people got out, all wearing ski masks.

They threw bricks through the windows of the store, shattering the glass. Then the smallest tossed a grenade. With a short flare, it exploded. Smoke poured out of the broken windows. The criminals piled back into the van. The smallest one followed last, but right before the van door slammed shut, the criminal pulled off their ski mask. It was Avery.

14

"*A*ustin!" I shouted across the bar. "Turn the volume up."

Austin reached up high to hit the volume button, and the news show blared through the pub. Everyone turned to watch the program.

"This is the first act of violence we've seen from the Whale Watchers since they reportedly freed Norman Beers from Oregon State Penitentiary a month ago," the reported said. "The butcher's shop they attacked stocked products from Brickston Farms. Investigators have identified one of the culprits—" The video froze and zoomed in on Avery's blurry face as she got back into the van. "The identity of this criminal has not been released to the public yet. We'll give you more updates as we receive them."

The reporter moved on to another story. Cade and I stared at each other, dumbfounded. Why would the Whale Watchers kidnap a no-name teenager from the small town of Doveport? And what the hell was Avery doing throwing grenades through shop windows?

. . .

AN HOUR LATER, I sat in the conference room at the sheriff's department while Edison, Agent Marioni, the locals cops, a detective, and a team of FBI agents argued about the new development in Avery's case. Their voices overlapped as they bickered about the best way to approach the situation, causing a ruckus so loud that the secretary poked her head through the door.

"I don't mean to be a bother," the woman. "But you all need to keep it down unless you want the entire damn town to hear about this investigation. I've got civilians out here with their ears pointed at this door, and you know how people in Doveport love to gossip."

"Thank you, Dolly," Sheriff Danvers said. "We'll do our best to."

As soon as Dolly shut the door, the commotion resumed.

"She should be charged as an adult!" one of the FBI agents shouted.

"She's thirteen," Edison yelled back. "Furthermore, she's obviously been coerced into acting for that group. Avery would never do that on her own!"

"Says the mother who didn't watch her daughter closely enough to keep her from being kidnapped," the no-name agent shot back.

Marioni grabbed Edison to stop her from lunging at the agent. "Hollstein, you're out!"

Agent Hollstein threw his hands in the air. "For what? Telling the truth?"

"Out!" Marioni roared. He set Edison aside to take Hollstein by the lapels of his jacket and throw him out of the room. "You're off the case."

Sheriff Danvers snapped his fingers. "Let's take a step back. Agent Marioni, I think our first order of business is recovering the girl. I don't care what crimes she's committed with the Whale Watchers. We have to believe that Edison's right. They probably coerced her to act for them."

Marioni ran his fingers through his hair, a difficult feat considering all that gel. "I agree. I want eyes on Avery as soon as possible. Track that van. Get me a location. And call up whoever's in charge of the Beers/Brickston investigation. They've gotta have information on the Whale Watchers. I want to know where they'll strike next so we can be there when they do."

Marioni's team of agents filed out to obey his orders. The sheriff and detective stayed behind.

"What can we do?" Sheriff Danvers asked.

"Find out if anyone in Doveport has a connection to the Whale Watchers," Marioni ordered. "Question every vegan and vegetarian in town if you have to. Detective, can I have a word? I'd like to go over the case with you. Wait for me outside, if you don't mind."

The detective nodded and exited after the sheriff. Once they were gone, Marioni turned his gaze on me. Short stubble covered his face, except for a bald, red patch on his chin. Marioni was so stressed that he'd literally been pulling his hair out. Edison watched from the corner as he converged on me.

"I noticed you didn't have a whole lot to say," Marioni spat in my face. "Why's that? Usually, you think your input is the most important."

"Like I could have gotten a word in edgewise with all you important men fighting for dominance."

Marioni planted his hands on the armrest of my chair and

loomed over me. "You expect me to believe you don't know anything about Avery's connection to the Whale Watchers?"

"Why would I?" I asked, staring up into his stupid face. "Because I stormed their campsite a month ago? Tell me something, Agent Marioni. Are you so desperate to find a lead on this case that you'll exploit whoever you want?"

He pushed away from me, sending my chair rolling backward. He glanced at Edison, who wore a legitimate look of fear. I wondered what had transpired between them during all of those candlelit dinners.

"This isn't over," Marioni spat, driving his pointer finger at me like he wished it was a gun instead. "I'm going to get to the bottom of this."

"You won't find me there."

He stormed from the room, leaving me alone with Edison for the first time in weeks. She tried to follow Marioni, but I rolled my chair to block her from reaching the door.

"Don't even think about it," I said. "Why the hell does Marioni think I'd know about the Whale Watchers?"

"Don't be ridiculous, Bex. Get out of my way."

She dodged left, but I blocked her again. Accidentally, I rolled over her toes with the chair. She lost her balance and fell back against the conference table.

"You told him, didn't you?" I demanded. "About my ability. How could you do that to me?"

"I didn't!" Edison cried. "I wouldn't ever betray you like that."

"Really? Because it feels like we haven't been friends in weeks." My chest rose and fell rapidly with my breath. "You'd rather hang out with Marioni. Why's that?"

"He's looking for my kid, Bex."

"So am I."

Edison pinched the bridge of her nose and closed her eyes. "Please don't make me discuss this with you. I've got enough on my plate as it is. Just let me go home. Cade's probably waiting for me."

"Cade's at my house," I said. "Apparently, you haven't been the guardian to them you promised you'd be when you took them into the program. Nevertheless, they're safe."

Edison swallowed hard. Questioning her parenting skills was a low blow, but I needed to make her listen to me. On the upside, she hadn't made another attempt to leave, and the defense shield she'd put up to block me was crumbling by the second.

"I have a feeling I know why you don't want to talk to me," I said. "It's because you're scared Marioni might realize he's asking the wrong person about the Whale Watchers."

The color drained from Edison's face. "I don't know what you mean."

"We are best friends," I reminded her. "I can read you like a book. You told Hollstein that the Whale Watchers *must* have coerced Avery into acting for them."

"So?" Edison snapped. "It's true. Avery wouldn't hurt a fly, and she certainly wouldn't throw a smoke grenade into a shop unless someone was holding a gun to her head."

"Really? She didn't look too bothered about it on the video."

Her jaw dropped. "How could you say that? You know her!"

I shrugged. "Do I? I thought I knew you too, but you won't tell me the truth."

"About what?"

"About everything!" I shouted. I sprang to my feet, and the rolling chair ricocheted off the wall with a loud bang.

"Do you think it's a coincidence that both you and your daughter were kidnapped as teenagers? Because I don't! This feels personal, Edison. I bet whoever took Avery *knows* who you are, and if you were straight with me, I might actually to get ahead of the FBI on this case. But you won't answer my damn questions. You never have, and it sounds like you never will."

Edison shook as she zipped her coat up. She cleared her throat. "If you'll excuse me, I have things to do today. I don't have the time to deal with your conspiracy theories. Send Cade home, will you? You might disapprove of me, but I'm her legal guardian. Not you."

"But I don't want to go!" Cade whined. They stood with their back to my bedroom door, preventing me from leading them out. "Edison's being a jerk, and stupid Marioni won't leave. The whole house smells like his cheap cologne."

"If it were up to me, I'd let you stay here," I said. "But Edison's right. I'm not your legal guardian. I don't want to piss her off. She's taking all of this out on me right now, for God knows what reason. I can't step out of line. I wouldn't be surprised if she already sent the police to come get you."

Cade rubbed their eyes. They were rimmed red with exhaustion and emotional distress. "I don't know if I can do this for much longer, Bex." The teenager slid down the door and sat on the floor. "I'm tapped out."

I pulled the blanket off the bed, settled next to Cade, and draped the comforter over our knees. "I've got your back. You know that, right? It doesn't matter if you're here or at Edison's house. I'm always there for you."

Cade sniffled. "Yeah, I guess."

"And Edison still cares about you."

They snorted. "Doesn't feel that way."

"You have to understand where she's coming from," I said. "Her daughter's missing, but I know if you disappeared too, she'd be twice as upset. She has a weird way of showing she cares about people, but don't give up on her. She loves you."

"Not as much as she loves Avery."

I had nothing to say about that. There were a few things that Cade didn't know about Edison and Avery, but I didn't have the right to share them. However, I did happen to know that Edison had the capacity to love more than one child, even if that child wasn't biologically hers. In fact, I got the feeling that Edison loved each and every kid that came through the Home Safe program. She was so deeply attached to them, and she knew every kid's story by heart.

"You've got it wrong," I told Cade. "Edison loves you all so deeply, but when it comes to Avery, there's more to it. Losing Avery is huge for her because she knows what it's like to be in Avery's position, and she's terrified of what Avery might be going through."

Cade wiped their nose on the blanket. "If I hadn't been around, maybe Avery wouldn't have disappeared."

"Whoa, don't blame this on yourself." I pulled the comforter away from Cade's face to look them in the eye. "This has nothing to do with you."

"I drew Edison's attention away from Avery," Cade pointed out. "That's why Avery never liked me." Their lip quivered. "All I wanted was to be her friend. I wasn't trying to steal her mom."

"Avery knows that."

"I'm not sure she does."

I smoothed Cade's hair away from their forehead. "Listen,

kiddo. Being a teenager is tough. It's even harder for you, given your past. No one should have to go through what you've gone through. You deserve people who care about you."

"But Avery—"

"Forget about Avery for a minute," I said. "This is about you. For me and Edison, it's not a choice between who to love. We don't have to pick between you and Avery. We can love you both as separate individuals. Your issues are different from Avery's and vice versa. Does that make sense?"

"I guess so," Cade sniffled.

"I will say that attention can shift at a moment's notice," I admitted. "That's why it feels like everything is about Avery right now. Edison's first priority is finding her daughter. Her second is taking care of you. That's how it is sometimes, but it doesn't mean she cares for you any less. Besides, that's why I'm here, to pick up the slack."

Cade leaned their head against my shoulder. Their breathing had calmed. "Thanks, Bex. It helps a lot to have you around, but what happens when you leave again?"

I patted Cade's knees. "I'm not going anywhere for the time being. There's too much to be done here."

AFTER DROPPING Cade off at home—and staring Edison down from the car in the hopes she would come to her senses and realize I was her best ally—I returned to my house. I pulled Mom's old car into the garage, rolled down the windows, and inhaled the familiar scent of comfort. I leaned the driver's seat back all the way and propped my head on my arm. I recalled the meditation techniques I learned in Nepal. Focus on your breath. Scan the body from head to toe. Focus the energy on different points in the body, starting with the feet and traveling up to the navel, diaphragm, chest, throat, brow, and to a point about six inches above the head.

That last point always baffled me when I first learned meditation. How was I suppose to concentrate energy and feel it in my body when the focus point wasn't a *part* of my body? It wasn't until one of my instructors taught me visualization that I began to get it. The exercise was to imagine a golden orb of light traveling through your body, almost like a miniature personal sun. When it reached the top of my head, a comfortable warmth spread across my body and radiated downward, but all of my attention remained on that spot six inches above me. In that moment, every part of me felt as if it were reaching up toward the sun. It was the most relaxed I'd ever been. My goal for my continuing meditation practices was to recreate that feeling. Unfortunately, it was much harder to accomplish in a cold car.

Several minutes passed, but I couldn't calm the racing thoughts in my head. I'd focus on the breath for a few seconds then let all my stressors come right back in, like someone had kicked down the door that kept them at bay. My fingers and toes twitched, unable to find stillness. I noticed every sensation: my toes sweating in my thick socks, a bird chirping loudly outside, the faint smell of exhaust. It was impossible to drown out the multiple distractions.

When someone tapped on the top of the car, I sat up so quickly that I hit my head on the top of the car. Rubbing the lump, I noticed my mother had come to join me in the garage again. She circled around to the passenger side and got in.

"My, it's been a while since I've sat on this side of the car," she said, rubbing her palms furiously against her thighs. She was dressed in jeans, a big coat, and boots.

"Are you going somewhere?" I asked.

"No, I just got back," she replied. "Melba dropped me off."

"From where?"

She gave a thin cough. "I—well, it's hard for me to say."

I levered my seat back to a sitting position. "What's going on, Mom?"

She was lucid. That much I could tell from the way she held her words back, seeming to examine her sentences in her head before she said them out loud. If she was stuck in the past, she wouldn't have a problem with blurting out whatever came to mind.

"Mom?" I ventured again after a minute of silence. "Is something wrong?"

"No, nothing's wrong," she answered. "I've been thinking about what you said to me that day on the porch, about treating you the way I treated you when you were a teenager."

A chilly breeze swept through the garage from outside, creeping into the car through the open windows. I shivered. Mom and I hadn't spoken much since the mentioned conversation. It was all polite hellos and goodbyes. Occasionally, I had breakfast or dinner with her when she was in a good mood. Otherwise, I steered clear.

"I know you've been avoiding me, and I think I have a better understanding of why than I did before." She nervously kneaded her hands. "Melba's been taking me to see a therapist."

A burst of surprise went through me. Despite her background in the medical field, Mom didn't trust doctors. She trusted mental health specialists even less.

"You're kidding me," I said.

"I'm trying." A note of pleading colored her tone. "I told the therapist about us and everything that happened between your dad's death and now."

"And?"

"And I understand why you don't want to stay in Doveport," Mom replied. "There's too much bad history here, and I was a big part of that. I'm taking responsibility for the way I treated you."

My equilibrium was out of whack. Had the universe turned upside down?

"I can't make you stay here," Mom went on. "But I'll try to do better from now on." She let out a derisive laugh. "Though I can't make any promises for my alter-ego. She's a bit of a bitch."

I mustered a watered-down smile. "I appreciate the effort."

"That's it?" Mom ventured. "Nothing else you want to say?"

I didn't know what she wanted from me, so I said, "Thank you for trying."

She looked disappointed. "All right, then. I'll see you inside."

If she expected more, I couldn't give it to her. Deciding to see a therapist was a huge step for her. She had made progress, but there was one thing missing from her emphatic speech: an apology.

15

_____

The following week, Edison called me to set up a lunch date. Putting aside my shock, I immediately agreed, and we met at our usual booth at Maxine's café. Maxine had made a fresh batch of croissants, so I ordered ham and cheese. Edison, despite the implication of lunch, didn't ask Maxine for food. She nursed coffee after coffee, until I lost count of how many times Maxine refilled her mug. She never got up to pee. I wondered at the size and strength of the bladder.

We chatted like two acquaintances who had run into each other and reluctantly agreed to share a table. Edison didn't seem particularly interested in covering any topics that were relevant to our lives, so we talked about trivial crap like the weather, Doveport High School's last football game, and a throwdown between two locals at the pub the other night. Awkward silence fell between subjects, so I filled them with the sound of my chewing.

"I haven't seen Cade in a few days," I mentioned off the

cuff, hoping to climb out of the pool of discomfort we were drowning in. "Are they on house arrest or something?"

"In a manner of speaking." The dainty, professional phrase sounded odd coming out of her mouth. I was used to Edison's casual, languid way of talking. This stiff woman sitting across from me wasn't my best friend. "I got a call from the school. Apparently, Edison's been skipping class for several weeks. I don't suppose you know anything about that?"

"Uh, no. They didn't mention it."

When I was kid, my mom said she could always tell when I'd done something wrong because my eyebrows would cinch together in the middle. The lines between them formed a V shape, like a crudely drawn seagull. It was my tell, and Edison knew it too.

"Liar," she said sharply. "How long have the two of you been doing this behind my back?"

"Is this why you wanted to have lunch? To bust my balls about Cade?"

"Well, if you're encouraging them to skip school—"

"I'm not!" I said hotly. A few faces turned to look at us, disturbed by the sudden rise in volume at our table. I lowered my voice. "Look, I caught them in the lie a week ago. I gave them a stern talking to. I didn't think they'd keep doing it."

"That was stupid."

I peeled the ham and cheese off the second half of my croissant and ate just the bread. "Cade's in a tough spot. You don't know what's going on with them."

Edison crossed her arms. "And you do? Please, enlighten me."

"When you were gone, I fell apart." I held Edison's gaze,

trying to see past the cold glare in her eyes. "I didn't know what to do with myself without you, especially knowing that you were in trouble. That's what Cade is feeling now, amplified by a hundred. They have to live with you, Ed. Whatever you're feeling about Avery gets projected outward, and Cade picks it up."

"So you're saying it's my fault that Cade is skipping school?"

With a groan, I sank into my chair and let my legs extend outward. "It's no one's fault. It's just the way it is."

Edison, wound up like a pretzel, glared at my boots where they grazed the leg of her white pants. To avoid a war, I pulled my feet back in. I leaned across the table, hoping to pull Edison closer to me.

"What happened to us?" I asked quietly. "You've been throwing me a lot of curveballs lately. First, you were mad at me because I *wouldn't* look for Avery. Then you got pissed when I did. I'm at a loss here."

Edison covered her eyes. Dimples appeared in her chin, a sure sign that she was holding back tears. I kept forgetting to take my own advice and cut Edison some slack. All of this weighed on her more heavily than it did on me.

"Hey." I slid a stack of clean napkins across the table. "Take your time. Everything's going to be okay."

She grabbed the whole wad of napkins and used them to mop her eyes. "You don't know that."

"It's what I kept telling myself when you disappeared," I said. "I was right. You came home safe and sound, and so will Avery."

"Not if we keep running around in circles." She dabbed her cheeks and took a deep breath. "Marioni hasn't made any progress. Neither have the cops. I don't understand how this could happen. They have Avery on video! How could they not find her?"

"Either Marioni and his team are too dumb, or the Whale Watchers are too smart," I replied. "Maybe a combination of both."

A hint of a smile appeared on Edison's face. She set aside the damp napkins. "I was furious when you went to San Junipero."

"I'm aware."

"Not for the reasons you might think," Edison said. "I wasn't mad at you for trying to track down Avery. I was angry because you took Cade with you instead of me."

This new development threw a wrench in my under-standing of Edison's emotions. "Cade helped me figure out where the Whale Watchers were. That's why I brought them."

"We'll get to *how* you found them later," she said. "What I want to know is why you didn't immediately inform the FBI."

"Well, I-I—you were—" I stuttered, attempting to come up with an excuse that made sense, but I didn't have one available. "I have no idea, Ed. Marioni was more interested in dating you than finding Avery. Tipping him off felt like a terrible idea."

The iciness returned to Edison's puffy eyes. "What about me? Why didn't you tell me you knew where Avery was?"

"Marioni had you in his pocket."

"Oh, for God's sake, Bex." She tossed her hands in the air. "I don't want to screw Rocco. I want him to find my kid, and if that means sucking up to him so he spends more time on my case than whatever else is going on in his life, then that's a sacrifice I'm going to make."

The sense of her statement washed over me. Why didn't I

see it before? Edison had always used her wiles to get what she wanted. I had a strong feeling it was how she managed to escape her own kidnappers, though she'd never filled me in on the details.

Edison snatched the half-eaten croissant off my plate. "I need this more than you."

"Go for it."

With a full mouth, she mumbled, "I asked you to lunch because I had to tell you I was wrong. You made more progress on Avery's case in a day than Marioni and his team have made all month. I've been an idiot. I want you to start looking for Avery again."

The truth was I *had* been looking for Avery. I combed through news stories and researched the Whale Watchers, but with my abilities playing hooky, I didn't have the same advantage from a month ago.

"I can't," I admitted.

Edison's face immediately wrinkled. "Why not?"

"Ever since that night at San Junipero, I haven't been able to—" I caught sight of an elderly couple one table over. The woman had her ear turned toward us. I cleared my throat. "I haven't been able to log into my accounts."

Edison stared at me. "What?"

"You know." I jerked my head at the older lady. "I haven't been able to *log in*. I seem to have forgotten my password." To get the point across, I tapped the screen of my phone.

Understanding finally flowed across Edison's expression. "Oh! I see. That's inconvenient. Isn't there some way to recover your password?"

"Not that I've found yet."

The café door flew open, rattling the bell overhead so violently that the patrons nearest to it ducked for cover.

Cade stumbled in, scanned the room, spotted me in the corner, and ran over. They bumped into the elderly couple's table as they passed, knocking over the woman's coffee. I didn't feel too bad about it. That was pure karma for eavesdropping.

"Sorry, I'm so sorry," Cade gushed, seizing a handful of napkins from a nearby dispenser and tossing them across the mess. They left the old couple to fend for themselves, in too much of a hurry to get to me and Edison. "Bex!" they gasped. "I need to talk to you." They glanced at Edison. "Alone."

"Really?" Edison said, hurt and annoyance clear in the tightness of her tone. "What about me?"

"Sorry, it's private," Cade stammered, "and Bex already knows about it."

"I don't suppose this has anything to do with you skipping so much school?" Edison pried.

"No," Cade said. "Sort of. It's a long story. Can I talk to Bex or not?"

I caught Edison's eye. All she wanted was to be included in whatever secret me and Cade shared together, but Cade's frantic attitude implied that Edison wasn't ready to know what Cade needed to tell me.

"I'll call you," I promised Edison as I picked up my coat. Cade hopped up and down on the balls of their feet, unable to contain their energy. "And I'll make sure Cade gets home safely."

It hurt to leave Edison alone at the table, her shoulders sinking into her chest as Cade and I abandoned her. I told myself it was for the best. We'd clue Edison in when it was appropriate to do so.

Cade led me through the back exit of the café, into the delivery lot. The trees hadn't been tended to in years. The old pathway from which Edison had disappeared was filled in with foliage. Still, the sight of it gave me chills.

Cade shook out their hands as if trying to rid them of a swarm of fire ants. I grabbed Cade by the collar of their jacket and forced them to stand still. They managed to squirm to and fro anyway.

"What's the matter?" I asked. "Are you hurt?"

"No, but I think Avery might be."

Dread circled the top of my head like a vulture, waiting for the perfect moment to descend. "What are you talking about?"

"I keep hearing her voice." Cade brushed my grasp from the front of my jacket and bounced erratically around the lot. "It hasn't stopped. It's almost constant. I can't sleep or eat. I can't focus in school, so I don't go anymore. I'm sure Edison told you that. Do you think they'll expel me? I can't get expelled. I have to graduate. I have to be a decent person. Do you think I'm a good person? Do you think—?"

When they passed me again, I grabbed Cade around the shoulders and hugged them as tightly as possible to my chest. I knew what anxiety looked like, and Cade's was spinning out of control.

They resisted at first. They tapped their foot and pushed against me. I held on tighter. Pressure was scientifically proven to reduce feelings of stress. It didn't work for everyone, but I had the feeling that it might work for Cade. I was right. After a minute, they relaxed against me. Their breathing evened out. Their muscles went slack. I held on.

"When I was a kid," I murmured, "and I was feeling particularly terrible about losing Edison, I'd wrap myself as tightly as I could in a blanket. Like a human burrito. It helped a lot."

Cade didn't lift their head from my chest. In a muffled voice, they said, "I needed that."

"I told you I got your back. You okay?"

They pulled out of the hug, visibly less shaken than they had been a minute ago. "I think so."

"Tell me about Avery," I said gently. "Did she say she was hurt?"

"No, not exactly," Cade replied. "It's still the same. I can hear Avery, but I don't think she knows I'm listening. Her thoughts aren't clear, so I get flashes of emotions instead. Mostly, she's scared and anxious, but not to a point that she can't handle herself." Cade took a deep breath, chest rising with the inhale. "But I was at the park just now, spinning on the carousel, and all of a sudden, I was terrified. Like running-from-a-serial-killer terrified. It felt like someone stabbed me in the heart and all my blood was running to that point. Then I realized *I* wasn't the one who felt that way. It was Avery."

Stomach acid inched up my throat and coated my tongue. "She's been hurt? Someone stabbed her?"

"No," Cade said. "She's okay physically. I'd know if she wasn't. But something scared her. Something big. Bex, if we don't find her soon, I'm afraid the Whale Watchers are going to kill her."

$\mathcal{T}$he first step to locating Avery—again—was to deal with my own problem first. Though my break from brain zaps had been refreshing, I needed them to start up again. I didn't have much chance of succeeding without my extra senses. I tried everything to trigger a brain zap. I spent hours in my room, surrounded by as many phones and tablets I could find, but no matter how much I focused, I couldn't get it to happen. It was like that pathway in my brain was closed off, and I no longer had access to it.

I couldn't venture into cyberspace anymore either. What once came so easy to me was now like pulling teeth. I posted a random update on Twitter to see if I could push it to the top of my followers' dashboard the way I usually did. It was no use. I couldn't get into whatever part of my head linked me to technology. The fact that I had no understanding of my powers didn't help. That was where Cade came in.

It was their idea to try and trigger a seizure. I wouldn't have volunteered for the task if Avery wasn't in danger, and I wasn't getting anywhere on my own. But when Cade showed up at my house with an armful of heavy-duty lights, I started having second thoughts.

"Do you have any idea what you're doing?" I asked Cade as I helped carry the equipment down to the basement, where we'd decided to do our experiment.

"I'm a fifteen-year-old with no prior knowledge of epilepsy," Cade called over their shoulder. "Nor have I ever studied brain anatomy. What do you think?"

I lifted my stage light higher so I wouldn't trip over the last step. "That's comforting."

Cade dumped their load of crap on the sofa with a grunt of effort. "Fear not. I've consulted the great Google and came up with a plan."

"Sure, as long as Google said it was cool. Where did you get all this stuff anyway?"

"Would you be mad if I told you I stole it?"

"Not mad," I said. "Concerned maybe. AV club?"

"All except for the stage lights. Got those from the drama club." The teenager grinned as they began untangling a rat's nest of extension cords. "Do you have a power bar? We're gonna need one. Maybe two. Oh, and turn on your sound system too."

I left Cade to set up in the basement and found Mom sitting at the kitchen table, reading a magazine. She glanced up as I passed.

"Babysitting again?" she asked.

"Yup."

She hummed and returned her gaze to the magazine. "I didn't think kids Cade's age needed so much supervision."

"I'm helping Edison out." I rummaged through a closet full of junk next to the basement door. "Do we have power cords anywhere?"

"Check the garage. Your dad kept a bunch in his hardware cabinets."

"Thanks. By the way, it might get kinda loud in the basement while we're down there," I warned her. "The kid wants to play some weird game. I'd steer clear if I were you."

Mom checked the time. "Melba's coming to pick me up soon anyway."

IN THE GARAGE, I unearthed a few power cords from Dad's collection and brought them back inside. When I returned to the basement, Cade had set up the lights and speakers in a semi-circle around the couch. The equipment was plugged into a control board Cade must have swiped from the sound booth in the school's gym.

"Perfect!" Cade said, relieving me of the power cords. They plugged the various lights and speakers into the walls and turned everything on. The subtle hum of power surged through the basement. "Take a seat, Bex. I'm ready if you are."

With every light pointed at the couch, the hot seat was brighter than the sun. "Can you kill the lights at least?" I asked, shielding my eyes. "They're blinding me."

"Kinda the point," Cade said, but they flicked a few switches on the control board to dim the area. "Come on, get to it."

I picked my way through the jungle of cords and wires, stepped over a low stage light, and sat on the couch. Despite being at my own house, I felt like I was in the basement of a government facility, about to be interrogated for information.

"Got your phone, right?" Cade asked. They sat on the old desk in the corner of the room, legs swinging freely as they balanced the control board on their lap. "You're gonna need it."

I dug the phone out of my pocket and waved it to show Cade.

"Cool, put it on your lap. This is how things are gonna work." They flicked a switch on the control board, and the lamp closest to me—a fairly subtle LED—came on. "We're gonna try with just like the lights first. If that doesn't do anything, I'll add sound. You ready?"

My fingers clenched the couch cushions. "I guess."

"Here we go."

Cade flicked another switch on the board. They'd programmed the lights to flash on and off at different times. I fought the instinct to close my eyes. The bright lights made them water, and the constant change from light to dark made things more uncomfortable. Cade slid a control bar on the board, and the speed of the lights intensified.

"Anything?" Cade asked.

"Other than annoyance? No."

"Damn. Okay, here comes the music."

They pressed another button, and a staticky tune played loudly over the speakers. I didn't recognize the song because Cade had altered it in every possible way. They'd cranked up the distortion and modified the pitch so that it sounded less like a song and more like a torture device. My teeth ground together as the noise and lights overwhelmed my system.

"It's not working!" I shouted.

"Where's your phone?" Cade hollered back. "Try accessing your stuff!"

With the phone in hand, I attempted to get into cyber-space, but the distractions around me were too much. My head felt like it was going to explode, and not in the same way as a brain zap.

"Turn it off!"

"What?" Cade shouted.

"Turn it off!" I bellowed, covering my eyes with my arms. "I can't take any more!"

Cade fumbled with the control board, and the lights and noise died off a moment later. Cade's shoulders slumped. They were disappointed.

"I was sure that would work," they said.

I rolled over and laid on my back, letting the floaters fade from my eyes. "That was terrible."

"You didn't feel anything?" Cade asked. "At all? No tickle in your brain?"

"No tickle."

"Well, that was only the first trial," they said. "Most experiments don't succeed on the first run. Let's try again."

I threw a couch cushion at Cade to knock their hand away from the control board. "It's not going to work. I can't concentrate with all of that crap flashing."

"You mean I stole this shit for nothing?"

I covered my face with the crocheted blanket from the back of the couch and groaned. "Ugh, I'm still seeing stars."

The couch sagged as Cade sat by my feet. I peeked through the blanket. They propped their chin in their hands and pouted. I nudged them with my foot.

"Come on, it's not your fault," I said. "It was a good idea."

"Not *the* idea," Cade replied. "We have to try something else. What triggered your abilities in the first place? Maybe we can work off that."

"We've been through this." I said, fending Cade off when they tried to tickle my socked feet. "I'm not a superhero. I don't have an origin story. Do *you* know why you started hearing voices in your head?"

Cade grimaced. "That's a fair point. But you told me that your abilities started shortly after Edison disappeared. That's something, right? Maybe it was triggered by necessity."

"If that's the case, why wouldn't it work now?" I asked. "I *need* to find Avery, but I'm out of luck."

"What about the phone?" Cade snatched it out of my lap and hit the button to wake it up. "Dude, the battery's dead. Stupid."

"What?" I grabbed the phone back to test it myself. Sure enough, the screen wouldn't power on. "I just charged this thing this morning!"

"Sure you did." Cade rolled their eyes. "How are you supposed to find Avery with a dead phone? No wonder your powers aren't working."

I plugged the phone into its charger in the nearest outlet. "I'm telling you, it wasn't dead before. Something must have drained it."

Cade's expression brightened. "Coincidence?"

Excitement stirred in my chest. "Maybe not?"

The phone chimed and turned on. Cade and I hunched over it. The cell service in the basement was shoddy at best. I only had one bar.

"Hang on, if your powers work off of phones and tablets, it probably has something to do with the cell towers and the strength of the signal, right?" Cade asked eagerly. "Maybe even the Wi-Fi?"

"I guess. Maybe. Why?"

"What if we could boost the signal?" they suggested. "Give you more of a chance to pick something up from it?"

"How are we supposed to do that?"

Cade hopped off the couch, dug around in their back-pack, and unearthed a plastic black box with an antenna attached. "Aha!"

"What's that thing?"

"It's a network extender."

"Did you steal that too?"

"Surprisingly, no." Cade plugged the network extender into one of the power bars. "I bought this with my allowance for Edison's house. Her Wi-Fi sucks upstairs. Let's see if we can get this to work—"

As soon as the network extender powered on, blinking to indicate it had connected to the existing Wi-Fi, an enormous wave of energy washed through my head. I felt like Franken-stein's monster as the creator waited for the bolt of lightning to throw the switch that would jolt me to life. My eyes rolled back in my head, my muscles tense and rigid. My phone rang over and over as new text messages flooded in.

Cade unplugged the network extender, and everything faded to a reasonable level. I slumped against the couch, utterly exhausted. My phone notifications slowed and even-tually stopped. Cade studied me, jaw dropped low.

"I'm so sorry," they said. "I had no idea it would be like that. How do you feel?"

"Like I sat through a round in the electric chair," I croaked.

"But it worked though?"

I groaned and forced myself to reach for my phone. One hundred new text messages waited for me to sift through them. It was like they'd been backed up in my head, unable to transpose themselves until my "signal" was boosted.

"It worked, all right."

Cade pushed off their knees and sat next to me on the

couch. "Anything good?" They peered at the phone screen over my shoulder. "What is this crap? It's just gibberish."

"It's not," I said. "Well, some of it is. Look here, though." I pointed to a message that read *jun1p3r0*. "That must have been right before we figured out where Avery was the first time."

Cade took my phone and scrolled through the newer messages. "A bunch of these are compass directions, but it goes all different ways. That doesn't make any sense."

"They're traveling," I explained. "The Whale Watchers. If we followed the latest messages, we might be able to find them."

They jumped to their feet. "Then what are we waiting for? This says west toward Portland! Let's go."

"Slow your roll, kid." I stretched my neck, hoping it might ease the leftover throbbing sensation in my head. "There's one fatal flaw with these dumb messages. They don't tell you how far you have to go. The Whale Watchers could be in friggin' Idaho by now."

Cade collapsed on the couch again, pouting. "What was the point of all this then?"

I waved them to scoot closer to me, so they had a good view of my phone again. Then I pulled up a browser and searched the Whale Watchers. A bunch of hits came up, including the video of Avery throwing the smoke grenade into the butcher shop.

"Here's the thing with groups like the Whale Watchers," I explained to Cade. "They *want* to be seen. They want people to know what they've done. They revel in attention. Guess what that means?"

Cade looked stumped. "I have no idea."

I clicked on a Twitter page, *@thewhalewhatchers*. It pulled up the organization's feed, complete with a link to the official website, an About page, and most importantly, a list of followers.

I grinned. "It means they have social media accounts."

I worked methodically. Most of the people who followed the Whale Watchers' Twitter account were not a part of the organization. Rather, they believed in the Whale Watchers' goals and overall mission. If you didn't know about the group's illegal activities, it would be easy to get behind them. According to their website, they fought for the ethical treatment of animals, just like PETA.

According to the About page, the Whale Watchers first came together in the early nineties but didn't adopt their official name until 2010, the year Tilikum the whale killed a trainer at Sea World. Apparently, the Whale Watchers were the most vocal group when it came to the issue of keeping whales in captivity.

"Check this out," Cade said. They'd taken out their laptop to join me in gathering information on the Whale Watchers. "I found this Wikipedia article that lists all of the Whale Watchers' riots. The first one was in March of 2010. They stood outside of the Sea World parking lot and shouted profanities at the guests. One of the Whale Watchers actually attacked a guest. The fight escalated. Eleven people were injured and one died in the hospital from knife wounds."

"You'd think people who were so passionate about keeping animals safe might have the same thoughts about humans," I muttered. "Does it say which Whale Watcher attacked the guest? Were any arrests made?"

Cade skimmed the web page again. "It was some dude named Whisper Collins. What kind of person names their kid Whisper?"

I Googled Whisper Collins. The first hit was an Instagram account. I bypassed it, looking for more information
on the arrest. A few links down, I found a news story from a
local online paper in Orlando, Florida. The journalist had
covered the incident more thoroughly than the Wikipedia
page did. I read part of the article aloud.

"Thirty-five-year-old Collins was not only arrested for
assault and battery during the incident," I recited to Cade.
"He was also charged for child endangerment due to the fact
that he brought his ten-year-old daughter to the riot.
According to police reports, the young girl broke her arm
during the fight and was hospitalized with the other victims.
It is likely that Collins will face time in prison and lose
custody of his daughter."

Cade scrunched their nose in disgust. "What an asshole."

"I guess stupidity ran in the family," I remarked. "Maybe
he was mad because his parents named him Whisper."

I returned to the search results, scrolled to the top of the
page, and clicked on the Instagram account I'd skipped over
before. The account was private, but the profile picture
showed a girl around nineteen or twenty holding a sign that
said "Veganism is a Humanism!"

I prodded Cade. "Look at this."

"No way," Cade muttered. "Do you think she's Collins's
daughter?"

"It would be one hell of a coincidence if she wasn't," I said.
"Not a lot of people out there with a name like Whisper
Collins."

"Too bad her profile is private."

A mischievous grin crossed my face. "Not for long. Watch
this."

Though an uncomfortable tingle crept through my head

as I accessed my version of cyberspace, I was happy to have my ability back. It felt like I'd been missing part of myself for the past few weeks. Not to mention, it was a pretty convenient talent to possess. I easily got past the wall that kept Whisper Collins's profile private, refreshed the page, and gained full access to the page.

"How the heck do you do that?" Cade demanded. "Seriously, how does it work?"

I shrugged and handed them the phone. "It's hard to explain. I visualize all these different colored wires, and each one leads to a person's profile or computer or whatever. So I zoom in, pick the wires I want, and re-route them for my own purposes. I can push my own posts into people's feeds so they always see my stuff first, regardless of whatever algorithms the website uses. I can make my content show up more often in search results. If I'm really feeling evil, I can put up blocks around other people's profiles so *no one* sees their stuff."

"Have you done that before?"

"Once," I admitted. "I met this insufferable girl in Taiwan who wouldn't shut up about how popular she was on Instagram."

"You're my new idol."

I rolled my eyes. "Let's see what Whisper Collins Junior is up to, shall we?"

Together, we scrolled through the girl's Instagram page. Her appearance was striking. She shaved her head and bore a prominently hooked nose. Her photos were mostly indulgent selfies, each with a long caption about fighting for animal rights, but there was nothing besides her name to link her to the Whale Watchers.

"Dead end?" Cade asked.

I studied the most recent selfie Whisper posted. She'd gotten a new tattoo, one of a bright-blue lightning bolt that covered the top of her forearm from the wrist to the elbow.

"Pull up that video at the butcher's shop again," I told Cade.

They did so. We watched through it a few times, but it wasn't until I slowed the video down that I saw it. As the Whale Watcher closest to Avery tossed their brick through the butcher's window, the sleeve of their black jacket rode up. Beneath it was a bright-blue patch of skin.

*O*nce we knew Whisper Collins Junior—or the Second, whatever you wanted to call her—had followed in her father's footsteps and joined the Whale Watchers, it was easy to trace her through social media. I followed every thread, checked on all her followers, and read each comment she'd ever posted. Using Collins as the focal point, we were able to identify more than thirty other possible members of the Whale Watchers.

Cade organized the information we gathered. They'd found a stack of poster boards and a box of magic markers leftover from my middle school science fair days. After hours of studying the Whale Watchers, the poster boards covered at least ten square feet of the basement floor as Cade drew a visual representation of how the members of the Whale Watchers were connected. I infiltrated private social media accounts, bank accounts, and hospital records, but the Facebook posts ended up being the most helpful. It turned out the Whale Watchers developed a simple code, so they could all communicate in public forums without being found out. Unluckily for them, Cade loved codes.

"It's called the Caesar shift," Cade said. They lay stomach-down on the floor with the Whale Watchers' Facebook page pulled up on the laptop in front of them. To me, each status update and post looked like a bunch of random letters, but Cade saw something different. "Caesar used it to send military messages. It's, like, the easiest cipher to figure out. All you have to do is substitute each letter with another one by shifting left or right in the alphabet."

I watched them scribble furiously on a spare piece of poster board. "I still don't get it."

Cade held up the poster board. On the top line, Cade had written the alphabet in order. Below each letter was a second one, though I had no idea how they corresponded.

"For this one, the Whale Watchers have shifted each letter four spaces to the right," Cade explained. "So an A becomes an E, a B becomes an F, and so on and so forth."

"How did you figure that out?"

They returned to deciphering the Whale Watchers' latest Facebook post. "I usually start with two or three letter words. 'It' and 'the' give away the key pretty quickly. Then you just have to fill in the blanks. Give me a few minutes. I'm almost done with this."

As Cade finished up, I examined the information sprawled across the poster boards. It was more than the police or the FBI ever hoped to figure out, but it was all theoretical. Though these people were connected to the Whale Watchers through the Internet, we couldn't prove that any of them—except for Whisper Collins—were involved with Avery's kidnapping.

I circled a familiar name in red marker: Norman Beers. Something about that guy irked me. Maybe it was that he didn't look like a criminal. We always pictured them as gross, dingy people with missing teeth and a lot of face tattoos, often forgetting that people like Ted Bundy got by on pure charm and handsome physiques. Norman Beers was like that. He smiled in his mug shot. He wore clean, ironed clothes. He had a strong jaw and soft, kind eyes. You *wanted* to like him, which was exactly why I didn't trust him. I believed in the humane treatment of animals, but murdering someone for not caring was a new level of crazy.

"Got it!" Cade shouted, hopping to their feet with excitement. "It's the plans for the next Whale Watchers' riot. They're going to hit an egg farm called Mellow Meadows in Tillamook. Supposedly, it's a cage-free facility, but the Whale Watchers think the owners are lying about how they treat their chickens. Looks like they're gonna sneak in at night and let all the chickens loose."

"That's pretty tame compared to the Whale Watchers' latest activities," I mentioned. "It's more like an elaborate prank than a riot."

"According to these comments, they also plan on tying the Mellow Meadows owner up in the field like a scarecrow," Cade added grimly. "So, and I quote, 'he knows how it feels.'"

"That's more on brand."

"What are we going to do?" Cade questioned. "Do you think Avery's going to be there? Do you think she's going to help? Should we call the cops?" They let out a groan. "Do we have to tip off the FBI? Stupid Agent Marioni is going to take all the credit for our work. Wait a second... did we just commit a crime? I mean, you're basically a hacker, right? We accessed a bunch of private accounts. Am I gonna go to juvie for this—"

"You're doing it again," I said loudly.

"What?"

"Babbling."

"Oh." Cade pointedly fell silent. For a second. "Okay, but what's the plan? What should we do?"

"*We* are not doing anything," I said. "After last time, I promised Edison I wouldn't involve you in anything dangerous."

Cade let out a growl of frustration. "No fair!"

"You want to get shot again? How's your leg?"

"So what then?" they challenged. "You're gonna tell Marioni?"

"No," I said. "But I am going to tell Edison."

THE WHALE WATCHERS' attack on the egg farm wasn't supposed to happen until Saturday night. That meant I had two days to come up with a plan. My first order of business was coming clean about our research session to Edison. I made sure Cade was at school when I did it. It was easier to explain things without the overactive teenager jumping in every other moment.

"You figured all of this out on your own?" Edison asked.

We sat at her kitchen table. I'd brought along the poster boards, since it was the easiest way to share what we had learned about the Whale Watchers. She examined them open-mouthed, eyes darting from one name to the next, unable to process it all at once.

"Cade helped," I admitted. "But I did most of the snooping. Once we found Whisper Collins, it was easy to track down a few others. Whisper, the younger one, was with Avery on the night they attacked the butcher's shop."

"This girl?" Edison asked, pointing to a picture we'd printed off Whisper's Instagram and glued to the poster board. "With the shaved head?"

"Yeah. My guess is the Whale Watchers paired her with Avery on purpose," I said. "They're only a few years apart, and most of the other members are guys. Maybe they thought Avery would feel more comfortable if she had another girl to talk to."

Edison stared at the profile picture, as if silently willing Whisper to take care of Avery. I cleared my throat.

"There are a few things that don't add up," I said. "First of all, we didn't find anything about the other missing girls, but it seems unlikely that the disappearances aren't related. Second, I can't figure out *why* the Whale Watchers would abduct Avery. Any ideas?"

"Perhaps they needed a martyr," Edison suggested.

"You haven't gotten any weird phone calls, have you?" I asked. "Or letters. Anything?"

Edison shook her head. "Do you think they would contact me?"

"I don't know," I replied. "But something feels off about all of this."

She flipped over the stack of poster boards so she didn't have to look at them anymore. "What do you plan on doing with this information? I know your pride would take a hit if you handed it over to Marioni."

"That's why I'm here actually," I said. "I promised you I'd find Avery, and this is the place she's likely to be on Saturday night. But it's *your* decision as to what to do with this information. Do you trust Marioni to get the job done?"

Edison gnawed on her bottom lip. "Honestly? I don't trust any of them. Not the FBI or the police. Sheriff Danvers is a great guy, but he hasn't made a dent in these investigations. Neither has that detective of theirs."

"So just to be clear," I said, "you want *me* to go after Avery?"

"Is that asking too much?" Her eyes begged me to say no. "You've already done it before. And you have a Taser, right? You can defend yourself."

Part of me had already decided that I was going to be the one to fetch Avery, whether Edison wanted to give the information to the officials or not. It was a stupid idea. I'd probably end up facing the wrong end of a shotgun again. Yet, a weird instinct—stemming from the same place in my brain that fed my ability—told me I needed to do this.

"I'll go," I told Edison. "But not to the egg farm."

MY PLAN WAS to find the Whale Watchers *before* their attack on the egg farm. With any luck, I could infiltrate their camp again. Without Cade to draw attention to us, I might actually be able to find Avery. However, I did need Cade for something.

"You will stay in the car." I emphasized the last four words as I briefed Cade on our mission for Friday night. We'd rendezvoused in my mother's garage to get our shit together. "I'm going to park—"

"Somewhere safe," Cade finished for me in a bored voice. "Out of the line of fire, miles away from the campsite. Blah, blah, blah. We've been through this a hundred times, Bex."

"Just making sure it gets through that thick head of yours."

"What did you tell Edison to get her to let me go with you?" Cade asked.

"The truth," I answered. "That you wouldn't go anywhere near the Whale Watchers or their campsite. Your job is to sit in the car behind that laptop. If you move, I'll kill you. Got it?"

Cade rolled their eyes. "Got it. Can we go?"

Tillamook was about an hour's drive from Doveport, maybe a little longer. After Cade and I loaded the car with the classic stakeout materials—binoculars, water, and snacks —we got on the road. Edison called us about fifteen minutes in.

"I've changed my mind about this," she said.

"Too late," Cade and I chorused.

"Really, you two should turn around," Edison went on. "We'll call Marioni instead. Please? I can't stand the thought of either of you getting hurt."

"We'll be fine, Ed." I smacked a packet of powdered donuts out of Cade's hands. "Those are for the stakeout, doofus. Don't waste all our food."

"Didn't your mom ever teach you not to smack another person's donuts?"

"It sure *sounds* like you'll be fine," Edison remarked, sarcasm tinging her voice. "Look, promise me you'll get out of there if it's too fishy. If Avery's not there, there's no point in making a scene."

"We'll keep you posted," I said, driving one-handed as I confiscated the donuts from Cade and popped two in my mouth at once. "Talk later, Ed!"

"Bex, don't you dare hang up—"

Cade pushed the End Call button for me. If Edison gave me heat for me later, I'd blame it on the teenager. They pulled up the navigation app on my phone and examined the coordinates for our destination.

"Are you sure this is where they are?" Cade asked. "It's in the middle of nowhere."

"It's only a few miles from Mellow Meadows," I replied, changing lanes to get around an ancient red pickup truck. "And it's a registered campsite."

Cade pulled up the website for the campsite. "For, like, hardcore prepper folks who want to practice for the end of the world. There aren't even latrines. You have to dig your own!"

"No one ever said fighting for animal rights was glamorous."

I'd tracked down the Whale Watchers campsite with the same method we'd used to find their Mellow Meadows agenda. Wandering into cyberspace, I first identified which members of the group were guaranteed to participate in Tillamook then wormed my way into a private group message. There, plain for me to see, were the details of where the Whale Watchers intended to camp that night. From what I'd gleaned, the Whale Watchers operated a bit like a traveling circus. They never stayed in one place, switched vehicles often to keep officials off their tails, and moved camp every night. Sometimes, despite their caution, a park ranger or random camper recognized who they were. They've had a few close calls, but since breaking Norman Beers out of prison, the group had managed to avoid getting booked.

Around ten o'clock at night, we approached our destination. As Cade observed earlier, there wasn't much to look at it. Tillamook was home to a few dairy farms, so a lot of it was huge fields, numerous cows, and a couple of factories. We kept driving until we hit the shadows of the trees. I slowed down as we approached the pin on the map. There was no sign for the campsite, only a skinny dirt road hardly large enough for one car. I wondered how the Whale Watchers managed to get their RVs through.

As planned, I drove past the campsite's entrance. With a little extra research, Cade and I had discovered a back way in, though the road was even smaller than the first. Branches snapped and cracked off the trees as the car rolled over the dirt.

"Stop!" Cade said, and I slammed on the brakes. They leaned over the dashboard and peered into the gloom. "I think I see something."

I put the car in park and rooted the binoculars out of the backseat. Through the lenses and a thicket of tall bushes, I spotted a familiar circle of RVs and tents.

"It's them, all right," I muttered. "I recognize that ugly monster truck."

"Let me see," Cade said.

I handed them the binoculars. "Remember the plan, right?"

"Yes," they said, exasperated. "Stop asking."

"It's more for my benefit than for yours. Remind me again what we're doing first."

Cade sighed. "Step one, stake out the area and locate the package. Step two, create a diversion to draw the Whale Watchers out of the camp. Step three, secure the package."

The package was our code word for Avery. Before we raised hell, I wanted to make sure she was actually here. That meant watching the camp for however many hours until she showed up. And it really was *hours*.

. . .

CADE FELL ASLEEP. I didn't blame them. The stakeout was incredibly boring. For the last four hours, I spied on the Whale Watchers as they loitered around the fire with seemingly no purpose but to waste time. It wasn't until midnight, as I slumped against the side of the car with my elbows propped on my knees to keep the binoculars in front of my eyes, that I spotted Avery.

"Cade!" I hissed, thunking the teenager with more gusto than I meant. "There's the package! The plan is a go!"

Cade snatched the binoculars from me. I squinted through the trees. Though the camp was a good one hundred yards away, I could see Avery as she emerged from one of the tents, approached the fire, and warmed her hands.

"Is it just me or does she seem okay?" Cade asked.

Avery didn't appear to be injured. She looked clean and well-cared for. She chatted idly with the other Whale Watchers, seemingly unconcerned to be sharing such close quarters with them.

"Yeah," I muttered. "I expected her to look more—"

"Tortured?"

A tall girl with a shaved head—Whisper Collins Junior—handed Avery something wrapped in a napkin. Avery bit into it. It was a hot dog.

"Are you kidding me?" Cade hissed, obviously appalled. "These dumb asses are making a huge fight over the treatment of animals but they're out here eating hot dogs?"

"Maybe they're tofu dogs?"

Cade pressed the binoculars tighter to their face. "No way. That's all beef, baby."

"Don't be weird."

"What are we going to do?" Cade asked, handing the binoculars back. "She looks fine."

I shifted in my seat and took another look at Avery. She chewed on her hot dog, laughing at something Whisper had said. "She's still a minor, participating in illegal activities. We're taking her home."

Cade fished something out of the back seat and presented the object to me. "Onward to step two then. Do you remember how to set this thing off?"

"It's not rocket science."

"Just make sure you get out of the way and run back to the camp as soon as possible," they instructed. "It won't be long before the Whale Watchers come after you with that shotgun. I'll be on the walkie talkie to let you know if the coast is clear."

"Now who's being repetitive?" I buttoned my coat all the way up to the collar and pulled a knit cap over my head. "Give me the thing."

Cade plunked the object into my hand. "Do you have the lighter?"

"No, I though *you* had the lighter."

"Oh, God." Cade rummaged around in the glove compartment and came up with a pack of matches. "Here. Don't lose those! Remember, check the wind before you set it, and—"

"Cade!"

"Okay, I'll shut up."

I tucked the object under my jacket, got out of the car, and dashed into the trees. I headed west around the camp, keeping the Whale Watchers' bonfire in my eyeline the entire time. The wind was hard to gauge beneath the trees, but at the top of the forest, it swept the dying leaves in a northerly direction. I found a patch of ground with a clear shot at the sky, got down on my knees, and planted the object in the dirt, making sure to angle it the proper way.

Then I struck a match, lit the fuse, and made a run for it. A few seconds later, huge fireworks exploded into the sky. If I set it up properly, the sparks would fall right into the Whale Watchers' camp.

ot a moment later, startled yells echoed from the camp. I grinned and put on a burst of speed as I hauled ass back toward the car. Overhead, a rainbow of colors decorated the sky. I'd found the fireworks in a weathered cardboard box in the garage. They were illegal to have in Oregon, but my dad had always been a huge fan of driving across state lines to get "the good ones." Shockingly, they still worked.

I yanked the walkie talkie out of my belt. "Status?"

The walkie fizzled as Cade replied in a staticky voice. "Worked like a charm. It's raining sparks in the camp. Everyone's making a break for it."

"What about the package?"

"Heading east. Looks like she's alone. Do you think she'll run?"

I leapt over a fallen log and dodged around a couple of bushes. If Avery was east of the campsite, I had a lot of catching up to do. There was also the issue of dodging the other Whale Watchers, who had darted into the woods in random patterns. Thankfully, it looked like most of them were heading toward the spot where I'd planted the firework, thinking they'd catch the culprit, but not all of them went that way.

"Got someone on your left," Cade hissed through the walkie. From their position in the car, they had a good view of the campsite and surrounding area.

I darted to the right just as a burly man in a camouflage jacket burst through the shrubbery. As his boots stomped over the ground, I dove behind a robust tree. He stopped short, his head lifted like a hunting dog's when he heard my sneakers rasp against the bark.

"Who's there?" he demanded in a deep, unsettling voice. "Is that you, Max? I'm not fallin' for your dumb tricks again."

The footsteps circled around the tree. Carefully, I stepped in the opposite direction, keeping the wide trunk between me and the Whale Watcher. A twig snapped beneath my shoe. I flinched, sure the man would catch me, but at the same time, someone hollered from the west side of camp.

"Found it!" someone called. "Check this out, guys!"

The large camouflaged man abandoned his hunt to join the others, who presumably had happened upon the firework rocket. I kept moving.

"Need an update on the package location," I murmured into the walkie.

"Where are you?" Cade returned. "I lost you."

"Right in front of you." I turned toward the car and waved. If you didn't know the vehicle was there, you wouldn't notice the metallic deviance in the forest landscape. I caught a flash of Cade's phone light in the distance. "Turn off the light. You'll give us away. See me now?"

The car went dark again as Cade replied, "Gotcha. The

package is about twenty yards west of your position, sitting between two forked trees. Approach with caution. I saw two others heading that way. Whisper Collins and someone else."

I took a daring dash across the empty campsite, hoping to shave a few seconds off my time. It wouldn't be long before the Whale Watchers abandoned the fireworks rocket and returned to camp. "Any identification on the other runner?"

"Didn't get a good look at the face," said Cade. The walkie talkie buzzed, as if I was getting too far out of range. "A little over six feet tall, slim, and short hair. Probably a dude."

"Great," I muttered, more to myself than Cade. "Let's hope I don't run into him."

But the woods were quiet as I kept moving toward Avery's location. Despite the chill, I was sweating under my knit cap. It dripped down my temples and into the collar of my jacket, going cold against my skin. I checked the time. It had been about four minutes since I'd set off the firework. It had long stopped raining sparks, and the Whale Watchers would soon abandon their romp through the woods.

"Stop!" Cade whispered suddenly.

I skidded to a halt, kicking up dirt. "What is it?"

"Ten feet to your right."

Moving slowly, I stepped over a huge boulder. My heart raced as I neared a space between the trees. When I spotted one of Avery's shoes, I had to keep myself from running full speed to collect her. I emerged into the clearing, opposite of where she was leaning against the forked trees. She looked up and spotted me. Consternation spread across her face.

"Bex?" she questioned.

"Avery." I raced across the clearing and smothered her in a hug. Then I held her at arm's length to examine her. "Are you okay? Are you hurt?" Her hair had grown out. The half inch closest to the roots was her natural color, and the black dye was beginning to wash out in spotty areas. Her cheeks looked thinner and her jawline sharper. "Have you been eating?" When I spotted gauze around her wrist, I pulled up her sleeve for a better look at the bandage beneath. "What is this? Did they hurt you? What happened?"

Avery pulled her arm out of my grasp and covered the bandage with her sleeve. "What are you doing here? How did you find me?"

"The same way I found your mom," I said. "Did you think I wouldn't come after you?"

Avery fixed me with a hard, cold look. "You shouldn't have." Her eyes widened with realization. "You're the one who set off the firework, weren't you? That was stupid. You know they'll kill you if they find you, right? You better go."

"I know, we're running short on time." I patted Avery's back and headed back toward the car. "Come on. Let's get out of here. It's cold." Halfway across the clearing, I realized Avery wasn't following me. I turned back. "What are you waiting for? I'm taking you home."

Avery scuffed the toe of her shoe in the dirt and avoided my eyes. "I'm not going home."

"What are you talking about? Of course you are. Let's go before the Whale Watchers come back."

She stubbornly stood her ground, lifting her chin in newfound arrogance. "I said I'm not going home, Bex."

I stared at her, dumbfounded. "I'm not leaving here without you, so get your ass in gear, kid."

When I reached for her, she yanked away, finally abandoning her spot between the forked trees to avoid my grasp. "Don't call me that," she said in a sharp tone I'd never heard her use before. "I'm not a kid anymore."

"You're thirteen!" I reminded her. "By legal definition, you *are* a kid. You literally have no say in this. Do you know how worried your mother has been about you?"

Avery rolled her eyes and crossed her arms. "Like she cares."

"Of course she cares!"

"She only cares about the Home Safe kids," Avery spat venomously. "I was basically invisible."

I let out a deep sigh. "Look, Cade isn't going to be living at your house forever. They're waiting for another foster home to open up."

"You think it's just Cade?" Avery asked. "This isn't the first time some weird, fucked-up kid has stayed at our house. I lock my door at night because I don't know what weirdo might come in while I'm sleeping. My mom doesn't care about me or my privacy. All she cares about is making herself look good with that stupid foster program."

I had never seen this side of Avery or heard this part of her story. She was so angry. It was all over her face. Her eyebrows were set, her jaw was clenched, and her hands had balled themselves into fists. She was serious. She truly had no intention of returning to Doveport with me.

"Did you run away?" I asked. "Did you intentionally seek out the Whale Watchers?"

"No, actually." Avery puffed her chest out proudly. "They were looking for me specifically."

"Oh, yeah? Is that why they tossed you into the back of a van and took you away from home?" I demanded. "Because that doesn't seem like a nice way to treat someone. What about the other girls, huh? Were the Whale Watchers looking for them too?"

Avery sneered at me. "I'm not going to tell."

"Avery, this isn't a game," I said. "Whatever the Whale Watchers told you, they're lying. No animal activist kills people to get their point across. It doesn't make any sense. I have no idea why they're kidnapping teenagers, but they are using you. You're not one of them."

"Shut up!" Avery's cheeks flushed pink. "You don't know what you're talking about!"

Behind Avery, something moved in the woods, maybe a big animal or one of the Whale Watchers. Either way, it wasn't good news for us.

"Why don't you get in the car and you can explain it to me?" I said, exasperated and desperate to get Avery out of here. "We can talk this out, but it's not safe for us to be here. Please, kid—"

"I told you not to call me that!"

"Shh!" I put a finger to my lips. "Be quiet."

"Why should I?" she demanded. "You're the one who's not supposed to be here, not the other way around."

"Avery, if you just—"

Whatever had been lumbering around in the woods finally appeared. Thankfully, it wasn't a bear or a wolf on the prowl. It was Norman Beers, the accused murderer. Despite wearing loafers and slacks, he moved over the uneven trees with alarming grace. Though his hair was longer, he looked the same as he had on TV. When he flashed a handsome smile, it completely threw me off.

"Ah, I see you've found our fire starter," Beers said. He draped a hand lightly across Avery's shoulders with a familiarity that made my lip curl. I expected her to pull away, but she didn't appear to have any qualms with Beers's touch. "Should we do introductions?"

"I know who you are," I snapped at him. "You're a murderer."

"I was *accused* of murder," he corrected me calmly. "They never had any proof."

"Oh, really? Then why didn't they let you out of prison?" I asked. "You're still a wanted man. I could tip off the FBI right now and make a quick buck."

Beers chuckled, unconcerned. "Now, now. Let's not do anything rash. I suppose we can skip the introductions. I know who you are too. Bex Lennon." He used his fingers to make air quotes. "The Wanderer."

"So you've seen my Instagram page," I said. "Big deal. Who hasn't?"

"Well, I know a little bit more about you than what you post on your Instagram," Beers claimed. "In fact, you'd be surprised if you knew how far back we went."

I rolled my eyes and ignored the bait. "Avery, come on. You don't have to stay here. Please come with me."

Beers's grasp tightened on Avery's shoulder. "She's not going anywhere."

"She's not yours to command like the rest of your brainless troops," I snarled at him. "She's just a kid, like the other two girls you kidnapped. Where are they, huh?"

"Safe," Beers answered. "For now, at least. Avery has a special place in my heart, so she gets a bit more freedom than them. Don't you want to know why?"

"All I want is to get Avery back to her mom."

Avery stepped behind Beers. "I don't want to go."

Beers pursed his lips. "You heard her. She doesn't want to live with her mother."

I let out an aggravated groan. "Avery, are you kidding me? This would be a lot easier if you were on my side. What's the point of staying here? Eventually, the FBI is going to track down this whole group, and everyone involved will go to jail. What's keeping you here, other than this dolt?" I gestured at Beers's outfit. His pressed collared shirt looked more fit for an office than the woods. "He doesn't even know how to dress for the outdoors. Why would you trust him to keep you safe out here?"

"Because he's my father!" Avery blurted out.

A stunned silence fell over the clearing. Beers's upper lip twitched, almost in annoyance, as if he wanted to be the one to reveal the butt of this joke. Avery's entire body quivered, but she stood firmly next to her supposed parent.

My gaze flashed between the two of them. When I looked at Avery, I usually saw the parts of her that resembled Edison. The same shade of brown hair, the delicate bone structure, their general stature. I ignored the things that separated the mother and daughter, like the slight difference in skin tone and the thick set of Avery's eyebrows. As much as I wanted to believe Beers had lied to Avery about this, there was too much evidence in their matching features.

"You?" I whispered. My breath had left my body, leaving me without wind to form words. "You're the guy?"

Beers's expression didn't change. He remained indifferent. "Is it so hard to believe I once loved Edison Maxx?"

I stammered, unable to piece together the information in a way that made sense in the head. "I don't understand. How did you meet Edison in the first place?"

"It was a bit of a tragic love story," he said conversationally. "You see, the Whale Watchers have been operating for much longer than the public suspects. When I was eighteen, they recruited me on my college campus. It was such a noble mission, one that I whole-heartedly believed in. Of course, we have certain techniques that many disagree with. When I was young, I didn't understand why we did some of the things we did. That's how Edison and I met."

"What are you talking about?" I asked through clenched teeth.

"I was part of the team that took Edison under our wing all those years ago," Beers explained. "It was my first big mission for the organization. I was the one who watched her day after day, tracking her every move so that we could find the perfect time to bring her aboard."

"You mean kidnap her," I growled.

"That depends on your perspective," he replied lightly. "We simply rooted out young people that we saw promise in. We took quick note of Edison." He cleared his throat and clasped his hands together. "I must admit our practices back then were a bit barbaric. My superiors—the ones I eventually took over for—were harsh on our new members. We hazed them, forced them to do all sorts of initiation challenges to be part of the group. Edison fought back harder than anyone else. That was why I fell in love with her."

"She was just a kid, you ass. You were legally an adult. You forced yourself on her."

"She was a woman," Beers snapped, exhibiting real emotion for the first time since he'd emerged in the clearing. "And perfectly capable of making her own decisions. I was the one who finally helped her escape. I was the one who forced the Whale Watchers to change their methods."

"Yet you're *still* kidnapping teenaged girls over ten years later," I reminded him. "What methods have you changed exactly?"

"Some things must be done for the greater good," Beers said firmly. "Avery understands that now. Don't you, kiddo?"

Avery planted her feet and came out from behind her father. "Dad cares about me more than Mom ever did. At least he actually wants to spend time with me."

"Avery, if he wanted to spend time with you, he would've tracked you down a lot earlier than this," I told her. "Whatever he's doing, whatever his reason is for reconnecting with you, it's not because he loves you like your mom does."

"Shut up!" Beers shouted. He took a breath to calm himself. "Don't you dare question my allegiance to my daughter. I have done nothing but care for her. If Edison had given me the chance to do more, I would have, but she never told me about Avery. I found out I had a daughter by chance."

"Poor you." I afforded him a mocking pout. "It must have been so tragic for you to skip out on childcare for thirteen years."

His nostrils flared, but he kept his composure. "Losing Edison was one of the hardest things I've done in my entire life. I refuse to lose my daughter too."

"That's too damn bad," I said. "Because she's coming home with me."

I rushed forward with the intention of grabbing Avery out from under Beers's protection before he realized what was happening. It was a stupid, thoughtless idea. As Avery dove behind her father, Beers's arm sprang straight out and whacked me across the chest. It knocked all the wind out of me, and I ended up flat on my back on the forest floor.

Beers drew a handgun. Where he'd been hiding it in his slacks, I had no idea. He pointed it right between my eyes.

"I'm not a killer," he declared. "The news has that wrong. However, I won't rule out the possibility of becoming one if it means protecting my family."

I scrambled backward, my palms scraping across dead leaves and twigs. "You wouldn't."

He cocked the gun. "I would."

"Don't!" Avery hung on Beers's arm, dragging the gun down and away from me. "Please. She had no idea what she was getting herself into. Let her go home."

"If she goes home, she'll tell everyone where we are," Beers said, taking aim again.

"So?" Avery's bottom lip jutted out, a classic maneuver from her childhood that could make anyone do whatever she wanted. "She found us at San Junipero, but we escaped the Feds anyway. We could do it again."

"It's too dangerous," Beers said.

"You said you're not a killer," Avery pointed out. "And she's my mom's best friend. It would hurt her too."

Beers's brow wrinkled in the middle. His finger twitched on the trigger. Then he held the gun with the barrel pointed upward, safely away from me.

"Get out of here," he ordered me. "And if you know what's good for you, you won't tip off the police *or* the FBI. If you do, I'll know."

I lurched to my feet, adrenaline coursing through my veins, but I couldn't leave without trying one more time. "Avery, please. Come home with me—"

Beers fired a warning shot past my shoulder. I yelled as the bullet flew through the trees. The sound of shattering glass filled the air.

The car. Cade was still inside.

houghts of Avery's safety went out of my head as visions of Cade with yet another bullet wound—a serious one—filled my mind. My priorities shifted from one teenager to the other within the blink of an eye. Avery could take care of herself. She was bizarrely comfortable with Norman Beers and the Whale Watchers, and I couldn't make her come home with me if she didn't want to. Cade, on the other hand, had no family to take care of them. Edison and I were the closest thing they had to parents, and I'd been doing a terrible job of stepping into the role.

Without a second thought, I did the last thing I expected to do that night and left Avery with her kidnappers. I sprinted from the clearing without looking back and dove into the forest. My heart pounded as I ran across rocks and roots. I tripped over a dark tangle of weeds and stumbled to the ground, scuffing my knees. When I picked myself up, I broke through the last patch of shrubbery to reach the car.

The windshield was gone. Bits of shattered glass littered the forest floor and the dashboard of the car, glittering in the moonlight. Cade was nowhere to be seen. I yanked open the door and found the bullet embedded in the headrest of the driver's seat. There was no blood. That was a good sign.

Cade crouched in the foot space beneath the passenger's seat, their head pressed against the glove compartment. They trembled with fear, the whites of their eyes wide as they peered up at me.

"Stay down," I ordered as I brushed broken glass off the seat and climbed in. Broken windshield or not, we needed to get the hell out of the campsite before Beers changed his mind. I threw the car in reverse and backed out of the woods. When space allowed, I made a tight three-point turn and sped off the campsite.

When I reached the highway, I pulled over to the side of the road and dialed the emergency roadside service. Cade was still huddled beneath the seat, drawing short, fast breaths.

"I need a tow," I told the person on the other end of the roadside service line. "Our windshield is broken."

After reporting our location and hanging up, I rounded to the passenger side to help Cade out. Their knees were drawn up to their chest so tightly that I damn near needed a crowbar to unfold the teenager.

"It's okay," I whispered, pushing Cade's hair out of their face. The color had drained from their skin, and their hands were too cold for my liking. "Everything's going to be okay. We got out of there, and a tow truck is on its way. We'll be home in a couple hours."

When Cade finally spoke, relief swam through my veins.

"What about Avery?" they croaked.

I cradled Cade against my chest, warming them with my body heat. "It's a long story. A really long story."

.   .   .

I CALLED Edison and filled her in. She ordered a car service to bring us home so we wouldn't have to ride in the tow truck. A few hours later, the service dropped us off at Edison's house. Thankfully, the driver hadn't been one of those pushy, talkative types. Otherwise, he might have asked why we were both chilled to the bone and covered in broken glass.

Edison was quiet as she pulled us into the house. She hugged us both fiercely. She didn't ask where Avery was. Our rounded shoulders and defeated attitudes told her everything she needed to know. Besides, I think she wanted to spare Cade further grief for the night. As Edison ran a bath for the teenager upstairs, I shook the glass out of my shirt and pants in the garage and vacuumed up the pieces.

As Cade bathed, Edison fixed me a glass of tequila on the rocks. I stared blankly at the liquor, swirling it around. The ice clinked against each other.

"You should drink it," Edison said. "It'll help clear your head."

I took a sip, for Edison's sake rather than mine, but the sharp bite of tequila and the sour spurt of lime juice did actually help me gather my thoughts.

"Do I dare ask what happened?" Edison said.

"Norman Beers."

I watched her carefully as I said his name, looking for any kind of reaction. But her face remained impassive. Too impassive.

"The guy who broke out of prison?" she asked. "What about him?"

"Is it true?" I didn't have the strength to beat around the

bush or go along with whatever game Edison wanted to play. "Is he Avery's father?"

She kept her mask in place for a second longer. Then her carefully-placed facade dropped all at once. Her lips trembled as she asked, "How did you figure it out?"

"He told me," I said. "Apparently, the two of you were in love. You didn't care to mention that part to me, huh? No wonder you never wanted me to know who Avery's father was. He's a lunatic."

"He wasn't back then," Edison replied, her voice quavering.

"What happened?" I asked softly. "Can you finally tell me?"

She drained the rest of her drink. "You know the first part. The Whale Watchers—though they weren't called that back then—kidnapped me from behind the café. They did it because my parents had money. The ultimate plan was to ransom me and all the other girls, but not before our parents were good and desperate to find us."

"Beers said they chose you because you showed promise with the group," I said.

"That's bullshit." Edison got up to pour another glass of tequila. "They weren't interested in letting us join them. They kept us in a trailer that they hauled behind a pickup truck, as if we were cattle. They beat us to keep us quiet and subservient."

"And Beers?"

She squeezed a lime with such force that the juice squirted across the floor rather than into her glass. "He was the only who took care of me. He stood up for me, didn't let the other group members torture me. He never cared about the other girls though. Just me."

"He was obsessed with you."

"Something like that," Edison said. "It wasn't long before Stockholm Syndrome kicked in. I was convinced Norman loved me. He convinced the others to let me sleep in his bed. He made sure I was cared for. I grew attached to him simply because he kept me safe. But no matter how much I pleaded with him, he refused to protect the other girls. Eventually, I realized he only made an exception for me because he was attracted to me. That was when I began plotting my escape."

I swirled the tequila around. The ice was beginning to melt. "He said he helped you escape."

"I tricked him into doing it." Edison stared deep into her glass. "I convinced him that I was madly in love with him. Maybe I truly was. I couldn't get past the other group members without his help. One night, I asked him to take me for a moonlit walk to celebrate six months together. The group bought it. We strolled into the woods. When we were far enough from the camp, I made a run for it and never looked back."

"What about Avery?"

She pinched a piece of salt off the rim off the glass and placed it on her tongue, then took a long swig from her drink. "Norman was the only boy who'd ever paid attention to me like that. You remember what my parents were like. Strict, overbearing. They treated me like a coworker rather than a daughter. I found myself missing Norman the more time I spent at home, so I contacted him. I dated him in secret. I never told my parents or you or anyone because I knew they would judge me. Then I got pregnant, and—well, you know the rest of the story."

"You didn't tell him," I said. "That you were pregnant."

"I was going to," she admitted. "But I thought about what

he had done with the group. Officially, he was a criminal. He had no intention of leaving the Whale Watchers. I couldn't raise Avery with a man who was constantly on the move." She ran her fingers along the condensation around her glass then brushed her forehead with the cool water. "Not to mention, my parents were unfathomably disgusted by the event."

"Did you ever tell them what happened?"

"No," she replied. "They tried their hardest to get the truth out of me. It was one of the reasons they sent me away from Doveport, other than preserving their supposed reputation. They were so furious that I wouldn't tell them who'd done it. Mom thought it was Johnny Clemmons."

"The quarterback?"

Edison flipped her hair over her shoulder. "Only the most popular boy in school would want to get me pregnant." The humor drained from her tone. "I went to live with my aunt and uncle willingly. I thought it would make it harder for Norman to track me down. Guess it never mattered in the end. He found out about Avery anyway. God knows how."

"Want me to guess?"

"No."

I brushed hair from my forehead. It was getting too long. "From the way he talks about you, he's still obsessed with you. He's probably been watching you since you got pregnant with Avery. He was just waiting for the perfect moment to strike."

"But why give us a heads-up?" Edison questioned, pacing across the living room. "He took two other girls before Avery. What's his end game?"

"He said the other girls were safe *for now*," I recalled.

"What happened to the other girls that had been kidnapped with you? I don't remember hearing about any ransoms."

Edison's face went a pale greenish color. She clutched her stomach, as if willing it to stay calm. "The Whale Watchers were mostly men back then. They used the girls however they wanted, and they weren't gentle about it. One by one, they vanished. I asked Norman what happened to them, but he never told me."

Bile rose in my throat as intrusive images flashed through my head. The Whale Watchers were scum, no matter what they claimed as their noble purpose. The entire organization was a scam.

"We can't let them have Avery," I said quietly. "He doesn't get to win."

Edison let out a small laugh, one without humor. "Don't you see? He got Avery on his side. He's already won, and it's all my fault."

"Hey." I intercepted Edison's pacing and took her arm to keep her still. "That's not true. Don't let him make you think like that. Avery's better off with you. You know that."

Edison's expression fell flat and numb. "I resented Avery. Did you know that? She looks like him. It was my decision to let Norman into my life. It screwed everything up. I love Avery, but from the day she was born, she has reminded me of the mistake that defined my entire life. She's right to be upset. She's right to hate me."

I tipped Edison's chin up so she would look at me. "Listen to me. You are an amazing mother. You have given Avery everything she needs to be successful. She's grown into an incredible young woman, and you have *never* withheld an ounce of love from her."

"I was detached," Edison countered, "and she knew it. She felt it. No wonder she went off with her dad."

"You know what we need do then, right?"

"What?"

"Get her back, so we can fix it."

IT WAS EASIER SAID than done. After our excursion to Tillamook, the Whale Watchers disappeared. The planned riot at Mellow Meadows never happened. Beers must have packed up his sycophants and moved out of the area. Though I hadn't tipped off the FBI, terrified of Beers's revenge, he wasn't taking any chances. All was quiet on the animal activism front. The news had to find other stories to report, drawing out the weather and traffic updates to fill up time, and the locals moved on to other gossip. No new tragedies came to light, and in a few days' time, the only people who remembered that girls had gone missing for no reason were their parents and the authorities.

To make matters worse, Avery had discovered a way to keep me out of her head. Though my abilities were turned on —I was able to manipulate my social media feeds and receive feedback as usual—my connection to Avery was somehow blocked. No brain zaps or texts. Nothing. And when I tried to force my way into Avery's consciousness, I found myself staring at a theoretical brick wall. Instinctively, the teenager had put up a firewall to stop me from reading her.

Cade was experiencing a similar block, though they were taking it a lot harder than I was. Without Avery updates, Cade's anxiety went through the roof about Avery's safety.

"A year ago, I would have been ecstatic to get rid of the voices in my head," Cade told me one afternoon at

Maxine's cafe. It had become a daily ritual for us to meet there each afternoon. "Now, I feel like my brain's betraying me."

"I don't think it's you," I countered. "I think it's Avery."

Cade tossed aside a piece of bread that had been sitting on their plate for so long that it was probably stale by now. "You think she knows we're in her head?"

"No," I said, "but maybe she felt it and understood she needed to block us if she didn't want to keep giving the Whale Watchers away."

"What does that mean for us?" Cade asked. "How are we supposed to catch them?"

I sighed and slumped in my seat. "You know, buddy, I'm not so sure we're cut out for this anyway. We've tried twice and came up short both times. I think I'm ready to turn this one over to the real investigators."

Cade's stare snapped up to study me. "You're giving up?"

"No, not exactly," I said. "I'd never give up on Avery, but it's a lot harder to do this when she doesn't want to be found *and* I don't have access to her feeds."

"Maybe not hers," Cade reminded me. "But you can access the other Whale Watchers. We can't let this keep happening."

I flagged Maxine down and gestured a request for another donut. Sugar made me antsy, but the way things were going these days, I figured I'd earned the right to a few sweets. "Norman Beers isn't stupid. Haven't you noticed the Whale Watchers are all quiet on the Western front? They're laying low because of us."

"That should excite you," Cade insisted. "He's scared of us. He can't figure out how we keep finding them. We need to take advantage of that."

"We *need* to figure out their next move," I said. "They

won't stay quiet forever. My bet is they're planning something big."

"Like what?"

I thanked Maxine as she dropped off the fresh donut then waited for her to return to the counter before I replied to Cade's question. "I don't know, but when it happens, we'll be ready."

As if things weren't complicated enough in Doveport, my mother began to take advantage of my downtime. While Cade was at school and Edison worked, I had nothing to do but attempt to repair my injured Instagram reputation. Since I had nowhere to work, I mostly stayed at home, manipulating my social media feeds from the comfort of the basement. The only problem was that Mom was always home too.

"Honey, can you take me to my doctor's appointment today?" she hollered down the stairs one morning.

"Where's Melba?" I yelled back, scrolling through another travel blogger's feed in hopes of finding inspiration.

"She's not coming today," Mom said. "She had a family emergency. Can you take me or not? It won't be long."

Since I had no excuse not to take her, I swapped my pajama pants for jeans, helped Mom into her coat, and led her out to the car. Thankfully, I'd gotten the shattered windshield replaced before she'd seen it.

Mom's doctor's visit didn't reveal any new information. However, since it was my first time meeting the physician, I got a long explanation as to what would happen to my mother as time went on. Her delusions would continue to worsen.

"She's going to need your help," the doctor said while Mom and I avoided eye contact.

We drove home in heavy silence. I couldn't think of what to say. To me, our relationship was irreparable, but the dreaded hold of family obligation reared its ugly head. To Mom, it was my duty to take care of her, despite her lack of care for me in the past.

As if to top the day off with a bitter cherry of weirdness, someone was waiting on our front porch as we pulled into the driveway. It was a hulking figure with a golden mane of hair and wearing an enormous backpack. I rolled the window down and gawked at the visitor with disbelief.

"Taj?"

In true Beard Guy fashion, Taj's face broke out in his signature smile. As he jogged over to the car, my mother sank into her seat, somewhat wary of this enormous, rugged man. Taj leaned down far enough to see inside, his eyes twinkling with glee and mischief.

"What's up, Lennon?" he said, his deep voice filled with more joy than Santa Claus. He threaded one massive arm through the window and yanked me into a complicated hug. "It's so good to see ya!"

I stuttered into the shoulder of his coat. "W-what are you doing here? How did you find me?"

"You left me a copy of your passport in case you ever went missing, remember?" He dug a piece of folded paper from his back pocket and showed it to me. It was a blurry black and white copy of my information, including the picture of me that was almost ten years old and my mother's address. "I figured since I hadn't heard from you in a month, that officially counted you as missing. Dude, you fell off the face of the earth. What happened?"

"It's kind of a long story." I glanced over at my mother. She was glued to the car seat, both hands planted to brace herself for whatever this large man might throw at her. "Let me pull into the garage, Taj. Then we can talk."

Taj saluted and stepped back from the car to get out of my way. I rolled up the window and eased the car forward. My mother craned her neck to watch Taj as he examined the apple trees in the front yard. He plucked a perfectly ripe one from a high branch and took a bite.

"Who on earth is that?" Mom asked, her voice octaves higher than its usual register. "He's gigantic!"

"I met him while I was traveling," I said, putting the car in park. "We've been to a few places together."

"What's he doing here?"

"Guess I'm going to find out. Is it okay if he comes inside?"

Mom peered through the back windshield. In the yard, Taj whistled to a song bird in the branches of the apple tree. "Are you sure he's not a criminal?"

"He's a thief," I said truthfully. "But he only steals from the rich."

"A regular Robin Hood, huh?" Mom grumbled. "Fine. Let him inside, but if one piece of china goes missing, I'll know."

"Mom, we don't have any china. I gave it all to the Salvation Army, remember?"

"Oh."

When I exited the car, Taj lifted me into a real hug, squeezing me so tightly that my ribs almost cracked. Mom lifted an inquisitive eyebrow.

I thumped on Taj's back. "Put me down, you oaf!"

His laugh echoed through the trees as he set me on my

feet and patted my head. I swatted his hand away. "I missed your insults," he said.

Mom cleared her throat.

"Uh, this is my mom," I said awkwardly. "Lydia."

Taj straightened his back, squared his shoulders, and bowed slightly over Mom's hand as he took it in his own. "Pleased to meet you, Mrs. Lennon."

Like anyone who became subject to Taj's legendary charm, my mother's reservations fell away and left her like a puddle of melted goo. "Oh, goodness," she giggled into her other hand. "It's just Lydia."

Taj patted her tiny hand with his enormous one. "Lydia, then. I'm so sorry to impose on you. I had no way of letting Bex know I'd be in town. It seems her phone wasn't accepting international calls or texts."

I grimaced. I'd turned off the international stuff when I'd gotten back to the States, hoping to save on cash. "Sorry about that, Taj. Can we go inside though? It's freezing out here."

Mom slipped into hostess mode at the blink of an eye. "Of course! Come on, dear." She took Taj's elbow, since that was the highest part of his body she could reach, and led him inside. "I'm sure you're tired from your trip. Where did you come from?"

"Sydney." Taj took off his massive boots before stepping off the welcome mat. My mother helped him out of his coat and hung it up in the closet. It was weird to see him in this house, as if my two worlds—the one in Doveport and the one everywhere else—had collided. "I figured I'd take a page out of Bex's book and visit my home as well. Wow, this is a beautiful house, Lydia."

"Oh!" She waved off the compliment like it was nothing,

but the blush rising in her cheeks gave her away. "Please. It's a mess."

"It's perfect," Taj said, flashing his signature smile again.

"Mom, do you mind if me and Taj catch up?" I asked. "Alone?"

Mom's grin slipped, but she kept it together. "Sure, honey. I'll make you kids a snack."

As Mom busied herself in the kitchen, I led Taj into the basement. He took a quick look around, poking his nose in my old belongings.

"Your mom's nice," he noted. "You never mentioned this was her house."

"I didn't exactly expect you to turn up here," I replied. "Which leads me back to my question from earlier. What are you doing here?"

Taj observed my tight shoulders and tense gaze. "I wanted to say hi. I missed my traveling buddy, and I thought it might be fun to surprise you." The lightness dropped from his attitude. "What's going on? Why are you acting like I'm some stranger you met once on a moped in Rome?"

"You wouldn't fit on a moped."

"Seriously, Bex. What's the deal?" He lowered himself onto the couch and stretched his arms to either side. His total wingspan had to be close to seven feet. "I thought this was gonna be a short trip for you. Do your high school career talk then meet me in Greece. Next thing I know, you've fallen off the face of the earth and disappeared from cyberspace. When was the last time you posted on Instagram?"

"A while ago," I admitted. "Things got crazy here. I wish I could explain."

"Why don't you?"

If there was anyone I wanted on my side at all times, it was Taj. I trusted him more than anyone, except Edison, and he'd always had my back in the past. So why didn't I want to share all of my grief with him?

I pushed aside one of his arms and sat on the couch beside him. "You are a part of my normal life," I began, choosing my words carefully to best describe my feelings. "When I'm traveling, all of this" —I waved my arms at the basement and the ceiling above us to indicate my mother and the rest of Doveport— "goes away. I'm not Bex Lennon from this tiny town in the middle of nowhere. I'm Bex Lennon, social influencer and world traveler. They're two completely different people."

Taj's beard bristled as he frowned with consternation. "Why is that?"

"Because this is the life I left behind to become the person I wanted to be," I explained. "But every time I come back to Doveport, I'm reminded of the person I *used* to be. I remember all the things that happened here that I'd love to forget."

Taj studied me quietly, his gaze focused on my face. After several long minutes, I shifted uncomfortably.

"So that's why I barely know anything about you," he said. "You were always running away from your childhood trauma."

I opened my mouth to protest but couldn't find anything truthful to say. Taj smiled gently.

"It's okay," he said. "You don't have to explain."

"You don't want to know what I've been running from?"

"It's your business, not mine," he replied. "If you want to tell me, I'm happy to listen. Otherwise, I'm happy to support you as you continue to run."

Anxiety crept into my throat like thick molasses. "What if the things I'm running from are starting to catch up to me?"

Taj's brow furrowed as he turned toward me. "Are you in trouble?"

"Not exactly," I said. "But someone I love is, and I can't figure out a way to save her."

"Tell me what I can do to help."

EVERYTHING CAME SPILLING OUT. It turned out that telling Taj was the one thing I really needed. I started at the beginning, with Edison's disappearance and reappearance, then worked my way through to Avery's kidnapping. Taj listened with an intense expression. For once, the laugh lines around his mouth didn't appear. He took me seriously, that is, until I tried to explain my abilities.

"Back up," he said. "You can do what now?"

"I can manipulate technology," I answered. "Well, kind of. It's not an exact science."

"I'm not sure I believe you."

"Give me your phone."

He dug it out of his pocket and handed it over. I opened it up to his Instagram profile. "Hmm, look at that. Only seventy-five likes on your last post. Not exactly impressive."

He rolled his eyes. "Sorry I don't use a million hashtags like everyone else. I'm not as well-versed as you are, Miss Thing."

His phone chimed repeatedly as notifications popped up on his feeds. He snatched it back from me, his eyes widening as he watched his latest post grow in popularity. I peeked over his shoulder. One hundred likes. One hundred and fifty. Two hundred and counting. Comments popped up like rabbits from the ground after winter thawed. *What a hunk!* and *God, I'd travel anywhere with this man.* Taj's follower count tripled.

"What the heck did you do?" he demanded, scrolling through the massive amounts of notifications. "I can't get anyone to notice my stuff!"

"I told you," I said, shrugging. "I have a gift. It does more than that. It helped me find Edison, and I've been using it to help me find Avery too. You can't tell anyone though. I don't want to be captured and studied."

Taj crossed his heart, though his gaze remained fixed on his growing Instagram presence. "I promise. Shit, this is amazing!"

I snapped in front of his nose to get his attention back. "Can you focus? There are more pressing matters at hand than your social media, remember?"

Right away, he tore himself out of cyberspace and set the phone far enough away so it wouldn't distract him. "Sorry. It's hard to get my head around this. You've got powers!" His eyebrows knitted together. "So how come you haven't been able to get Avery back? You surely have the upper hand."

"Part of the problem is that she doesn't want to be rescued," I said. "She's got it in her head that she's daddy's little girl, but I have a feeling Beers is using her. He's got to have an angle, right?"

Taj stroked his beard, thinking. "Men like Norman Beers have a reason for everything. He's too self-righteous not to. You said the Whale Watchers have gone quiet?"

"Yeah. We haven't been able to figure out their next

move." I unearthed a file box from beneath the coffee table and showed the contents to Taj. It was all the information Cade and I had gathered on the Whale Watchers before we'd attempted to rescue Avery from Tillamook. "My connection with Avery has been severed, and I haven't been able to find any members in cyberspace. They wiped their social media feeds, the Facebook groups, and the members' Instagrams. They finally wised up and realized they were leaving a trail for me. I got nothing."

Taj sat on the edge of the couch to rifle through my research. "There's gotta be something," he muttered. "It's not like this guy suddenly stopped making trouble. Let me see your computer."

I handed over my laptop, and we got lost in the search for the Whale Watchers' whereabouts. Mom ventured into the basement at some point to feed us Philly cheesesteaks and crackers, like we were two elementary school kids having a playdate. Taj didn't find much new information. Rather, he caught himself up on the Whale Watchers' antics so far.

"Hey, come look at this," Taj said after two hours of fruitless searching. He beckoned me over and pointed to the laptop screen. "It's a thread on Reddit."

"More like a sub thread," I said. "A sub-sub thread."

"Whatever." Taj scrolled slowly through the comments on the thread so I could skim them for myself. "The chat initially started about veganism a couple days ago." He waved the mouse halfway down the page. "Read that and tell me what you think."

I squinted at the screen and read aloud, "Vegan goods for sale in DP on Saturday. Don't miss out." I looked at Taj. "They're having a bake sale. So what?"

"DP," Taj said. "Doveport?"

"Uh-huh. We have vegans here too."

"But what if it's not a bake sale?" Taj asked. "You said the Whale Watchers used a code, right? A buried Reddit thread is the perfect place to set up a new method of communication between group members."

I pressed my lips together. "This might be pushing it. It's a stretch."

"You really want to take that risk?"

"The Whale Watchers aren't stupid enough to come back to Doveport," I told him. "If they did, they would be easy pickings for the FBI. It doesn't make sense."

"They've evaded the Feds for this long," Taj pointed out. "What if they're coming back here because of Avery? What if Beers has something else up his sleeve?"

"Give me that."

I took the laptop from him and read the entire thread for myself. It started off innocently enough, with a user called VeganBaker2006 asking other Redditors for advice on egg replacements. As the thread progressed, the conversation turned to the one thing all vegans usually agreed on: the unjust treatment of animals. If I didn't know anything about the Whale Watchers, I'd pass off the thread as no big deal. However, the thread had garnered a lot of attention in the few days since it had been posted, and over fifty other users had participated in the conversation. Farther down, the group began making plans to meet up, and the supposed vegan bake sale was supposedly their first opportunity to do so.

"VeganBaker2006," I muttered under my breath as I clicked on the person's profile. Vegan Baker had no other interests and had not posted to any other threads to ask for advice. "Avery was born in 2006. Think it's a coincidence?"

"Is there such a thing?" Taj asked wryly.

I shut the laptop with a snap. "Guess we're going to a bake sale on Saturday."

WITH A LITTLE MORE DIGGING INTO VeganBaker2006's short Reddit history, we discovered the "bake sale" was supposedly being held outside Doveport's one and only bookstore. It wasn't an unusual place for vegans to gather since the bookstore's owner was adamantly against eating animals herself. The store also doubled as a venue for open mic nights, which made it all the more confusing when we pulled up outside. Apparently, along with the bake sale, the bookstore was also hosting a poetry reading. Every hipster within driving distance had showed up, complete with strangely-shaped mustaches, tortoiseshell glasses, and flannel shirts. The line to get in led down the sidewalk.

"Park here," I said, forcing Taj to pull over on the curb before we got any closer. "Let's keep an eye out for a few minutes."

One by one, the hipsters filed inside the bookstore. I didn't see any evidence of vegan baked goods. It didn't make any sense. Why would the Redditors dedicate an entire thread to meeting up and then not show?

"Whoa, got one," Taj said, tapping me on the wrist rapidly to get my attention. He pointed through the windshield. "Nine o'clock."

To our left, a nondescript tan sedan pulled into the parking lot across the street. It wasn't exactly what I expected the Whale Watchers to pull up in, but after I'd gotten a look at their trucks and RVs, they needed a fresh vehicle that the Feds didn't know about. Sure enough, as the driver got out of the car, I recognized the buzz cut.

"Whisper Collins."

Taj lifted an eyebrow. "Her name is Whisper?"

"Yup, and she's a Whale Watchers legend," I told him.

Whisper wasn't alone. Two others—presumably Whale Watchers as well—had come along for the ride. Avery, however, wasn't among them. I felt disappointment and relief all at once. Whatever meeting was happening inside the bookstore, Avery wouldn't be taking part in it.

"What's the plan?" Taj said, his hand hovering over the key in the ignition, ready to turn off the car and jump the Whale Watchers as soon as they crossed our paths. "Should we intercept them before they get inside?"

I laid my palm on Taj's shoulder to keep him from leaping out of the car. "No, let them go in. We'll follow in a few minutes. I want to see what's happening in there."

Taj's jaw clenched as he tracked Whisper and her two comrades across the street and into the bookstore. Once they were inside, I signaled Taj to follow them. We got out of the car and trotted as casually as possible up to the bookstore.

"Doesn't smell like a bake sale," Taj said, opening the door for me.

It wasn't a bake sale. It was a setup. The hipsters had been shunted off to one side, crowded together near the small stage. An FBI agent stood between each shelf, armed and ready for a protest. They had already detained Whisper Collins and the two other Whale Watchers.

Agent Rocco Marioni sauntered up to me, a thin smile on his wicked face.

"Hello there, Rebecca," he said. "Isn't this a surprise?"

2 1

*M*arioni's face was far too smug for my liking. He planted his hands on his hips, fingering a set of handcuffs there. I glanced behind him, catching the eye of Whisper Collins. She mouthed, "Way to go." The agent in charge of her gave her shoulders a shake to command her attention.

"What's going on?" I asked Marioni warily. I stepped away from Taj, making the distance between us clear. "What are you all doing here?"

"I'd like to ask you the same thing," Marioni said, grinning. He slipped his hands into his pockets. I hated how casual he looked. "You see, Rebecca—"

"No one calls me that."

"Ms. Lennon—"

"No one calls me that either."

Marioni shot me a look of frustration. Apparently, he wasn't accustomed to being interrupted during one of his dumb monologues. "You won't be so chatty when you're sitting in a jail cell."

I laughed outright. "First of all, you're wrong. Second, why would I go to jail?"

Agent Marioni gestured to Whisper and her cohorts. "You and your little buddies here replied to a coded thread on Reddit. *We* started the thread. It was a ruse to get a few of the Whale Watchers behind bars."

"You're VeganBaker2006?" I asked in disbelief.

"I do love me some biscuits." Marioni mockingly smacked his lips. "Worked like a charm too. I had a hunch you'd show up, but the other guys didn't believe me." He turned to address the rest of his team. "What do you think, boys? You all owe me lunch."

"Look, I don't know what you think is going on," I began, "but I'm not a part of the Whale Watchers. Where have you been for the past month and a half? I've been trying to catch the Whale Watchers and find Avery, not join them."

Marioni picked up a small glass orb that the bookstore was selling as a paperweight, tossed it up, and caught it in his hand. The hipsters watched the drama unfold from the stage. Almost all of them had their cell phones out to record the incident. Nothing like this had ever happened in Doveport before.

"It's an odd cover," Marioni said. "I'll give you that. But I think that's exactly what you were going for. Admit it, Bex. You've been with the Whale Watchers since before you returned to Doveport. Don't you think it's an awful coincidence that Avery disappeared just a few days after you came to town?"

"It *was* a coincidence," I growled. "I don't have anything to do with the Whale Watchers."

"Then why reply to the thread?"

"Because I was trying to catch them!" I pointed at the

three younger Watchers who had been duped into meeting at the bookstore. "Whisper Collins knows where Avery is. You should be questioning her."

Marioni glanced over his shoulder. Whisper raised her hands.

"I have no idea what she's talking about," she said innocently. "I just came here for some muffins and a book on Sartre for my philosophy class."

"Oh, please," I scoffed. "You can't possibly buy that."

Marioni sucked his teeth and gestured to Taj with the glass orb. "Who's your hulking friend, Bex?"

I took another step away from Taj. Likewise, he retreated toward the other hipsters. Like Whisper, he lifted his hands and attempted to look as innocent as possible. At his height and weight, it was a difficult feat, but Taj had a way of expressing integrity through his eyes.

"We don't know each other," Taj announced. "I have no idea what's going on."

Marioni studied Taj with a wry gaze. "But you came in the same car?"

"She said she needed a ride," Taj replied, the lie so effortless. "And I'm not the type of guy to leave a woman on the side of the road. Besides, vegan bake sale and poetry sounded right up my alley."

Marioni wasn't stupid, but without proof, he had no choice but to accept Taj's story. Good for Taj. Not so good for me.

The bookstore owner—a petite woman with a head of curly gray hair—got to her feet on the stage and grabbed the microphone. "Excuse me, FBI guys? I don't mean to be rude, but I need you to be on your way. The only reason I agreed to let you set this up here was because you promised me it wouldn't interfere with our poetry reading. Perhaps you haven't noticed, but this is *definitely* interfering."

The other hipsters murmured in agreement. Taj nodded firmly and planted his hands on his hips. Marioni rolled his eyes.

"Fine, lady," he said. "We're getting out of here. Julian?" He waved over one of the agents on his team. "Let's get Ms. Lennon in handcuffs. She can ride with me."

"What the hell?" I said. "You can't arrest me!"

"Watch me," replied Marioni with a smirk.

Julian, a skinny guy whose plump cheeks didn't match his thin stature, grimaced as he pulled his handcuffs off his belt and approached me. "Sorry about this," he said, gently taking my hands behind my back to secure me. "It's my job to follow orders."

"Yeah, the Nazis were just following orders too," I shot back. Though fighting back crossed my mind, one look at Taj made me forget about it. Taj shook his head slightly, pursing his lips. I knew what that meant. If I fought back, it would give Marioni another reason to detain me. Going quietly was my best bet. They couldn't hold me for very long when I hadn't done anything wrong.

As Julian escorted me past Marioni, I made sure to step on Marioni's shiny leather loafers, leaving a dirt print on them.

"Whoops," I said, shrugging. "Didn't you see there."

Since Doveport was miles away from any official FBI offices, Marioni drove me to the Doveport police station. The entire way there, I berated Marioni for his choices. He didn't deign to reply, but I did catch sight of him clenching his teeth through the rearview mirror. At the very least, I'd gotten on his nerves.

The Doveport police station was relatively small. As Marioni escorted me inside, the local cops glanced up from their desks. They raised their eyebrows, asking silent questions about my arrest. Sheriff Danvers came out of his office.

"Whoa!" Danvers stopped the agent in his tracks. "What's going on here, Marioni? Why have you got one of my civilians in handcuffs?"

"Your civilian replied to a trap we set to catch those involved with Avery Maxx's kidnapping," Marioni said, lowering his voice to sound more authoritative. "I need to hold her here until I figure out what to do with her, and I've got others coming in as well. I hope your holding cells are empty."

"We've only got one," Danvers replied gruffly. He eyed me from beneath his receding hairline. "Are you sure you got the right person? I've known Bex since before she was born. Don't think she'd kidnap her best friend's kid."

"See?" I surprised Marioni and jerked out of his grasp. "The sheriff trusts me."

Marioni clutched my shoulder tighter than he needed to. "Sheriff, I have proof that she's involved with this crime."

"No, he doesn't," I interrupted dryly.

"I am permitted to hold her for at least twenty-four hours," Marioni said loudly, drawing the attention of every officer in the building. He pulled his badge out and flashed it around the room. "Do I need to remind you small-town flatfoots who I am? I have federal jurisdiction. I *outrank* you."

Sheriff Danvers planted his hands on his belt. "I don't give a damn what kind of jurisdiction you say you have. This is my town. Bex can stay in the bullpen, *uncuffed*, until you get me an official warrant from the FBI."

Marioni turned to one of the agents who had followed us into the station. The agent handed Marioni a file folder, from which Marioni extracted a piece of paper. "Here you are," he said, handing it to Danvers. "It gives me permission to arrest anyone who replied to our online summons. That includes Ms. Lennon here."

Sheriff Danvers read the official document, his nose wrinkling. He gave it back to Marioni and shot me an apologetic grimace. "Sorry, Bex. I can't argue with that."

"No problem, Sheriff. I'll be out of here in no time."

"Holding cells?" Marioni asked smugly.

Danvers jabbed his thumb over his shoulder toward the back of the building.

"I can make it there on my own," I told Marioni when he attempted to take my elbow. "I don't want any more of your palm grease on me."

Marioni bit his lip as if holding in a nasty retort. "Move it then."

Grudgingly, I made my way to the holding cell. It was located in a short hallway at the rear of the station. The emergency exit was at the other end of the hall. If I was bold enough, I could make a break for it, but knowing Marioni, he had agents stationed outside in case I was stupid enough to try something.

Marioni yanked on the barred door. It was locked. He hung his head and muttered some choice swear words under his breath.

"Relax, man," I said calmly. "Take a deep breath."

"Shut up," he snarled. Then he hollered into the bullpen, "Danvers! I need the damn key!"

Sheriff Danvers' grin made it obvious that he'd kept the key from Marioni on purpose, but as he moseyed in, he said, "Sorry about that, Marioni. Gettin' forgetful in my old age."

Sheriff Danvers made a show about fitting the key into the lock, fumbling it twice on purpose then pretending he couldn't figure out how to unlatch the handle. I did my best to contain the laugh building in my chest. The sheriff knew damn well how to operate the holding cell. He was intentionally messing up to drive Marioni nuts. It was working. Marioni looked like he was about to burst at the seams, his face red as a beet.

"Maybe you should retire," Marioni snapped when Sheriff Danvers finally got the door open.

Sheriff Danvers wiped his forehead. "Whew! Maybe you're right, Marioni. Law enforcement's getting a little too dramatic for me, if you know what I mean."

"Give me the key," Marioni ordered as he shoved me into the cell.

"No can do," Danvers replied. "You can use my facilities, but I'm still the boss here. You need access, you can come to me and ask for it."

Marioni's teeth gnashed together with such force, his pearly whites almost cracked. "Then stick around until my agents bring in the others."

A few minutes later, Julian and another agent escorted in Whisper Collins and the two other Whale Watchers that had been stupid enough to fall for the FBI's Reddit thread. They shoved the group members into the cell with me, and Marioni gestured for Sheriff Danvers to lock the door. He did so, but as he followed the agents out of the room, he caught my eye and winked.

With Marioni and his agents gone, I was all alone with

the Whale Watchers for the first time since the campsite. I turned toward them.

"We haven't met properly," I said cheerfully. "I'm Bex Lennon. Your psychotic leader abducted my best friend's kid."

Whisper Collins harrumphed. "It's not kidnapping if she's his daughter."

"Actually it is," I corrected her. "Because he never had custody over Avery. Who are your friends? We might as well get to know each other."

Whisper shrugged, leaving it up to the others to introduce themselves. They were both boys in their late teens or early twenties. Both of them kept their gaze on Whisper as she paced the short distance of the cell.

"Brock," said the first.

"Brady," added the second.

"Aren't you adorable with the alliteration?" I patted Brock's chunky cheeks then clapped my hands together loudly. "Here's how this is going to go, idiots. I'm betting you three want to get out of here as much as I do, so we're going to make a deal."

"No way," Whisper said. "I'm not making any kind of deal with you."

"Would you shut up and listen?" I leaned against the bars, letting the coolness of the steel seep into my skin. "I'm betting Norman Beers won't be too happy when he hears three of his people are being held by the FBI. You're not getting out of here scot free. Something's gotta give. You guys are gonna spend a lot of time in prison for the things you've been involved in, and Beers isn't gonna rescue you like you did for him."

Whisper stopped her pacing and lingered on the opposite

side of the cell with her arms crossed. "Am I supposed to trust you?"

"Momentarily," I answered. "You want to get out of here or not?"

Whisper glanced at Brock and Brady, both of whom nodded furiously at her. "Fine," she said. "What did you have in mind?"

I opened my mouth to reply, aware that whatever came out would be a crock of crap. The only reason I'd offered in the first place was in the hopes of getting information about Avery's situation. It turned out I didn't need to. The door to the hallway burst open, and Marioni marched in.

"What the hell is this?" he demanded, holding his phone up for us to see. He was shaking with fury, which made it hard to focus on the screen.

I grabbed the phone through the bars and brought it into the cell.

"Hey!" he yelled.

I ignored his protests and focused on the phone. The reason I'd grabbed it was obvious. The screen showed Avery, alone in a concrete room with gray walls. She was tied to a chair. Her face was bloody and bruised. Someone had shoved a bandana in her mouth to stifle her yells. Tear tracks cut through the dirt and blood on her face.

Without thinking, I took Whisper Collins by the throat and pinned her to the wall. Brock and Brady stood up, unsure what to do as Whisper gagged and fought against my hold.

"Where is she?" I bellowed.

"Who?" Whisper choked.

I held up the phone. "Don't tell me you don't know anything about this."

"I don't!"

I tightened my grasp, and Whisper's face turned bright red. Marioni banged on the cell, rattling our cage, but without the key, he had no power to stop me from strangling Whisper.

"Try again," I demanded.

"P-please!" she sputtered, spit flying from her mouth as she gasped. I let up enough for her to speak, and she drew a raspy breath. "I didn't know anything about this! He was treating her like a goddamn queen! I didn't think—"

"You have two seconds to tell me where this is," I said.

"Let her go, Lennon," Marioni yelled. "You're on thin ice as it is."

"I want to know what's going on!" I roared.

He threw a metal chair against the bars. The resulting crash was so loud and jarring that it made me flinch. I lost my grip on Whisper, who ducked under my arm and ran to Marioni.

"Get us out of here!" she howled. "She's crazy!"

"Shut up," Marioni spat. "You probably deserved it. If you haven't figured it out already, the Whale Watchers are holding Avery for ransom. Apparently, they want twenty-two thousand dollars for her safe return to Doveport."

"Twenty-two thousand dollars?" I paced across the cell, studying the video of Avery. Her eyes darted back and forth, as if keeping an eye on someone out of sight of the camera. "That's how much Edison made at the last Home Safe fundraiser—oh my God." I covered my mouth in shock. "It's my fault."

"What is?" Marioni barked.

"The reason Norman Beers knew about Avery," I muttered, more to myself than to Marioni. "I promoted the

Home Safe fundraiser on social media. I posted a live stream of Edison's closing speech. That's how the Whale Watchers knew she had the money. *Oh—*" I buried my head in my hands and pulled my hair. "I boosted Avery's Instagram! No one knew her before, but Beers must have seen her page. No, no, no—"

"Are you done spiraling?" Marioni snapped. "I don't care whose fault it is. I've only got twenty-four hours to figure this out before my career gets yanked out from under me."

"Twenty-four hours?"

"Yeah," Marioni said. "The Whale Watchers were pretty clear. They want the money by tomorrow, or they'll kill Avery."

ime passed in the cell without a way to track it. Marioni refused to let me out, though I was sure he knew I wasn't involved with the Whale Watchers. Whisper Collins, on the other hand, deteriorated with every passing second. The longer she stayed in the cell, the more withdrawn she became. As the long hours ticked by, her eyes sunk into her skull and her cheeks grew sharper, as if she were starving right before my eyes. Her cohorts, Brock and Brady, were likewise concerned with their possible incarceration, but neither one of them appeared to have enough individual thought to do or say anything about it.

Fear ate away at me. The image of Avery tied up in that concrete room circled in my head like hair in a clogged shower drain. The room looked familiar. I sat in the corner of the cell and forced myself to remember every detail about the footage I'd seen. The room hadn't been dark. Pinkish light poured in from the top and cast an angled shadow across one of the walls. Was it sunlight? Did the room have a large window? The floor was concrete too, and if I concentrated enough on the memory, I recalled lines painted across it beneath Avery's chair. What was this place?

Every twenty minutes or so, Sheriff Danvers made an attempt to get into the hallway that led to the holding cell. Every time he tried, he was shot down by the FBI agents outside the door who had been tasked with guarding us. The arguments floated into the cell.

"This is my station!" Sheriff Danvers kept saying. "I have the right to check on the citizens in the holding cell."

"Sorry, sir—"

"It's *Sheriff.*"

"Sheriff," the agent corrected himself. "Got my orders. Can't let anyone in, including you."

It didn't stop Danvers from trying repeatedly to access the holding cell throughout the night. I appreciated the effort. I needed to talk to someone sane, not Marioni or the other goons who were too obsessed with cracking Avery's case to see reason.

The fear grew more pronounced as the night wore on. The cell grew dark without any natural light to illuminate it. Whisper Collins curled up in a ball between her henchmen and went to sleep. Hours had passed—crucial hours to Avery. How much time did we have left before Norman Beers went all Norman Bates on her? Did it matter to him that she was his daughter or did it simply sweeten the deal? Maybe all he wanted to do was hurt Edison.

Though Avery was in trouble, I worried about Edison too. She had already been through so much, but neither of us expected the past to haunt us like this. Surely Marioni had already told her about Avery's ransom. Knowing Edison, she would surrender several million dollars to get Avery back, but the FBI didn't like to give terrorists what they wanted. I actually agreed with that tactic. The Whale Watchers deserved a lifetime in prison, not twenty-two thousand dollars to continue kidnapping, looting, and vandalizing.

My mind whirred through a million possibilities per minute. I needed to get out of here, but I had no way out. I had to figure out where Avery was, but I was fresh out of clues. I needed to talk to Edison, but—

The door to the hallway flew open, and Edison marched in. Her face was red with tears and stress, but she didn't let that stop her from powering through the FBI agent guarding the door.

"I will punch you!" she hollered, pulling her fist back as if she was about to undercut the agent's crotch. "Don't tempt me!"

"Ma'am, I'm not supposed to let anyone through—"

Edison slammed the door in his face. He peered through the window, obviously annoyed, to keep watch on us.

"Edison!" I gasped, grabbing her hands through the bars. "Ed, I'm so sorry. I'm such an idiot. I don't know why Marioni—"

"Because he's an ass," Edison finished. She wiped tears from her cheeks as fresh ones fell. "Listen to me, Bex. I'm doing my best to get you out here, but I don't have the resources. I called Raven—she's a lawyer now—and she's working out what to do."

"Forget about me," I said. "What about Avery? What's Marioni doing to save her?"

Edison let out a phlegmy scoff. "He's trying to negotiate with the Whale Watchers. He says his guys are working behind the scenes to figure out where she is, but since all of them are sitting on their butts *here*" —she gestured to the station beyond the door— "I don't have a whole lot of faith in them. That's why I brought you this."

She glanced toward the door, where the FBI agent was still spying on us. Then she threw back her head and let out an anguished howl. The agent, startled, drew away from the window. As soon as his back was turned, Edison turned off the agony and passed Avery's cell phone through the bars.

"Cade gave it to me," Edison explained as I tucked the phone into my pocket before the agent spotted it. "They were sure you could find Avery if you had it."

"Avery's been blocking me," I said. "I haven't been able to access her."

"If this isn't some elaborate game that Norman's playing with me and Avery is truly in trouble," Edison began, "she's sure to reach out. I don't know how your magnificent brain works, but I *do* know that you have the advantage over those idiots twiddling their thumbs out there." She checked the time on her own phone. "I have to go. I'm meeting Raven. Hopefully, we can find a loophole to get you out of here."

I grabbed her hand and squeezed it. "I'll do everything I can to find her, Ed."

She smiled grimly. "I know you will." She set her face in a tormented expression and opened the door so quickly that the agent outside almost fell through it. "Excuse me!" she shouted through tears. In another second, she was gone.

The agent closed the door, leaving me alone with the Whale Watchers once more. I kicked Whisper's shoe, jolting her awake. As her eyes opened blearily, I knelt down to be on her level.

"You're diabetic, aren't you?" I asked, examining her shaking body. "Don't you have any insulin?"

Brock answered for her in a gruff voice. "Beers has it."

"Why?" I asked.

"He gets it for her," the other guy, Brady, added. "She couldn't afford it on her own. Beers has pharmaceutical connections."

"That's why Whisper works for him," Brock said. "She has no other way to get insulin. She was homeless before the Whale Watchers. She would've died if he didn't find her."

"What about you two?" I asked. "What's your excuse for joining?"

"We were stupid kids," Brady said. He knocked Brock on the shoulder in a friendly way. "We're brothers. When our parents got divorced, we dealt with it the only way we knew how. We broke shit, vandalized our town, or stole. If it was a petty crime, we did it."

Brock ran his fingers over Whisper's buzz cut. "We went to juvie twice, but we pulled a dumb stunt when we were eighteen and got charged as adults. We were supposed to do ten years in jail."

"But?" I prompted.

"Norman Beers found us," Brady said. "He offered us a deal. Work for him, doing the same shit we always did, and never get caught. At the time, it seemed like the best option."

I was starting to understand why Beers's followers were so faithful to him. He took advantage of youths in need, presenting them with a way out of their predicaments. In a sick way, it was the same as what Edison did, though she didn't use the teenagers from Home Safe for her own perverse needs.

"What if I could get you three out of the Whale Watchers?" I said. "What if I could find a way to have you all pardoned of your crimes? Would you help me?"

Brady shook his head. "It's impossible. There's no way you could do that."

"You could testify against Beers," I told them. "You could say he coerced you to do those things. It's the truth, isn't it?"

Brock and Brady exchanged a look of uncertainty.

"Look at it this way." I rested a hand on Whisper's leg. She might have thrown me off—if she had the strength. "If you three stay with the Whale Watchers, you *will* eventually get caught. You'll go to prison no matter what. All you're doing now is prolonging the inevitable. But if you agree to help me, I'll be on your side from now until forever." I caught Whisper's eye as she gazed up at me. "I can get your records wiped, and I can make sure you never have to rely on Norman Beers for your insulin ever again."

Whisper looked at me for a long minute, her eyes boring into mine as if she were trying to dig out my true intention. I held her gaze. She wasn't a bad person. She had gotten sucked into the Whale Watchers because of her crappy father and a condition she couldn't control. She was no different than Cade or any of the kids in the Home Safe program. Brock and Brady deserved another chance too. Clearly, their parents hadn't cared enough about them to begin with.

With the last of her strength, Whisper nodded. "Do it," she said in a raspy voice. "Whatever you're planning. Get us out of here, and I'll help you find Avery."

I nodded firmly. "First of all, I need you to pretend to pass out. No matter what happens, don't stir. Got it?"

"Think I can manage," Whisper joked weakly. She could hardly move. If she didn't get insulin soon, she would go into shock.

"Time for the show," I muttered.

The metal chair in the hallway was within arm's reach. I

275

grabbed it by the backrest and slammed it against the bars. Once, twice, three times. The loud bangs echoed through the hallway.

"Hey!" I bellowed between the crashes. "Hello, is anyone out there! This chick is dying! YO, FBI IDIOTS!"

Marioni came through the door. "Shut up!" he roared. "Haven't you done enough? We're trying to save a girl!"

"So am I!" I hollered back. I moved over to reveal Whisper, lying limply between the brothers. Brock and Brady were doing their part too. The terror on their faces—fear for their friend's health—couldn't be faked. "She has diabetes. She needs an insulin injection."

Marioni sneered at Whisper's unmoving body. "I can't do anything about that. She should be prepared to care for herself."

"If she dies in here, it's your fault," I spat at him. "Think about it, Marioni. She's in your custody. If she dies, the story will blow up across the nation. The FBI will need a scapegoat, and guess who they'd pick?"

Marioni's jaw clenched as the truth landed. He knew I was right. If Whisper died, it might mean the end of his career. "I'll see what I can do," he snapped. "In the meantime, shut the hell up."

"Hurry up!" I shouted right before he slammed the door in our faces again.

MARIONI, of course, took his time. As the minutes dragged on, Whisper's condition worsened. She broke out in a cold sweat and lost any remaining energy to speak or move. Brock sat with her head cradled in his lap while Brady wiped her forehead with the hem of his T-shirt. Clearly, the brothers cared for her. It made me more determined to get the trio out of this damn cell. Like Cade and Avery, they were all victims of shitty circumstances.

"She's gonna bottom out soon," Brock said, feeling Whisper's forehead. "What are we supposed to do if they don't come back with the insulin soon?"

I texted furiously on Avery's phone. "Don't worry. I'm working something out."

"That's what you said ten minutes ago," Brady replied angrily. "You tracked us down twice without any help from the Feds. You could do that, but you can't get us out of this stupid cell?"

"Doing my best, Brady. Hold your horses."

Despite their skepticism, I *was* working something out, but the details had taken a little longer to arrange than I expected. According to my clock, twelve hours had passed since Norman Beers posted the livestream of Avery in that concrete room. Half the time to save her was already gone. I'd done my part. Now, I had to wait for backup. It was agonizing.

Another quarter of an hour passed. Whisper was the same color as a ghost. Brock and Brady had started losing hope. When they started yelling at the agents beyond the hallway, I pulled them back and shook my head.

"Don't draw attention to us," I commanded.

"She's dying!" Brock said. "What are we supposed to do?"

"Give it a few more minutes."

"We can't wait any longer—"

Before Brady had finished his sentence, the emergency exit door at the opposite end of the hallway popped open, but no alarm was triggered. An enormous man stood illuminated against the streetlight outside. It was Taj, in all his heroic glory.

He held his finger to his lips then lifted something into the light for all of us to see: the key to the holding cell. I punched the air in silent victory while Brock and Brady watched, dumbstruck, as Taj freed us from confinement.

"Quietly, quietly," he murmured, ushering me from the cell. He gestured to the boys. "Get in the car and wait for me."

Brock and Brady refused to move from Whisper's side.

"What about her?" Brady asked.

Taj checked to make sure the agent outside was distracted. Then he ducked into the cell and picked Whisper up with ease. She looked so small cradled in his massive arms. As he carried her out through the emergency exit, Brady and Brock followed.

My mom's old car idled out back. Sheriff Danvers stood beside it, surveying the shadows for threats with one hand on his gun. When we spotted us, he opened the back door and helped Taj get Whisper inside. Once Whisper was settled, Taj handed the cell key back to the sheriff.

I threw my arms around Sheriff Danvers. "Thank you."

"For what?" Danvers said gruffly. "I'm just a small-town flatfoot. What do I know about breaking criminals out? One more thing—" He pulled a filled syringe from his uniform pocket. "I heard you needed this. Upper thigh, abdomen, butt, or outer arm."

Brock grabbed the insulin shot from the sheriff and ducked into the backseat with Brady. "We can take care of it. I've done it a hundred times."

As Taj got into the driver's seat, the sheriff grabbed my arm. "Don't go home or to Edison's. They're swarming with agents." He dangled another key for me. "Go to my house instead. My wife will take care of you. She knows you're coming."

I pocketed the key and gave the sheriff another quick hug. "I won't forget about this."

"Don't act like you're dying, Lennon," he grunted, shoving me toward the car. "Get outta here."

As soon as I got into the passenger seat, Taj put the car in drive and pulled a U-turn. Carefully, so as to not attract attention, we drove right past the front door of the station—where several agents poorly kept watch—and got onto the main road.

I twisted around in my seat to get a better look at Whisper. "How's she doing?"

Brock pulled the cap off the insulin pen with his teeth, rolled up Whisper's shirt, and gently pinched the skin of her abdomen. Then, with no hesitation whatsoever, he stuck the needle in and depressed the plunger. When he removed the needle, he pressed his palm to the injection site and counted under his breath.

"She'll be okay," Brady said. "But she needs something to eat too."

"On it," Taj said. "We'll be at the sheriff's house in a few minutes."

"You guys owe me," I reminded the brothers. "Don't forget that."

Neither one of them replied, too busy with making sure that Whisper recovered properly.

Taj tapped my hand. "Are you okay? You're quiet."

"Just worried about Avery," I said. "I have no idea where she is, and I don't know how to find her. My abilities—" I lowered my voice in case the brothers were listening in. "I might be able to locate her, but I need to focus."

Brady leaned on the passenger seat. "I've got an idea."

We pulled up to Sheriff Danvers's house. Like my mother's, it was set behind a thicket of trees, far enough from any neighbors that it looked and felt like an official safehouse. The sheriff's wife was already waiting outside, with Edison at her side.

23

*A*fter we got Whisper settled in the sheriff's favorite arm chair with her choice of candy bars, we got down to business. Taj pulled the dining room table into the living room so Whisper could be involved with our planning while Cheryl, the sheriff's wife, warmed up leftovers to feed us.

"Thanks," I said as she sat a plate of homemade roast beef in front of me. "I don't know how to thank you."

Cheryl smoothed the hair on the back of my scalp, like a mother comforting her child. "Find Avery and those other girls. Get them home safe. That's the best thanks you can give me."

"We'll do our best," I promised.

"First order of business," Taj announced. Edison handed him her phone, and he showed it to all of us. It played the livestream of Avery in the concrete room. "We gotta find out where Beers is holding Avery. Only a few people have access to the livestream, including Marioni and Edison. Beers wants to keep this quiet, so I say we blow it wide open. Force him to tell us where he is."

"It might be easier than that." I took Edison's phone and studied the video of Avery. Like before, it jogged my memory, but I still couldn't place the scenery. "Let me try something."

The room went quiet as I laid the phone flat in my palms and closed my eyes. It was easy to dive into cyberspace—I'd been practicing a lot lately—but it came with warning signs. As I navigated the intricate map that laid invisible wires through the real world, sharp pains shot through my head. I ignored them, following the livestream from Edison's phone to its source. But when I reached the point of origin, something stopped me from seeing where the video was being streamed from.

"Damn it," I muttered, tossing the phone across the table. It almost landed in the bowl of leftover mashed potatoes. "They must have a ton of security features in place. I can't pinpoint the location of the livestream."

Whisper raised her hand. A bit of color had returned to her cheeks, and her body had stopped trembling. She looked much better than she had in the holding cell.

"If I may," she said coolly. "I can probably narrow down the possibilities."

Despite the promises we'd made with each other, I was hesitant to involve Whisper, Brock, or Brady too much in our plans. They could always default back to the Whale Watchers out of fear of Beers's retaliation. Still, if we were going to find Avery, we needed their help.

"Well?" I prompted. "Are you going to tell us or what?"

"I need a pencil, a piece of paper, and a map. Oh, and a laptop."

I grabbed a sheet of clean paper out of the printer on a nearby desk. Cheryl, who listened to the conversation from the dining room, disappeared into the garage and returned with a map of Doveport. When Whisper had everything she needed, she navigated to a secure web page with no title on Cheryl's old laptop.

"Beers isn't as stupid as he looks," Whisper said, typing a username and password into the login bars. "The social media stuff was my idea, not his. He was against it. He thought someone would use it to track us, and what do you know?" She smirked at me, and if I wasn't mistaken, the expression was laden with respect. "You did. I can't say I'm sorry about it. Anyway, Beers had a different way of communicating with the people he trusted most... like my father."

Brock and Brady's eyes went wide as Whisper hit enter and the web page reloaded. It was an official Whale Watchers' site, no doubt buried deep in the dark web, and it plainly stated the group's motto.

"Sorry, boys," Whisper said to the brothers. "I hope you understand why I kept this a secret. I couldn't afford anyone knowing that I'd stolen my dad's login information."

"What happened to your dad anyway?"

"He's dead," Whisper answered shortly, her sharp tone warding off any further questions. "But Beers doesn't know that. He thinks my dad's acquiring new recruits in California." She waggled her eyebrows mischievously. "But all this time, Beers has been talking to me instead."

"You've been trying to take the Whale Watchers down from the inside," I guessed.

"Trying is the key word." Whisper typed and clicked so furiously, it was hard to keep up with what she was doing on the website. "No matter what I did, I couldn't find a way to take down the entire group for good. Not until Avery showed up. And you."

Edison leaned on the arm of Whisper's chair to look over her shoulder. "What happened between you and Avery?"

"I did what I needed to do," Whisper said. "I figured out who Avery was pretty quickly and did my best to get her on my side, but Beers is a better manipulator than I am. We became friends, but Avery mistrusted me. After you stormed our camp at Tillamook, we had orders to disappear. Erase all social media and communications. Wipe everything that had to do with the Whale Watchers out of our lives temporarily and hide out until Beers contacted us. He never did. That's why I fell for the FBI's stupid Reddit thread. They were using the same code Beers usually did to communicate with us."

"You guys ever heard of burner phones?" Taj asked.

"Too much hassle," Whisper said. "Anyway, I figured Avery told Beers that I shouldn't be trusted. That's all he wanted from her, other than to torment you, of course." She nodded at Edison. "He wanted someone he could trust to root out the moles in his organization. After the job was done, he didn't need Avery anymore. Now, he's just milking it."

"He thinks I'll give him the money," Edison said.

"Won't you?" Whisper asked. "When we're down to the wire, and he's ten minutes from killing your daughter?"

Edison's face went pale. "I can't. I don't have the money anymore."

"What?" I said, dread creeping in. "Where did it go?"

"The fundraiser was over a month ago," she said. "I've already distributed those funds to expand the Home Safe program. The money's gone."

"Then I guess failure isn't an option," Whisper said. She

turned the laptop around so we could all see the screen. "Do you guys know what this is?"

"Coordinates," Taj and I said at the same time.

"You're right and wrong," Whisper said. "If someone outside the Whale Watchers attempted to locate these coordinates, they'd find themselves in some pretty random places, like the middle of the Amazon rainforest."

"Then what are they doing on this top-secret website of yours?" Edison asked in a dry voice.

Whisper picked up her pencil. "Once again, it's code, but not with words. Numbers."

As we watched, Whisper plugged the coordinates into a complicated formula and did the math by hand, filling up the entire front page of the paper. Then, when she'd gotten the answers, she plugged the new numbers into another formula and kept going. After two more sheets of paper, she finally lifted her head from the work and circled the final numbers.

"Here," she said, handing me the new set of coordinates. "Twenty bucks says they're all local. Beers likes to play close to home."

As Taj and I rushed to look up the locations on the map, Brock and Brady ogled Whisper.

"How did you figure out all those formulas?" Brock asked.

"I'm smart," she replied shortly.

"Hell yeah, you are," Brady said, high-fiving her.

Taj and I crouched over the map of Doveport, carefully matching the longitudes and latitudes up. Whisper had given us four sets of coordinates.

"What do we got?" Taj asked me once we'd circled all the locations.

"The high school, Dove's Pub, Maxine's Cafe, and the police station," I said, tracing the map with my fingers. "That doesn't make any sense. None of those places have a concrete room."

"What's directly in the middle of those four points?" Whisper asked. Under her breath, she added, "*Idiots.*"

I drew a line to connect the north and south points, and another one to connect the east and the west. Then I pinpointed where the lines intersected. "It's the recreational park in your old neighborhood, Edison."

Edison squeezed in between me and Taj to look at the map herself. As her fingers traveled across the wrinkled paper, her lips parted. "The racquetball court."

As soon as she said it, the image clicked into place. *That's* why I recognized the concrete room. It wasn't a room at all, just an alcove to play a sport in. We'd been there a bunch of times as teenagers. The park was a popular place for teenagers in the neighborhood to hang out at after school. To Edison, it held even more weight.

"It's where we used to meet," she said. "Norman and I. No one was ever there late at night."

Whisper wrinkled her nose in disgust. "How you ever found him alluring is beyond me."

"Hush," I commanded Whisper. To Edison, I asked, "Is this a trap? He knew you'd recognize the place and come looking for Avery."

"It could be," Edison said. "Or he wanted me to know where to drop off the money."

"Uh, guys?" Taj said.

I paced across the room. "We need to be careful about this. If we march in there with guns blazing, Beers will make sure we can't get to Avery. We can—"

"Guys?" Taj said again, this time louder. He had Edison's

phone in hand, his brow furrowed in worry. "You need to come look at this."

We rushed over to him as he turned up the phone's volume. Two people stood beside Avery, each holding a racquet and wearing a canvas bag with cut-out eye holes. It was a terrifying picture. One of them spoke.

"We are unhappy with your progress so far," the man announced, his voice muffled beneath the canvas sack. "Since you have not offered us a deal in return for the girl's safety, we must assume you don't care for her."

The men raised the racquets. At the same time, they swung at Avery. The blunt edges of the racquet—rather than the harmless plastic webbing—slapped against her skin. She yelped in pain, but the noise was dulled by the gag in her mouth.

"Oh, God!" Edison turned away and covered her eyes. "I can't watch this."

The men turned toward the camera again, leaving Avery shaking between them as she waited for another blow to land.

"You have one more hour to bring us the money," the speaker said. "At two a.m., we will kill your daughter."

The livestream cut off. Edison stifled a sob. I touched her shoulder, but she shrugged away.

"I'm sorry," she said. "I need to be alone."

She enclosed herself in the sheriff's office, leaving the rest of us to figure out what to do without her.

"Well?" I asked the younger trio. "What's up with Beers' quick trigger finger?"

"Any chance he figured out you escaped from jail?" Whisper asked.

The home phone rang. Cheryl grabbed it off the wall and

answered. "Hello? Hi, hun. Yes. Mm-hmm. Okay, I'll tell them." She hung up and faced us. "Marioni's looking for you. All of you."

"Surprise, surprise," Whisper grumbled.

"What do we do?" I asked, addressing the entire room. "We've got fifty-eight minutes to rescue Avery, and the rec park is probably crawling with Whale Watchers."

Brock crossed his arms. "Count on it. We aren't the only ones Beers has been blackmailing. He'll have an army to protect Avery."

"We don't have an army," Taj said.

Cheryl marched into our midst. "Damn straight you do! My husband may not be in charge of Avery's disappearance anymore, but he's still the sheriff of this town. The recreation park is under his jurisdiction. The Whale Watchers are no match for his officers. Even the rookies are the best batch I've seen in a while."

"Call him back," I told Cheryl. "Let's get ready for a battle."

WE TOOK twenty precious minutes to figure out our plan. It would take ten more to drive to the recreation park, leaving us with half an hour to free Avery from the clutches of Norman Beers and the Whale Watchers. Everyone had a role to play, but it all came down to whether or not we were brave enough to pull it off.

Before we left, I took Edison aside and helped her zip up her coat since her fingers were shaking so badly.

"Are you sure you can do this?" I asked her in a low voice. "I can do it—"

"No," she said firmly. "I'm ready."

"If you say so. Where's Cade?"

Edison drew her hood up. "They're safe. That's all that matters."

"Good. Let's go."

Outside the sheriff's house, we parted ways. Whisper, Brock, and Brady would stay here since Whisper wasn't strong enough to get herself out of trouble if things went south. Edison went off on her own, while Taj and I took a different route to the recreation park.

"Are you sure this is a good idea?" Taj asked. "We can leave it up to law enforcement."

"We can't ensure they'll show up," I said. "Let me try to get Avery out of there first."

"I got your back, Bex. Just like always."

The parking lot for the recreation park was across the way from the racquetball courts. The streetlights were out. Anyone passing by would never know that a teenage girl was being held hostage between the concrete walls in the center of the park.

"Are we sure she's here?" Taj wondered aloud as he peered into the darkness. "I don't see anyone."

A brain zap hit me. I was back in business. I checked my phone. *H3r3.*

"She has to be," I said.

Warily, we stepped out of the car. As we walked across to the racquetball courts, I kept my eyes peeled for movement. There were a hundred trees and bushes the Whale Watchers could be hiding behind as they waited for the perfect chance to jump us. There were three racquetball courts, each one separated by one of those concrete walls. With Taj right behind me, I checked the first one. No sign of Avery. We darted across to the second, but she wasn't there either.

She had to be in the last court. She had to be.

But she wasn't.

"Damn it!" I pounded my fist against the concrete wall.

"Maybe Whisper got the coordinates wrong?" Taj suggested. "Could she be at a different court?"

"No." I scuffed my toes against the floor of the court. There were four smudge marks where the legs of Avery's chair had been, along with smeared droplets of blood. "She was here. They must have just moved her. They knew we were coming."

"Wasn't that the point?" Taj asked dryly.

Norman Beers stepped into the court. Taj immediately pushed me behind him, but it wasn't the smartest move. It forced us against the back wall of the racquetball court. We were cornered. As usual, Beers wore a pressed shirt, slacks, and loafers. Today, he'd added a long black overcoat and black leather gloves to ward off the cold.

"Bex Lennon," he said. "We meet again. I was rather hoping Edison would show up with the money, but I suppose this is a decent second best."

"If I were you, I'd take a step back," Taj growled.

Norman studied Taj without fear. "I see you brought your bodyguard. I have a few of mine scattered around as well."

From the shadows, more Whale Watchers emerged, but I hadn't met these folks before. They were all roughly Taj's size, and each of them carried a baseball bat or some other homegrown weapon. One of them squeezed the trigger of a handheld Taser. The electric buzz made my heart jump.

"Where's Avery?" I demanded.

"She's around." Norman picked a fleck of dirt from beneath his nails. "I thought it might be best to separate her from the hubbub until we've settled our deal. Where's the money?"

Taj tossed a black duffel bag onto the concrete, and Norman gestured for one of his henchman to pick it up.

"Open it," Norman ordered the Whale Watcher.

I grimaced as the man obeyed and got an eyeful of pepper spray. We'd filled the bag with rocks and rigged the zipper, hoping Norman would be the one to open it. Alas, the best plans…

Norman clicked his tongue as the henchman yelled and clutched his face. "I see we're here to play dirty. That's all right." He stepped toward me, but Taj spread his arms to prevent Norman from getting any closer. Norman peered around Taj. "Do you remember when I told you I wasn't a killer? I lied. I quite like it actually. It makes me feel alive. Killing Edison's daughter won't haunt me at night."

"She's your daughter too," I reminded him.

He waved off this statement. "She's no more than a pawn. I have no use for her and no attachment to her either. In fact, this is the best and only revenge I could take against Edison for breaking my heart the way she did."

"Oh, did I break your heart, baby?" a mocking voice asked.

Edison stepped *through* the henchman to join us in the court. None of the Whale Watchers had realized she wasn't one of them, her face covered by her hood. My heart pounded as she raised a gun—the gun she'd kept locked in her office safe since moving back to Doveport—and pointed it right at Norman's face. The Whale Watchers surged forward, but Norman halted them with a snap of his fingers.

"Hello, Edison," said Norman softly. "How are you?"

"Where's my daughter?" she snarled.

"I'm afraid I can't tell you that," Norman said. "Not until you hand over the money."

"I don't have the money," Edison replied. "And you won't get out of this alive."

Norman gestured to his henchman. "If you shoot me, you won't get out of here alive either."

Edison's gaze flickered toward the wall of Whale Watchers that prevented all of us from escaping the racquet-ball courts unscathed. Her finger lingered on the trigger. "Maybe I'm okay with that."

"Edison," I warned. "This isn't what we planned."

"Shut up, Bex! I'm thinking."

Norman laughed and clapped his hands. "Oh, this is perfect. I can't wait to see how the show ends."

"With your blood on the pavement," Edison growled at him. "And the Whale Watchers dismantled."

He spread his arms as if to give Edison a better shot. "Go ahead. Shoot me. Shoot the only man who ever loved you." When Edison didn't rise to the bait, Norman laughed again. "You can't do it, can you? No, of course not. Come here, baby. Let me love you. You know you need me."

He stepped toward her, arms reaching out to embrace her. Edison lowered the gun as Norman clasped her to his chest. All at once, chaos broke loose.

Sirens blared and lights flashed as police cars careened over the grass and into the park. The Whale Watchers yelled and scattered like cockroaches, determined not to be caught. A gunshot went off, and a body crumpled to the ground. In the mayhem, it was impossible to tell who had fallen.

The most intense brain zap I'd ever felt rushed through my head. It was strong enough to topple me over. Above me, Taj punched a Whale Watcher with enough guts to try and grab me. As the man fell over, I yanked my phone out of my pocket.

Und3rw@t3r.

"The lake!" I screamed at Taj. "Get me to the lake!"

Taj pulled me to my feet, and we ran off. Taj cleared a path through the crowd, punching every black-clad Whale Watcher who dared to get in his way. The police—who'd arrived with batons and anti-riot shields—left us be. They had strict orders from Sheriff Danvers to let us do whatever we needed to do.

The lake was far from the main brawl, but it wasn't free of Whale Watchers. One of them, a stocky man with enormous biceps, stood at the edge of the dock.

"It's too late," the man called, chuckling as we sprinted toward him. "She'll have drowned by now—"

Taj barreled past me and sank his fist into the Whale Watcher's nose. The man fell backward into the lake. I dove off the end of the dock and plunged into the dark water.

The icy chill shocked my senses. I kicked away from the Whale Watcher and swam deeper, opening my eyes to look for Avery. It was a different world from the one above it. Moonlight streamed down, illuminating the lake floor. A few feet away, I spotted the back of a folding chair. The water thrashed and bubbled around it. Avery was fighting to free herself.

I swam over, but I had nothing to cut the ropes with, so I hooked the chair around my elbow and kicked upward, dragging Avery along with me. When we breached the surface, Avery took a great gasp of air. The chair threatened to pull her under again.

Taj appeared out of nowhere and grabbed Avery. With powerful strokes, he pulled her to shore. I followed weakly. Even though Avery was alive, something felt wrong.

"Bex?" Taj called, scanning the water.

My muscles felt heavy. I started sinking. My vision clouded.

"Bex!" Taj shouted again urgently.

All at once, my head exploded. It was like getting a hundred brain zaps at the same time. It rattled my bones. My body was no longer under my control. It shook and trembled as I sank beneath the lake's surface again.

Everything went black.

24

ONE YEAR LATER

$\mathcal{T}$he plane ride from Greece to Portland was eons long. When I finally made it into the taxi that would take me to Doveport, I almost sighed with relief. I hated breathing recycled air, especially after spending a month and a half on the perfect island of Mykonos. I rolled down the windows and let the fresh, misty air of the Pacific Northwest wash over me. Visiting Doveport no longer felt like an arduous chore to me. In fact, I was beginning to cherish my time in the small town, though I no longer called it home.

When the taxi pulled up to Edison's house, it wasn't Edison that came running out to sweep me up in a bone-crushing hug. It was Taj.

"I've missed you, Bex!" he yelled joyfully, swinging me around in a circle. "It's been too long!"

"It's only been three months," I reminded him. "Put me down and help me with my bags!"

He obliged and emptied the taxi's trunk, slinging my

duffel bag over his shoulder. He paid the cab driver and escorted me into the house.

"Here we go," he said, dropping the bag onto the couch. "Edison would probably make you take your shoes off. That's her new thing. Do you want some water or a snack?"

I playfully knocked his shoulder. "Wow, aren't you the host with the most? Dating Edison's turned you into a little homebody, hasn't it?"

Taj blushed, and for the first time since I'd met him, I could actually see his cheeks turn red. He'd shaved his beard. "It's been going so great, you know?" he said. "I don't want to be away from her."

"You're so cute."

"Shut up or I'll let you starve."

Despite the statement, he led me into the kitchen and pulled out the ingredients for guacamole. In the last year, he and Edison had gotten to know each other. I'd never seen either of them happier. As he chopped avocados, tomatoes, and onions, we got to chatting about our latest adventures.

"How was Greece?" he asked. "Did you try the baklava?"

"I ate so much baklava that I never need to eat it again," I admitted. "It was great. I'm thinking about going back after this. Or I might hit Sardinia next. I'm really into Mediterranean islands right now."

"How are you getting along without me?"

"Oh, I found another large, handsome man to protect me from thieves and other bad men," I joked.

Taj threw the slimy avocado pit at me. I caught it and tossed it into the trash.

"How are things going here?" I looked around the quiet, empty house. "Where is everyone?"

"Edison had to drop something off at the bank," Taj said.

"And Avery and Cade are at band practice. They finally found a bass player who doesn't suck."

I chuckled and shook my head. "I've been following their band page on Instagram. They need a better name."

"What, you don't like The Wasted Youth?" he teased.

"It's so *emo.*"

"That's their brand." Taj glanced at the clock on the stove as he squeezed limes with his bare hands. "They should be home soon—"

The front door banged open. Cade and Avery's voices filled the living room. As usual, they were arguing.

"Learn to tune your guitar between every song," Avery was saying loudly over Cade's protests. "We're wasting time asking you to do it every time."

"Well, *excuse* me," Cade shot back. "Not all of us are married to our instruments like you are. Half the time, I expect you to start making out with your snare drum."

"Shut up!"

"No, you shut up!"

"I missed you too!" I called from the kitchen.

In a flurry of dropped backpacks, guitar cases, and drumsticks, the teenagers stampeded across the room to smother me with hugs.

"You're back!"

"We missed you!"

"Did you bring us anything from Greece?"

"As a matter of fact, I did." I dug two objects, both wrapped in brown paper, out of my bag and handed them to Cade and Avery. "There ya go."

They tore the paper off, unwrapping a beaded bracelet for each of them. I'd chosen blue for Avery and yellow for Cade.

"They're called kompoloi," I explained. "Or worry beads.

The Greeks use them to ward off bad luck, or you can play with them to reduce stress."

Cade slipped the bracelet onto their wrist and held it out for Avery to see. "My kompoloi is cooler than yours!"

"No, it's not!"

They ran off and stomped upstairs to wash off the school day. I widened my eyes at Taj as he set the bowl of fresh guacamole in front of me and poured tortilla chips out of a bag.

"Is it always like that?" I asked him, digging into the snack.

He wiped his hands on the kitchen towel and joined me. "Pretty much. I think it means they like each other?"

The front door opened for a second time, though it didn't ricochet off the wall like when the kids had come home.

"Babe!" Edison called through the house. "Hey, do I have time to take a shower before Bex gets here?" She put on a sultry voice. "And would you like to join me?"

I poked my head out from the kitchen. "Ew. Please, keep it to yourself."

Edison flushed bright red, but her excitement quickly drowned out her embarrassment. She threw her arms around my neck and gave me one of her classically-aggressive hugs. I lived for those hugs. It meant everything to see my best friend alive and healthy, especially after the events of last year.

The night we'd rescued Avery was still a blur. After Taj pulled me out of the lake, I was totally out of it. The seizure was the worst I'd ever experienced, and the medics who treated me warned that I might have lasting brain damage because of it. They were half right. Since that night, I hadn't had a single brain zap or wayward text message. My ability was gone. Thankfully, it didn't take my career with it. Once I got back on the road, my faithful followers regained interest in me, and I'd been able to maintain my social media fame without cheating.

Edison kissed me rapidly on the cheeks and forehead. "Ah, I love you! I love when you come to visit."

"All right, enough!" I warded off her love so I could take another bite of guacamole. "What did you have to do at the bank?"

"Some stuff for Home Safe." Edison stole my loaded chip and popped it into her mouth. "We're officially a nationwide non-profit!"

Taj and I cheered loudly, clapping and roaring as if our imaginary team scored the winning goal at a championship match. Taj kissed Edison's forehead.

"I'm so proud of you," he said.

Edison kissed him back, and I beamed at them. She looked so happy in his arms. There was a point where I thought Edison might never be able to trust a man enough to love him, but Taj was sweet, kind, and understanding. Fate, also known as me, had brought them together.

"I better be the best man *and* the maid of honor at your wedding," I told them.

"Absolutely," Taj agreed.

"We'll see," Edison said. She detached herself from Taj and pulled me aside to talk to me alone. "Any updates?" she asked in a low voice.

"You really want to know?"

She chewed her lip then nodded.

"No progress," I told her. "It's starting to look like he'll never recover."

The fateful gunshot that changed all of our lives was

Edison's doing. Caught in Norman's embrace, she'd pulled the trigger without being fully aware of where she was aiming. The bullet had grazed Norman's head, taking a decent chunk out of his brain. Somehow, he survived, but his wretched personality didn't. The man didn't even know his own name. We all spent a lot of time in courtrooms after that, but ultimately, it was decided that Edison had acted in self-defense.

Without a leader and with many of their members in prison, the Whale Watchers disbanded. This led to the rescue of the two other girls that had been abducted from Doveport. Police found them in a storage garage in Portland and returned them to their families. Those who had been coerced into joining the Whale Watchers—like Whisper, Brock, and Brady—had managed to escape jail time. Instead, they had several years of community service to look forward to.

Edison changed the subject. "Are you going to visit your mom while you're stateside?"

"Yeah," I said. "She's starting to forget who I am, but the nurses say she's always in a better mood when I come see her."

"The home's nice?"

"Nicest in Oregon," I said. "And the most expensive. That place is practically a resort spa. I wish I could stay there."

"I wish you didn't have to sell your house to afford it."

Six months ago, Mom's health had gotten to a point where she could no longer live on her own. Since Melba wasn't available to look after her full time, I'd made the decision to sell the house and use the cash to pay for the best care in the state.

"It's okay," I told Edison. I pointed to a picture frame

above the fireplace, the one of me and my dad that used to hang beside the fridge in our garage. "You've got the most important part of the house right there. That's all that matters."

Made in the USA
Middletown, DE
19 December 2019